A Lady's Guide to Monsters and Moonlight

Julianne Sharpe

This edition published by Silver Thistle Press Ltd in 2026.
Silver Thistle Press Ltd., 272 Bath Street, Glasgow, UK G2 4JR

The characters and events portrayed in this book are fictitious. Any similarity to real persons, living or dead, is coincidental and not intended by the author.

ISBN: 978-1-917794-14-5 (Paperback)
ISBN: 978-1-917794-11-4 (Ebook)

Cover design by a human designer at GetCovers / Miblart.

For all inquiries, please email hello@silverthistlepress.com
www.silverthistlepress.com

Printed in the United States of America

To my mother,
who shared her love of reading with me at a young age
and so set the course for my life.

And to Jess and Liz,
for daring me to write this story
and then encouraging the heck out of me when it became,
like, an actual book.

one

"This is the second funeral we've attended this week," I whispered in Uncle Gerald's ear.

He gave me the look that served as chastisement when I was a child, but it had lost its power over the years.

"Don't you find it odd?" I asked.

He lifted his fingers to his mustache and muttered into his hand. "Catherine, *please*. We are at a *funeral*."

"Exactly." I ignored the disapproving stare of Mrs. Witherpoole and gazed at the open grave before us. Sunlight filtered through the trees onto the cemetery grounds, its warmth brushing against my shoulders as leaves swayed in the wind. Behind us, the simple stone church marked the center of the village, with the graveyard on one side and the village green across from it. It was a beautiful morning, which made the funeral even sadder.

Just visible in the depths of the grave lay the coffin that held young Ann Claybrook. Next to the grave's edge, Mrs. Claybrook stifled a sob with her handkerchief. Mr. Claybrook looked stunned. He'd worn the same expression for two days now, and I feared he'd wear it a while longer.

Three nights ago, I saw Ann Claybrook at the Richardsons' party. Talked to her, watched her dance and laugh.

She was only sixteen.

That night, according to the Claybrooks, Ann walked ahead of them on their short journey home. It was too fine a summer night to waste in a carriage. Ann turned the corner of the lane that led to their house, and when the Claybrooks followed a few moments later, she had disappeared from view.

They thought nothing of it at first—Ann had run ahead, cutting through the Fredericks' garden as she often did. But when they reached the house and still could not find her, a search party was formed.

They found her four hours later, beneath a hedge on the far side of the Fredericks' property.

The vicar cleared his throat and resumed his liturgy. I watched his mouth as he spoke. I would have this service memorized soon if these strange deaths kept occurring. Sixteen-year-old girls did not inexplicably drop dead beneath hedges. Nor did young tailors mysteriously die in ditches.

I seemed to be the only person in Harwick convinced of this fact.

The service was short, and Uncle Gerald and I followed the other villagers as we shuffled through the cemetery gate and into the lane. It felt wrong to bask in the sunlight when Ann Claybrook was dead, but I couldn't help myself.

An arm slipped through mine, and I lowered my face from the sun's rays to smile at my friend Mary Hayworth.

"It's far too gorgeous today for a funeral," she said. "Poor Ann."

I nodded. We slowed our pace, letting the crowd pass us and disperse to their homes. After a quick look over his shoulder to ascertain my intentions, Uncle Gerald walked ahead, no doubt thinking about dinner and whether or not Polly, our cook and housekeeper, had remembered to sweep the mud from the foyer.

Peter Amherst, the shopkeeper's son, walked by, and he and Mary gave each other secret smiles. We turned down the shaded lane that led to the Andersons' orchard, and I gave Mary's arm a squeeze.

"Why don't you just run away together?" I asked, as I always did.

"You know why." She leaned her head against my shoulder. "I couldn't bear to disappoint Mother and Father."

"If you want to be with him, I'm not sure you have much choice."

She dropped my arm and drifted to the side of the lane, pretending to look for wildflowers. "It's not that easy."

Mary and Peter had been secretly engaged for two years, but her family was the richest in thirty miles. Her father owned half the farmland surrounding the village, and her mother boasted wealthy family connections throughout northern England. The Hayworths would never allow their daughter to marry a common man who'd have to work his entire life.

I decided to change the subject. These arguments never accomplished anything.

"Don't you find these deaths strange? So many of them in such a short time?"

Mary looked at me, but I could tell her thoughts were still on Peter. "Perhaps it's the heat."

I laughed. "The world will end before it gets hot enough in Harwick to do a person harm."

"What do you think, then?"

I watched my feet rise and fall on the path for the space of a breath before answering. "I think someone killed them."

Mary stopped and gaped at me. "Catherine! You can't be serious."

"I am. Three people found dead in two weeks! It can't be natural."

"Three? You can't include that soldier. He didn't live here."

"He died here."

She didn't reply, just continued walking. I followed. We were quiet for several minutes before she spoke again.

"I think you're overreacting. It's strange, yes, but a murderer in Harwick? I can't imagine anything more far-fetched."

Neither could I, but nothing else made sense.

∞∞∞

I sat with Uncle Gerald in the parlor that evening and pretended to read, though really I was planning my attack.

Our home had a simple layout, with a parlor, my uncle's small study, a dining room, and the kitchen on the main floor, and four modest bedrooms on the upper level. It felt too big for just Uncle and I these days, though when I was growing up with my three cousins, the house felt full to bursting with our antics. The difference was stark, when I let myself think about it.

For now, I had more dire things to ponder. Before he retired two years ago, Uncle Gerald had been Harwick's doctor. He still consulted with the village surgeon, Mr. Haviland, on a regular basis, and I was sure they'd discussed the recent deaths. I wanted the details.

When a violent illness took my parents and Uncle Gerald's wife eight years ago, it left me in his care. Having had three sons, he had no idea how to relate to a twelve-year-old girl. In the end, he decided to treat me like one of my cousins, which meant he indulged my interest in medicine rather than discouraging me as a woman would have. I'd read all of the medical texts in Uncle's study, and during winter evenings, he used to quiz me, giving me symptoms and seeing if I could diagnose the illness. By the time I was eighteen, he could no longer stump me.

The question was whether he would be willing to discuss a real case, not just mere theory.

"Uncle," I said, laying my book across my lap, "I'm disturbed by Ann Claybrook's death."

He looked up from his newspaper and peered at me over his spectacles. "It's very sad. Poor child."

I nodded and ran my fingers along the spine of my book. "Does Mr. Haviland know how she died?"

Uncle lowered his newspaper, and the look he gave me was much sharper than a moment ago. "Catherine, you're not starting in on this suspicion of yours again, are you? Miss Claybrook's death was perfectly innocent. A tragedy, but nothing could have been done to prevent it."

"But how does Mr. Haviland know it was her heart?" I asked. "I mean, what were the signs? The symptoms?" I hoped that, by casting my questions in the vein of our old game, Uncle Gerald would share his knowledge.

It didn't work.

"Catherine." He sighed. "I can't discuss this with you. Even dead, patients have a right to confidentiality. You shall just have to trust my word and that of Mr. Haviland."

"I do. Of course I do. I just wondered how you identify such an invisible illness, that's all."

"That's just the trouble." He rubbed his temples with

his fingers. "You can't identify it until it's too late." He looked out the window. "Too late."

He drifted into his thoughts, and I didn't have the heart to push him further. Despite his steadily receding hair and thinning cheeks, it was only in moments of unguarded emotion like this that he looked his age. I swallowed my guilt as he seemed to shrink in on himself. After a few minutes, he hoisted himself out of the chair, patted my shoulder, and left the parlor.

I retired to my room shortly after, frustrated. I didn't like casting my uncle into a melancholy. I should have realized my questions would turn his mind to his wife and my parents. On the other hand, I desperately wanted to know if there were any strange circumstances surrounding Ann Claybrook's death. When she was first discovered, one of the Claybrook servants went into hysterics, screaming in Gaelic. She was promptly silenced with the threat of dismissal, according to gossip, but I couldn't help my curiosity.

I wanted to know what had frightened her.

two

The next afternoon, Mrs. Ellerby invited me over for tea. She lived in a cottage across the lane and had taken it upon herself to act as my confidante and mentor since my parents died. I didn't tell her I was a twenty-year-old woman and thus capable of choosing my own confidantes and mentors, though sometimes I would have liked to. She meant well, and I didn't want to hurt her feelings. Besides my deep—if often exasperated—affection for her, she also made the best tea cakes in Harwick.

Her husband had died about six years before, and I was surprised—but glad—she hadn't set her cap at Uncle Gerald. With a pleasant plumpness and her hair still more black than gray, she was a handsome woman—but far too silly for my uncle. Fortunately, she seemed to have no interest in remarrying.

I dragged Mary to tea with me, as Mrs. Ellerby was less likely to lecture me in company. She was always delighted to have Miss Hayworth in her home but never felt she could invite Mary herself.

"So tragic, this affair with the Claybrooks." Mrs. Ellerby eyed us eagerly over her teacup. "Losing their youngest child that way."

"Ann was a sweet girl." I took another cake. "A lively presence in any gathering."

"Indeed," Mary said. "She will be missed."

"Yes, of course." Mrs. Ellerby leaned forward and set down her cup, a sign she was ready to reveal her best morsel of gossip for the week. "Have you heard about our newest arrival? A gentleman from Edinburgh has taken a room at the Black Swan."

"Why on earth would he come to East Yorkshire from Edinburgh?" I sipped my tea but couldn't help feeling mildly intrigued. Harwick rarely had visitors, and the Black Swan Inn, which boasted two rooms, slept only a dozen or so guests a year.

"A *young* gentleman," Mrs. Ellerby continued, ignoring my question. "Mr. Brock met him outside the inn. Apparently his father is a wealthy business owner, looking to settle in the country." She paused and straightened in her chair. "A tradesman isn't ideal, of course, but money is money. If they were to move here, it would be a great opportunity for Harwick. In more ways than one."

I wondered if she meant him to marry the entire town, but the way she smiled at Mary revealed her intentions.

"More tea?" Mary asked desperately.

"Come now, Miss Hayworth," Mrs. Ellerby chided, adopting a persuasive, intimate tone. "You've turned down every gentleman in Harwick. You must want to marry."

"I do," Mary said, gazing at her hands.

"I'm sure the gentleman will only be in town for a few days at most," I said, trying to quell Mrs. Ellerby's matchmaking instinct before it could take firm root. "He'll conduct his business and go back to Scotland, and we'll never see him again."

Mrs. Ellerby gazed out the window behind me, her eyes dreamy. "But if he decided to stay..." She gasped. "Oh! The old Markham place! It would be perfect."

The poor man had been in Harwick for less than a day, and already she had planned out his whole life.

"Think of it, Miss Hayworth," she breathed, a hand pressed to her chest. "Being mistress of such a home."

Mary looked at me, her teacup clenched tightly in her hands.

"Perhaps I will marry him," I said loudly, sacrificing myself.

Mrs. Ellerby scoffed. "Don't be silly, Catherine. Everyone knows you're going to marry Freddie Martin. It would be indecent to put yourself in Mr. Hale's notice."

"I'm not engaged to Freddie," I protested, though it did no good. Neither Mrs. Ellerby nor Uncle Gerald—nor anyone else in town, for that matter—believed me when I told them this. They wished me to marry my cousin Freddie, and so I would. It had been this way since I was six years old. The only thing that had saved me so far was that everyone was so sure it *would* happen that no one had thought to *make* it happen. "Perhaps this Mr. Hale and I will fall desperately in love."

Mrs. Ellerby looked at her ceiling, silently imploring it for help. Mary cast me a grateful look, and I placed another tea cake on her plate.

"You cannot have two husbands, Catherine. Stop talking nonsense." Mrs. Ellerby turned to Mary. "By all accounts he is a very agreeable gentleman and quite handsome. I hope someone has a party soon so that we can meet him." She smiled. "We must show him the best of Harwick's hospitality."

Mary pushed the tea cake around her plate. Mrs. Ellerby continued talking.

"A lovely pair you'd make, I'm sure. And if he plans to stay in Harwick, you would even be close to your family! A winter wedding. Oh! Wouldn't that be lovely, Catherine?"

I took a bite of cake, letting it sit on my tongue, but even the miracle of Mrs. Ellerby's baking could not soothe my vexation.

"I despise winter weddings." I set my cup in its saucer with a sharp *clink*.

Mrs. Ellerby sat back in her chair as though I'd slapped her, and I instantly felt guilty.

"I prefer spring," I offered in weak amends.

Mary saved me. "Mr. Hale? He doesn't sound Scottish."

Mrs. Ellerby beamed at her as though she had just recited the whole of *Pilgrim's Progress*. "His father, I am told, is from London. His mother was Scottish."

"How nice."

Our hostess took this as proof of Mary's interest in the gentleman and counted the round as won.

"I'm so sorry," I said as soon as Mary and I were safely away from Mrs. Ellerby's parlor and in the street. "If I'd known an eligible young bachelor had appeared in town, I never would have forced you to come."

Mary swung her bonnet at her side as she walked. "I should be used to it by now. It doesn't usually affect me so badly."

I took her arm. "You should focus on basking in the irony, like I do. You, who have a secret fiancé, are hounded on every side to get married, whereas I, who would very much like to be courted, am never even considered because of my fictional betrothal."

Mary laughed. "Do you talk this way in front of Freddie?"

"Absolutely. He has no more intention of marrying me than I have of marrying him."

She smiled and squeezed my arm. "You'll get your courtship. The trouble is finding someone worthy of you."

I scoffed. "That's hardly the problem. The problem is finding someone willing to look twice at me."

"Don't be silly."

"I'm not being silly. I'm being realistic. Uncle Gerald, Freddie, and I live comfortably, but not so comfortably that I can provide a dowry to attract attention. I therefore have only my beauty and my mind to recommend me, and as I have too little of the first and too much of the second, I am doubly damned."

Mary stopped walking and gave me a stern look. "Catherine Chase, you *are* beautiful."

"Not as beautiful as you," I said, speaking truth. No one was as beautiful as Mary. She was perfection from the top of her golden head to her delicately trim ankles, and everyone in fifty miles knew it.

She waved my words away. "For all the good it's done me. But that's not the point here. The point is that you are pretty *and* clever, what many men would call the best kind of wife."

I looked around. "When you find one of these men, introduce me. I wish to meet him."

An evil look crossed Mary's face, a look I was convinced only I had witnessed. "Perhaps Mr. Hale is such a gentleman."

"Please!" I threw up my hands. "Anything but him. Mr. Hale has only existed in my world for two hours, and already I've had enough of him for a lifetime."

We laughed and took a turn through the neighborhood, not yet willing to give up the afternoon or each other's company. When we turned back onto the lane that led to Uncle's house, we saw a gentleman on a chestnut horse coming toward us. He stood in his stirrups and waved, and I returned the gesture with a girlish enthusiasm I usually pretended I'd left behind me.

"It's Freddie!" I cried.

I clasped Mary's hand in one of mine, scooped up my skirt with the other, and ran. Mary trailed behind me, laughing, the ribbons of her bonnet floating along like the tails of a kite.

We ran to Uncle's house, where Freddie had pulled his horse to a stop and swung down from his saddle. I let go of Mary's hand so I could throw my arms around my cousin as soon as he was in reach.

He lifted me off the ground, just as he did when we were children, and set me down with a warm chuckle.

"I'm glad to see at least one person in Harwick has missed me," Freddie said. "How are you, cousin?"

"Very well," I gasped, out of breath from my run. "Especially now that you're home. How's university?"

"I'll be a doctor before we know it."

I narrowed my eyes and made a show of scrutinizing him. "We'll have to work on your accent. You sound positively southern. Have you no northern pride?"

He grinned. "I'm sure I'll be cured in a few days." He turned to Mary and bowed. "Miss Hayworth. Delighted to see you are well."

"Thank you, Mr. Martin," she said with mock formality, her grin giving her away. "It's been too quiet in town. I'm glad you've returned to liven up our dull parties."

"Such flattery!" he cried. "I'll never leave home again."

We walked with him as he took his horse, Bishop, back to the stable and settled him next to Belle, Uncle's ancient carriage horse. The noise we made in the street had alerted half the town to Freddie's presence by that point, including Uncle Gerald. He met us at the back entrance, the largest smile on his face I had seen in months.

"Freddie, my boy." He embraced his youngest son and then held him at arm's length, patting his shoulders and examining him as though he had been gone years rather than a handful of months. "I didn't think you'd be home until next week. This is wonderful."

They turned to go inside, and Mary quickly took her leave from me and disappeared around the corner of the house. I followed Uncle and Freddie into the dining room, where we had an impromptu afternoon meal, and Freddie regaled us with stories of his exploits—exaggerated, I was sure—from the term.

In turn, we told him of the tragic death of Ann Claybrook and the others, of the parties, the engagement of Miss Stewart and Mr. Horton.

It was hours before I had Freddie to myself, as we had to wait until Polly left for the evening and Uncle retired upstairs before we could speak freely.

"Are you engaged yet?" I asked, smiling.

Freddie made a comically sad face. "I'm afraid not. I did try, you know. Those blasted classes keep getting in my way."

I laughed. "I'll never be free of you if you can't trick some poor, innocent girl into marriage."

"Ah, that's where you're wrong, cousin. You'll never be free of me even when I am married. It's your lot in life to put up with me until one of us dies."

"I shall manage admirably, I'm sure."

Freddie leaned toward me. "You looked fairly bursting with news earlier. Are you ever going to tell me?"

I scooted my chair closer to him, and his expression changed from one of teasing to intrigue.

"It's these deaths," I said. "Don't you find it odd that three seemingly healthy young people would die in such a short amount of time? The tailor's apprentice and now young Miss Claybrook. Also, a soldier on his way back to York from Easington. They can't all be natural."

Freddie considered for a moment, and I wanted to hug him for not dismissing the thought out of hand.

"Tell me more," he said. "How were they found? What does Mr. Haviland say killed them?"

"The tailor's apprentice, Michael Smith, they found in a ditch near Henderson's Field. The soldier they found a few days ago in the Marxtons' well. It is thought he got drunk and stumbled into the well in the dark, which is plausible, I admit, but when coupled with the other deaths, it becomes suspicious."

"How did they die?"

"When it comes to Miss Claybrook and Mr. Smith, Mr. Haviland says their hearts gave out."

"What, both of them?" Freddie sat back in his chair and looked at me while he thought. "It is odd," he said at last, "but if Mr. Haviland made such diagnoses, there must not have been any outward proof of their death. Unfortunately, this makes it nearly impossible to prove they *didn't* die from failed hearts."

I sighed. "I know. It just feels wrong to me. I know

Uncle was brought in as a consultant on the two most recent cases, but he refuses to discuss it with me."

"I'll try him tomorrow. I may have better luck."

I nodded, grateful. "Don't mention we discussed it. He thinks I'm being melodramatic."

Freddie smiled. "You probably are." His smile faded. "Just so I'm clear, you're suggesting that something unnatural killed these people? Something external?"

I hesitated, but there was no way to avoid admitting it. "Yes. Something or someone."

Freddie's gaze drifted to the window and the blank darkness of the night beyond it. "Then I'm very glad I'm home for the summer. If, God forbid, you're right, I could never bear it if you or Father were hurt."

His uncharacteristically serious words made my throat feel tight, and I stood to cover my emotion. "I'm going to bed. Perhaps tomorrow we can go for a walk, and you can point out all the things that have changed since you were last here."

Freddie's smile returned. "Perfect."

I bent and kissed his forehead. Without meeting his gaze, I walked from the room.

three

Mary's parents threw a party that weekend, and I went to the Hayworths' home early so we could plan our strategy for the evening.

"At least there won't be any dancing," Mary said as her lady's maid, Williams, twisted her hair up onto her head. Williams worked deftly, her mouth full of pins.

"Don't rest your hope on that," I warned. "There's a piano forte in your drawing room, and Mrs. Witherpoole will be in attendance. If she's not allowed to play, she'll feel snubbed."

Mary frowned, thinking. "We'll have to get to her early and plant the idea of a somber piece." Her eyes brightened. "In honor of Miss Claybrook." She turned in her chair to look up at me, and Williams had to lurch sideways to keep her hold on Mary's half-pinned hair. "Or is that horrible, using poor Ann's death so that my mother can't force me to dance with whatever gentleman she currently has her hopes set on as my husband?"

"No one needs to know your true motive. Asking Mrs. Witherpoole to play for Ann is a generous, noble thing to do. Everyone will think you eight times more perfect than you already are."

Mary slumped in her chair, and Williams quickly stuck

in several pins. "But *I'll* feel terrible."

"Then I'll do it. I could use some goodwill. And as I am doing it for you, I won't feel guilty." Mary's eyes met mine in the mirror. "At least not much," I admitted.

Mary turned her head from side to side, examining Williams's work, then grinned her approval.

We went down to the drawing room just as the first guests arrived and were soon caught up in conversation. I took Mrs. Witherpoole aside as soon as I could and told her my idea. Tears filled her eyes, and she patted me tenderly on the cheek. I stood speechless, having never seen Mrs. Witherpoole bestow affection on anyone other than her nephew.

"You always were a good girl, Miss Chase," she told me, sniffing. "Even brought up among men as you were."

I nodded and thanked her, then retreated to Mary's side, where I intended to stay for the rest of the evening.

Half an hour later, a hush fell over the gathering, and I turned toward the front of the room to see what had captured everyone's attention.

A gentleman stood in the doorway, eyeing the room with a touch of nervousness. He smiled hesitantly, and Mr. Hayworth hurried toward him. As I had never seen him before, and Harwick was not a large village, he could only be one person.

"Mr. Hale!" Mr. Hayworth said, clearly delighted. "I'm so glad you've come. Please, let me introduce you around."

Mr. Hayworth began the introductions with his own family, which meant Mr. Hale was led straight to where Mary and I stood side by side. Mrs. Hayworth joined us.

"These charming women are my wife and daughter," Mr. Hayworth said with a pride I found touching.

Mr. Hale bowed. "Delighted to meet you, Mrs. Hayworth, Miss Hayworth. You have a lovely home." His accent, though prominent, was not as thick as I expected, and I wondered if he was educated at an English university.

"Thank you, Mr. Hale," Mrs. Hayworth returned.

Mr. Hale looked briefly at Mary and then turned expectantly to me.

"Mr. Hale, this is my dear friend, Miss Chase," Mary explained.

I curtsied, Mr. Hale nodded, and then Mr. Hayworth whisked him away to meet the Fredericks. Mrs. Hayworth moved off in the other direction to commiserate with Mrs. Witherpoole, who waited in readiness at the piano forte, and Mary and I were alone.

"I'd forgotten about him," I whispered. "I didn't think he'd still be in town." I gave her a long, measuring look. "But you didn't forget, did you?"

Mary sighed. "Father called on him this afternoon to extend the village's hospitality. I wasn't sure he'd actually come, as Father never got a straight answer out of him, but I knew it was a possibility."

"Well, your fear was for nothing. He obviously didn't fall instantly in love with either of us—though I'm surprised he was able to resist you. We're safe."

"Safe from Mr. Hale, perhaps, but not from my parents." Mary watched her father escort Mr. Hale around the room for a moment, then turned to me. "I'm thirsty. Let's get some punch."

We stood in the corner, as unobtrusive as possible, and watched the guests gossip and acquaint themselves with Mr. Hale. He appeared a few years older than Freddie. They were about the same height and had the same lean build, but I preferred Freddie's unruly mess of dark blond curls and freckles to Mr. Hale's neat appearance, every strand of his brown hair perfectly in place. He seemed pleasant and polite, but the most striking thing about him was the angry scar across his cheek and nose.

It was not jagged, as villains always had in novels, but smooth, though it curved slightly, stretching back toward his ear. It was a recent wound, though it had healed well. Even as I wondered how he came to have such a scar, I realized every other person in town would wonder the same, and all I'd hear for the entirety of Mr. Hale's stay was how mysterious and dangerous he must be.

Mary tugged on my sleeve. "Such a terrible scar," she whispered. "You don't suppose he's some sort of ruffian, do you?"

I closed my eyes. "No doubt. He's probably a highwayman."

She tapped my arm. "You're teasing me. I'll punish you by monopolizing Freddie's attention for the evening, now that he and your uncle have arrived. You'll have to stand all alone in the corner or else talk with Mrs. Witherpoole."

"You are cruel." I turned toward the room's entrance and watched my uncle and Freddie take their turn with Mr. Hale. Freddie still had his hat in his hands, as they'd just walked in the door. "But I thought you needed me to protect you," I said to Mary. "How can I shield you from your parents' intentions regarding Mr. Hale if I'm not nearby to outshine you with my considerable charm?"

Mary smiled. "If he speaks to me, I'll simply respond in the silliest way possible."

"With Freddie as your guide, I'm sure you can be very silly, indeed."

"You've caught on to the brilliance of my plan."

She left me with a smirk, and I was about to follow when I spotted Mr. Haviland near the punch bowl. Despite Freddie's best efforts, Uncle Gerald saw through his motivation to discuss Ann Claybrook's death and refused to tell him anything. Our entire childhood, Freddie and I performed mischief after mischief under Uncle's very nose, and *now* he had developed the ability to see through our plots. His timing was astounding.

I watched Mr. Haviland fill a cup with punch and made my decision. Mary and Freddie stood on the other side of the room, so I set my cup of punch on a nearby table and approached the surgeon unseen.

"Mr. Haviland," I said. "So good to find you well."

He smiled and dipped his head, and as he was not much taller than me, I could see the balding spot on his scalp. "Miss Chase. Are you enjoying the party?"

"Oh, immensely." I reached for another cup of punch, and Mr. Haviland leapt forward to fill it for me. "But I must confess to being concerned for you."

He spilled a bit of punch, and it ran down the glass and onto the tablecloth. "Oh, bother," he said, his normally ruddy complexion turning a deeper shade of red. He looked for a napkin with which to wipe up the punch, and I handed him one from the stack near the sandwiches. He patted at the stain. "Why would you be concerned for me?" he asked, glancing up through the graying hair that fell across his forehead.

"It's just these deaths. It must be extremely hard to deal with so many tragedies in such a short space of time."

Mr. Haviland abandoned the stain. "Indeed, indeed. Most exhausting. It wears on one's spirit, you know."

I nodded, a sympathetic look on my face.

"The blasted futility of it all!" he exclaimed and then looked stricken. "Oh, do forgive my language, Miss Chase."

I smiled and cocked my head, praying Freddie and Mary weren't watching. "Don't trouble yourself, Mr. Haviland. You forget I grew up with the Martin boys. Despite the reputations of sailors, I imagine Freddie could win a swearing contest in his sleep."

He chuckled. "Yes, but a good lad. He'll make a fine doctor."

I resumed nodding.

"But these deaths! Nothing could have been done, of course, but it's still a shame." He shook his head and gave the punch stain a doleful pat with the napkin.

"You must be very clever to identify an invisible illness," I said, leaning toward him and lowering my voice. "Is it true there are no external signs whatsoever?"

He looked surprised, and I rushed to explain.

"I can hardly avoid talk of medicine with Uncle Gerald and Freddie in the same house. They've so praised your conduct and professional insight in this matter." I hesitated a moment, then lightly placed my hand on his jacket sleeve. "Was it *very* difficult?"

Mr. Haviland cleared his throat, and his ears turned pink. "Well, it's true that heart conditions such as the one that afflicted Miss Claybrook and Mr. Smith often have no outward signs in life, but in death one can find certain clues."

I removed my hand from his arm and nodded, my eyes wide with what I hoped was fascination.

"For instance," he continued, "she was very pale, unnaturally so, a sign her heart had stopped beating. Also, she had several cuts on her arms, neck, and shoulders, which shows that her affliction came upon her quite suddenly."

"How so?"

"She did not have time to sink to the ground in dizziness or pain. Nor did she cry out. Her heart stopped, and she fell into the nearby greenery, which gave her the cuts. She had the most serene look upon her face. I assure you, Miss Chase, she did not suffer at all."

I wanted to ask how, if Ann Claybrook's heart stopped so suddenly that she had no time to react, she was found three acres away from the lane she walked at the time. But Mr. Haviland was gauging my reaction to see if I was as amazed as I should be, and I rose to the task.

"Oh, Mr. Haviland," I gasped, one hand at my throat. "How truly extraordinary that you can pull such conclusions from such trifling symptoms."

His chest swelled, threatening the already strained buttons of his waistcoat. Good-natured to a fault, the surgeon was well-liked and often invited to dine with the residents of Harwick. In the last five years, the effects had begun to show.

"Extraordinary," I repeated, my voice rising in pitch. I could see Freddie moving toward us. "Do excuse me, Mr. Haviland," I said, cradling my forgotten cup of punch in both hands, "but I must greet my cousin."

I turned, ready to intercept Freddie before he reached the surgeon, but he was too quick for me.

"Mr. Haviland!" Freddie said brightly. "How good to see you. And you, Catherine." He gave me a sly look. "Ignoring me, I see. The two of you must be having a fascinating conversation."

I was tempted to throw my punch at him, but Mr. Haviland was delighted to have another person to appreciate his medical genius.

"I was just explaining to Miss Chase how I diagnosed Miss Claybrook's cause of death."

One side of Freddie's mouth twisted upward. "Really? Fascinating indeed. But, Catherine, whatever brought on such a morbid curiosity?" His face was the perfect mix of innocence and concern.

Mr. Haviland looked startled, having not considered my motives until now. He turned to me, and I was just able to erase the glare from my face before he saw it.

"Well," I said, setting my punch on the table so I didn't spill it on my favorite gown, "it makes one consider one's own mortality. I mean, if bright, young Miss Claybrook can die so suddenly, with no warning, why not me? Or you, dear cousin?" I narrowed my eyes a fraction, and Freddie did not miss my implied threat.

Mr. Haviland chuckled. "Dear girl, I'm sure you have nothing to fret over. You're the very picture of health."

"Wasn't Ann?" I challenged.

Freddie touched my arm. "Catherine, if he says you're fine, then you're fine. Now, if you'll excuse us, Dr. Haviland, I was sent here by Miss Hayworth to fetch my cousin. Our hostess is in dire need of Catherine's advice."

"Of course." Dr. Haviland ducked his head, and Freddie returned the gesture.

I slipped my hand through Freddie's arm and dragged him away as discreetly as I could. "You're horrible," I hissed.

He laughed. "Me? You were the one batting your eyes to get information. I saw you put your hand on his arm, you vixen."

My cheeks warmed. I straightened my shoulders and asked in a cool, disinterested voice, "What does Mary need?"

Freddie laughed again and patted my hand. "Good try. Nothing. She's holding her own, quite brilliantly, against her mother's attempts to pair her off with Mr. Hale, though I can't see why. He seems pleasant enough." He looked at me. "I don't suppose you'll tell me someday why she's so picky about men?"

I gave him an apologetic look and said nothing.

"I didn't think so. Did you get what you wanted out of Mr. Haviland?"

I smoothed my dress. "Yes and no. I'm still convinced Ann died from something unnatural, but I'm no closer to knowing what."

"We'll figure it out eventually."

I looked up at him, sure he was teasing me, but his face was sincere. I decided not to pinch him after all.

Mary stood in a small circle with her mother and Mr. Hale. The gentleman seemed attentive, but there was a distinct distance to his manner. I could tell from Mary's relaxed stance that she saw it too. Mrs. Hayworth's rapt, hopeful gaze, however, had missed it entirely.

"Catherine!" Mary smiled when she saw me and pulled me to her side. As my hand was still tangled in Freddie's arm, he came too. Mrs. Hayworth's forehead furrowed slightly at our intrusion, and Mr. Hale looked as though he was trying to remember my name.

I smiled. "What a lovely party, Mrs. Hayworth. Beyond compare, as always."

Mrs. Hayworth's forehead cleared. "Thank you, Miss Chase. Did you find the punch refreshing?"

"Oh, yes," I lied. Freddie made a sound in the back of his throat, and I took back my decision not to pinch him.

He yelped, and Mrs. Hayworth's alarm caused the

feather in her hair to bob. As Freddie assured her he was well, Mr. Hale gave me a knowing look, one corner of his mouth twitching.

"So you're from Edinburgh, Mr. Hale," I said loudly, maintaining my innocent expression with ease. I had years of practice, growing up with Freddie.

Amusement flashed over Mr. Hale's face, but then he was all politeness and composure once more. "Yes, that's correct."

"And how long do you plan to stay in Harwick?"

"I'm not sure, but I doubt it will be too much longer."

No one else stepped into the conversation, and I knew it was because they had taken part in it already. Mr. Hale's face wore the strained patience of someone who had answered the same questions multiple times, but I had nothing else to talk about.

"Do you have business in the area?" I asked. Freddie shifted his weight, twitching his elbow in just such a way that it prodded my ribs, but I didn't know if he meant to stop my desperate repetition or simply inform me he hadn't forgiven me for pinching him.

"Of a personal nature," Mr. Hale responded, and we all nodded.

"Well, you've picked the best time of year to visit Harwick," Mrs. Hayworth said with the mix of authority and enthusiasm she applied to everything in her life. "June is our loveliest month."

Mr. Hale opened his mouth to say something equally bland in response, but before he could, Susannah Brock insinuated herself into our circle. I had never seen such an ill-tempered look on Mrs. Hayworth's face, but Mary looked jubilant. Susannah Brock, with her shining black hair and willowy height, was generally regarded as the second-prettiest girl in Harwick after Mary, now that Miss Ashton had married. No doubt Mrs. Hayworth saw her as Mary's main rival for Mr. Hale's affections.

"Mr. Hale," Miss Brock said, "my brother has just informed me that you love to ride. You must come out with us one morning while you are here. The orchards are particularly lovely this time of year, and there are some magnificent views from the bluffs just beyond our land." She smiled at him much the way I attempted to smile at Mr. Haviland five minutes before.

Mr. Hale inclined his head. "That's most kind. Thank you."

"You wound me, Miss Brock," Freddie said, dropping the arm I held so that my hand slid free and placing his other hand upon his chest. "You know how I've admired you from afar for so many years, and yet you invite another man to go riding in my presence."

I took a small step backward, watching with amusement as Miss Brock's forehead creased. Freddie had teased her in this manner since we were teenagers, ardently declaring his love one moment, then ignoring her for the rest of the night. The poor girl had no idea what to do with him, and usually I felt sympathy for her. Tonight, however, I planned to take full advantage of her confusion to make my escape.

"Oh, Mr. Martin, I didn't mean to offend. I only meant to—"

"No, never mind," Freddie said loftily, adjusting the sleeves of his jacket. "I see your true feelings for me and cannot be consoled with your pity. My dignity won't allow it."

Mr. Hale coughed—to cover a laugh, I was sure—and I looked away to hide my smile. Miss Brock recovered and apologized, managing to secure Mr. Hale's acceptance of her invitation at the same time. If Mary were at all interested in Mr. Hale, Susannah Brock would make a cunning rival, indeed.

Mary moved to my side, having spotted the opportunity for escape as well. "Catherine, I've not yet spoken with Mr. and Mrs. Lacey. Will you come?"

"Yes, of course."

As we moved off, I looked over my shoulder to see that Miss Brock had fled, and Freddie and Mr. Hale were in animated conversation. Freddie's ability to befriend had served him well throughout his life, and I was pleased he might have a friend in Harwick's visitor. So many of his childhood companions were gone, and I lacked the energy required to be his sole entertainment.

Mr. Hale laughed, a brief, unrestrained sound, drawing my eyes, and I wondered what personal business had brought him to Harwick.

Then it was time to greet Mr. and Mrs. Lacey, and I didn't think about the Scottish stranger for the rest of the evening.

∞∞∞

I sat in my room, tucked onto the window seat with my knees to my chest, running a brush through my hair as I watched the clouds race each other across the moon. It was a bright, lovely night, full of stars, and I was too awake from the party to go to bed.

I tried to puzzle out what I had learned from Mr. Haviland, but my medical knowledge was too limited. I didn't think spontaneous heart failure had killed her, but

I didn't know what had, either. I was unable to get Freddie to myself once we returned home, as Uncle Gerald, in a wine-induced bout of misplaced patriarchal responsibility, insisted on seeing both Freddie and I to our bedchambers. I would have to wait until morning to ask his opinion.

I couldn't make sense of Ann Claybrook's death, but that only strengthened my certainty that something terrible had happened to her.

A breeze twisted through the back garden, and I watched the hydrangea bushes dance in its wake. My window looked down upon the path that led from the back door of our house to the stable, and from there down a short slope to the small, wooded creek that ran through the village. It was a narrow, cheerful stream, content with its unimpressive existence. I'd been able to jump over it by the age of twelve, but Freddie and I still spent hours there as children, chasing tadpoles and minnows, returning muddy and flushed with pleasure when Polly called us in for dinner. My parents lived on the other side of the village, only a five-minute run when I was young, but I spent most of my free time in Uncle Gerald's back garden. Its openness left plenty of room for games, and with the woods and stable so close at hand, we never lacked hiding places or secret lairs. My parents' garden was small and surrounded by a rock wall as tall as my father. My mother filled most of the space with flowers, which gave off a lovely fragrance in the warm months but cramped my need to frolic.

I missed my mother's garden sometimes, especially in the spring when Mrs. Ellerby's roses bloomed. I knew nothing about flowers. My mother tried to teach me, but I had no patience for such things at age ten. Now I would never learn.

My hairbrush lay forgotten in my lap as I watched the hydrangeas sway, their blossoms brushing against the side of the stable. A cloud's shadow covered the back garden, and my eyes followed the moonlight as it fled into the woods.

Something moved in the trees, and my hairbrush slid onto the floor as I straightened.

A figure stepped to the edge of the wood's shelter and stopped. A man dressed in dark clothing. I couldn't breathe.

The cloud passed, and in the renewed light, I recognized him. He gave our garden a long, careful look, then drifted backward into the darkness of the woods.

In another second Mr. Hale had disappeared, and I was left to ponder, hands shaking, if I had imagined the whole thing.

four

Uncle Gerald frowned at me. "Catherine, be serious."

"I am!"

He shook his head and took a bite of bread. "You imagined it."

Our cook and housekeeper, Polly, set a plate of ham in front of me. Polly was older than Uncle Gerald by ten years and beginning to show it. In the last few years, she'd slowly become more and more unable to keep up with the daily demands of the house, which meant fires at times remained unlit, bed linen unchanged. We couldn't afford another maid, and Polly was too dear to let go, so I'd taken to quietly performing a few of the household tasks every day. This meant Polly now spent much of her time entering a room, intent on lighting the fire or sweeping the floor, only to discover it'd already been done. She was half-convinced a benevolent faery resided in the house with us.

I shouldn't have found it as amusing as I did, since my interference probably caused more confusion than assistance, but I couldn't help myself. Freddie's bad influence, Uncle would have said.

Polly eyed my empty plate and moved the ham toward me. "Nice and hot, miss. Eat up."

"Thank you, Polly." She bobbed and moved back to the kitchen, and I twisted my napkin in my lap. As soon as she was gone, I said, "I saw him. Mr. Hale was in our woods last night."

"You're sure?" Freddie asked, a frown sitting oddly on his face.

I nodded, hoping he could see the sincerity in my eyes.

Uncle Gerald sighed and rubbed his right temple. "Then perhaps he was lost or looking for his cat. Please, Catherine, eat your breakfast and try not to talk so loudly. You're far too animated for this time of day."

It was nearly noon, but Uncle Gerald did not recover from parties as quickly as he used to. I spread some marmalade on a slice of bread to appease him and busied myself cutting a slice of ham into ever smaller pieces until he stood and announced his intention to read the newspaper in his study.

He left the room, and Freddie stood to follow, but I grabbed his arm and pulled him back into his seat.

"You believe me, don't you?" I asked.

He nodded slowly. "You certainly saw something."

"It was *him*."

Freddie sat back in his chair. "Say it was. Why do you think he was in our woods?"

I paused. I had a theory for this, but even I had to admit it seemed farfetched. "What if..." I licked my lips and gave the slice of bread on my plate a nudge with my finger. "What if he has something to do with these deaths?"

Freddie's eyebrows rose. "However did you reach that conclusion?"

I lifted a fork and pointed it at him. "Have you got a better one? Why else would he be out in the middle of the night?"

"Maybe he has insomnia and takes walks to ease his mind, and he accidentally stumbled into our back garden while following the creek. It runs behind the inn, remember. Or maybe he has a lover and, being new in town, got lost on his way to their assignation. Or maybe, like Uncle Gerald said, he lost his cat or dog or horse or camel." He counted each point off on his fingers. He reached his pinky and wiggled it. "Or perhaps, as you think, he's a murderer. All equally plausible?"

I crossed my arms and slumped in my chair in a manner that would have given Mrs. Ellerby fits. "I suppose I deserve that, but you must admit it's a little suspicious. And he doesn't seem the type to keep a cat."

Freddie put both hands flat on the table and pushed himself to a standing position. "Let's find out, shall we?"

"How?"

Freddie gave me a look and left the room without answering. I scrambled out of my chair and followed. He strode out the back door and down the lawn, ignoring my increasingly insistent questions. When we were within a few yards of the line of trees that marked the creek's path, he stopped and turned to me with his arms crossed.

"Well? Where was he?"

It took me a second to realize who he meant. "Mr. Hale?"

"Yes, Mr. Hale. Or have other gentlemen been seen lurking in our woods?"

"No, just the one," I said stiffly, turning to face the woods. I pointed to the large, gnarled oak to our right. "He appeared there, near the Bulbous Tree."

The corner of Freddie's mouth twitched at my use of our childhood name for the large tree. Its trunk was distorted and swollen by strange growths, its limbs more twisted than those of its neighbors. Dark wizards and witches always lived within it in our youth.

"Then he must have been here for some evil purpose," Freddie said, nodding with mock severity. "His association with the Bulbous Tree is proof of his character."

"I'm never taking you into my confidence again," I declared. "All I get in return is mockery."

"Only when you deserve it." Freddie moved toward the Bulbous Tree, his eyes on the ground.

I followed, scuffing my shoes in the grass. Freddie slowly circled the tree, then moved further into the small wood, half-bent as he scanned the leaf-strewn forest floor.

"Are you doing what I think you're doing?" I asked, crossing my arms, certain he was teasing me.

"Perhaps," Freddie called back. "Especially if you think I'm doing something brilliant."

"I think you're doing something ridiculous. When did you become such a great hunter that you feel you can track a man through a wood? You've never even killed a pheasant."

Freddie straightened and glared at me. "Just because I don't enjoy shooting doesn't mean I don't know a footprint when I see one."

My arms fell to my sides. "Do you see one?"

"Well, no," Freddie replied, and my annoyance rose. "But I would know one if I saw it."

I waited for him to tire of his search and return to me. When he did, it was with a shrug.

"I see no sign anyone was here last night."

"Which means nothing," I said. "We've already established that hunting and tracking are in no way your specialties."

"*You* established, you mean." Freddie looked at the sky and then back at me. "But you have a point. Just because he left no visible sign—a convenient apple core or monogrammed handkerchief, for instance—doesn't mean he wasn't here."

"*Thank* you."

"So where does that leave us?"

I pushed a wayward lock of hair behind my ear. "Standing in the garden like idiots?"

Freddie nodded. "Precisely."

We turned and headed toward the house.

"You know," Freddie said, "if Mr. Hale were connected with these deaths, wouldn't he have had to arrive *before* they happened? It's rather hard to kill someone if you're in a different country at the time."

My steps faltered. "Oh." I could feel Freddie's smirk, but I refused to look at him. "That's a valid point."

"I rather thought so when it came to me. University must be doing me some good after all."

"*That*," I said, poking him in the arm, "remains to be seen."

Instead of fading, his smirk grew. "You know, if you're so curious about Mr. Hale's nightly habits—"

"I am not!"

"I'm riding with him tomorrow. Why don't I just ask?"

I felt my eyes widen. "Don't you dare."

"You want to know, don't you?" He raised one eyebrow in challenge and lengthened his strides.

I lifted my skirt and gave chase. "Freddie, don't! Please!" He kept walking, ignoring me, and I tripped over my shoes, barely catching my balance. "Freddie, don't you dare! Freddie? *Freddie!*"

∞∞∞

I sat curled in my window seat that night long after Freddie and Uncle Gerald were asleep, my eyes scanning the edge of the woods for movement. I had no particular reason to believe Mr. Hale would return, but I had no reason to believe he wouldn't.

I couldn't decide if I wanted to know what he was doing or not. A terrible certainty sat in my stomach, and despite Freddie's logic, I couldn't escape the feeling that Mr. Hale's strange behavior and these deaths were somehow connected.

Time passed, but I couldn't tell how much. My eyelids felt heavy, and I leaned against the window. Its coolness seeped through the thin fabric of my nightgown, but soon even that was not enough to keep me from sleep.

A noise woke me some time later, and my body jerked away from the window. My knuckles hit the glass with a sharp rap, and the sound brought me fully alert. Feeling foolish, I shifted my legs, intending to abandon the window seat for my bed, when I heard a horse whinny. Again, I realized, as that must have been what woke me.

I paused, one foot on the floor, and looked out the window. It was a swift, casual glance. I expected to see nothing but darkness, the vague mass of the stable and forest. Instead, the sky was clear, the moon was bright, and I could see the stable doors, the hydrangea bushes that ran along its side, the path that led to the creek.

And the woman standing in the open area just before the woods.

She wore an old-fashioned dress, almost medieval, the

kind one saw in Arthurian paintings. The moonlight reflected off her skin, and she seemed to glow. Despite the distance between us, I could feel her gaze on my window. On me.

Longing filled me, a desperate need to be with her.

Before I could examine my impulse, I stood and walked to my bedroom door, easing it open, then moved down the stairs as quickly and quietly as possible. My bare feet would have been noiseless if the stairs themselves didn't creak. Once on the main floor, I raised my nightgown and ran on my toes through the dining room and into the kitchen. I knew the layout by heart, every rug, every piece of furniture. The stove, the basin. The longing within spurred me on, and despite the dark, my fingers found the bolt of the back door on their first try.

I couldn't open the door fast enough. The need to have her gaze upon me made my legs shake.

The latch turned, the door opened, but my run was checked before it began.

The woman was not alone. A man stood a few yards from her.

Mr. Hale.

The woman looked at him, and I felt the loss of her attention like a blow. My chest tightened, cutting off my breath.

Mr. Hale reached one hand behind his back, his movements jerky, and the woman lifted an arm. In a movement made of grace, she turned her hand palm up and beckoned to him. His hand dropped. He straightened, seemed to relax. The woman beckoned again, and he took a step forward.

The last of the longing deserted me, replaced by a wave of fear. The tightness in my chest cracked, and air rushed into my lungs. I stepped forward, nearly tripping over my dread, and screamed.

"Mr. Hale!"

He flinched, and the woman turned toward me. Her eyes met mine across the distance, and the longing returned with such force that I swayed.

Mr. Hale shouted something I didn't understand. The woman's eyes left me, and I sagged against the doorframe. A hunting knife appeared in Mr. Hale's hand.

The woman and Mr. Hale looked at each other for several breaths. He shouted, but I couldn't make out the words. The woman moved toward him, gliding, her hand outstretched. Mr. Hale seemed to waver, but then he slashed at her with the knife, and she fled. After a quick glance toward me, Mr. Hale followed in pursuit.

I sank to my knees, and each breath I took felt as though it scoured my lungs. I didn't understand what I had just witnessed, if I had saved a life or allowed one to be taken. I wondered if there would be another dead body in Harwick tomorrow, and the thought made me sick.

The floor behind me creaked, and I lifted my head to see Freddie frozen in the kitchen doorway. As soon as my eyes met his, he gasped my name and rushed forward. He took my shoulders in his hands and pushed me upright.

"Catherine, what happened? Are you hurt? Are you all right?"

I closed my eyes and shook my head, unsure which question I was answering. I couldn't speak.

He wrapped one arm around my shoulders, pulled me to my feet and away from the door. As he fumbled the ill-tempered latch closed with one hand, I leaned my forehead against his shoulder and breathed. The latch clicked, and Freddie shifted against me. Before I realized his intention, he slipped an arm behind my knees and lifted me off the floor. We were halfway up the stairs before I found my voice and protested.

"I'm not hurt, Freddie," I said, my assurance weakened by the fact that I lay limply against him, my hands clinging to his nightshirt. "You can put me down."

"I will. On your bed. And then you're going to tell me what happened."

He moved quickly but quietly past Uncle Gerald's room and slipped through the open door of my bedroom. I expected him to drop me on the bed as though I were a stack of linens, but he set me down gently, and his tenderness broke the last barrier inside me. I began to cry.

Freddie knelt before me, his hands wrapped firmly around mine, and said, "What happened, Catherine? I've never heard you scream like that."

I couldn't decide which I wanted more: for him to believe me, or for him to tell me I had imagined it all. I met his gaze, about to tell him what I saw, but something in his eyes stopped me, a protectiveness I'd never seen before. I realized his fear for me had awakened within him the instinct to fight.

And I knew with sudden, unshakeable certainty that if I told him what I had witnessed, he would go out into the night and search for Mr. Hale and the woman, and that if he did, it could be his body we found tomorrow.

I gripped his hands as though I could anchor him there, and he watched me, expectant.

"I thought I heard something," I said, bringing every ounce of truth I could muster into my voice. "I went downstairs to see if perhaps it was Mr. Hale. I...I'm afraid I had worked myself into quite a state by the time I reached the door, and when I opened it, I startled a fox, and...

well..." I looked away, feigning embarrassment. "It was rather useless of me, and now you'll tease me about it for the rest of my life."

Freddie narrowed his eyes. "Really?"

I faced him. "Yes."

He studied me for a moment, then sighed and released my hands. He stood and said, "And you're really all right?"

"I'm fine, Freddie. But thank you."

"Then perhaps tomorrow you will tell me what really happened."

I looked at my lap. "Perhaps."

"Goodnight, Catherine."

I watched his feet move into the hall. My bedroom door shut, and I was alone.

I lay back on my bed and covered my face with my hands, seeing again and again the strange encounter between Mr. Hale and the woman. I felt the fear as she beckoned him toward her, the longing when her eyes met mine, the lurch of dread when Mr. Hale pulled a knife and gave chase.

I didn't sleep until sunlight brushed my window.

five

The next morning at breakfast, I could hardly hold my silverware. Every time Uncle Gerald or Polly spoke, I jumped, anticipating news of another death in the village. Freddie watched me, but I couldn't discern if the look on his face was one of concern or knowing amusement.

No news had come by the time I finished my tea—no frantic knock on the door, no suddenly remembered tidbit from Polly, who heard it from her son Daniel, our gardener and stable hand, who heard it in town that morning. This only served to heighten my nerves.

Freddie followed me about the whole morning as I beat rugs, swept the parlor, and dusted Uncle's bookshelves. At first he talked to me about his lectures at university, the way he and his friends passed their weekends and the rare free evening, but when I continued to ignore him, focused on my tasks, he lapsed into silence. Which, coming from Freddie, was nearly as unnerving as what I had witnessed the night before.

When I ran out of things to occupy my hands, I made the mistake of catching his eye.

"Are you going to tell me yet?" he asked, arms crossed.

I straightened a candlestick so that it lined up with its

mate. "Freddie—"

"No, Catherine. Tell me."

For a moment I couldn't speak, as I'd never heard him sound so stern. I was afraid to look at him. "I can't tell you what I saw when I'm not sure myself."

He took my shoulders and steered me to the sofa, then pushed me down onto it. I looked up at his face, but I couldn't tell what he was thinking.

"I didn't ask you to tell me what it *means*, Catherine, just what you saw."

I nodded, smoothing my skirt over my knees, and told him about Mr. Hale, the woman, my fear, the knife. When I dared to look up again, Freddie wore every emotion I had felt in the last twelve hours upon his face, and I felt as though I could breathe for the first time since I woke up that morning.

"My God," he said, staring at me. "No wonder you've been in such a state."

"I have not," I protested, but it was so weak Freddie didn't even bother arguing with me. He stood and paced the room, and I watched, glad to let someone else bear the weight for a while.

"I'm to go riding with him this afternoon!" Freddie cried.

"You won't now, will you?" I asked, my fingers twisting together.

He stopped and faced me. "There was no news this morning, no woman found dead. Perhaps…"

We stared at each other for several slow ticks of the grandfather clock, possibilities traveling unspoken between us.

I shrugged. "I am open to any guidance you have. You know everything I know."

Freddie resumed his seat next to me and glared at the rug. "The problem," he said at last, "is that we don't really know anything at all. About Mr. Hale or the mysterious woman."

I waited, afraid I knew what he meant to do.

"There's nothing for it." He stood and looked down at me, his arms crossed. "I'll have to go riding with him after all."

"Freddie—" I started to stand, but at his look I sank back onto the sofa. "Please. He saw me. He'll have no reason to think you don't know everything."

"With good reason, obviously," Freddie said with a sudden flash of grin. "But surely standing him up would make it apparent I do, indeed, know he spent last night chasing women around with a knife. If I go, his certainty will be shaken. He'll wonder. He'll probably spend as much time trying to get information out of me as I will out of him." He paused, considering. "Sounds rather fun, actually."

I felt my shoulders sag. There was a logic behind his reckless decision, and I could tell by his stance that his mind was stubbornly set on playing detective. Nothing I could say would dissuade him.

"Very well." I stood. "While you're riding, I'll call on Mary and go to the shops. Perhaps I'll hear some news."

He smiled his approval, and the clock struck the noon hour.

"Lunch!" he shouted, pulling me toward the dining room as though we were in danger of missing the meal. I made him pause at the study door so I could wake Uncle Gerald from his nap, then allowed myself to be dragged to the table. By the time Freddie deposited me in a chair, I was laughing so hard my sides ached.

An hour and a half later, in a flurry of coattails and a frantic, last-minute search for the proper hat, he was gone.

∞∞∞

"Have you heard?" Mary asked the instant she saw me.

The ground seemed to swoop beneath my feet. "Heard what?"

She gripped my arm. "Joseph Reep was found dead this morning, half a mile outside the village."

"The innkeeper?"

She nodded.

I closed my eyes, reminding myself to breathe. I'd never fainted in my life, but I felt dangerously close to it. Mr. Reep, owner of the Black Swan Inn, where Mr. Hale was staying.

"Catherine?"

I forced my eyes open. Mary peered into my face with concern.

"You've gone pale. Are you feeling all right?"

"Yes. No. I'm not—" I raised a shaking hand to my forehead.

"You're ill," Mary said firmly. "I'm taking you home."

"No!" My outburst startled us both. I took a deep breath. "I think the walk will be good for me."

Mary gave me an uncertain look but started for the High Street. I walked beside her, my mind churning with guilt and horror. I'd seen Mr. Hale the night before, clearly threatening a strange woman with a knife, and I'd done nothing. And now Mr. Reep was dead.

I stumbled. Freddie was riding with Mr. Hale today.

Was probably already far from the village, alone with the other man.

I reached for Mary and clasped her arm to my side. "Distract me. Please."

She stopped. "What is it? You look terrified. Tell me what's wrong."

I shook my head. "Please, just distract me. Tell me about Peter. Anything. I just need to think about something else."

"Mr. Reep's death has you this upset? You were hardly close."

"Mary, please."

She sighed, let me resume my hold on her arm, and started walking again, her pace brisker than before. "Fine. Don't tell me." Before I could protest or beg further, she continued, her tone clipped. "Peter's fine, though I haven't seen him in almost three days. It's been terrible."

I forced a laugh. "Three days! How tragic."

"Just wait," she said in a threatening voice. "Someday you'll know how this feels, and you won't be so quick to make fun of me."

We reached the High Street and headed to the Amhersts' general store. Half a dozen other people filled the store, but Peter seemed to sense Mary's presence. He looked up from the counter and his eyes found her immediately. Somehow, without moving a muscle of his face, his entire countenance warmed. Mary smiled and ducked her head, and then we were surrounded by excitedly dismayed villagers.

Mary and I did our best to listen to the five versions of the discovery of Mr. Reep's body that came from the five matrons in front of us, led by Mrs. Ellerby.

"Heart failure!" my neighbor declared, her eyes wide.

Like Michael Smith and Ann Claybrook before him. I was not at all pleased that my theory about the deaths seemed to be correct. Three people suffering the same unpredictable and unpreventable affliction within a fortnight could not be a coincidence.

"The inn will have to close, of course," Mrs. Ellerby said, "Mr. Reep being without family. Poor Mr. Hale will be on his way, I suppose." She brightened, her gaze landing on Mary. "Perhaps your family could put him up, Miss Hayworth! Your parents have always been most generous, and it wouldn't do for the village to let the poor man be without a roof over his head."

Mary made a noncommittal noise, and I stiffened at the mention of Mr. Hale. It sounded as though Mr. Reep hadn't been stabbed, and I knew of no way Mr. Hale could forcibly induce heart failure, but that didn't change the suspicious and threatening nature of his behavior the night before. His purpose in town could not be good, whatever it was.

Mrs. Witherpoole entered the shop, and Mrs. Ellerby and her friends descended on her, allowing us to escape. Mary pulled me toward a display of buttons. Peter joined us almost immediately.

"Can I be of service?" He nodded at me and smiled, and I managed to give him a warm smile in return.

"Horrible news about Mr. Reep, isn't it?" Mary asked.

"Indeed, Miss Hayworth. Very tragic." His eyes slipped toward the shelf. "Are you in need of buttons?" I could hear the smile in his voice.

"These small black ones," Mary said, pointing at a jar. "How much are they a dozen?"

Peter dipped his head, as though to hear her better. He was tall and built like a sapling, but I had seen him lift hundred-pound sacks of grain above his head as though they were full of air. The top of Mary's head was even with his shoulder, and she lifted her face to his. They were a matched pair, with their golden hair and blue eyes. Their children would be exquisite.

I turned and pretended to be engrossed in a selection of sewing needles as Mary and Peter whispered to each other. With nothing to distract me but a basket of needles, my mind swung back to Freddie. Surely he was all right. Mr. Hale wouldn't try something in broad daylight, only hours after another death had been discovered in the village. But if Freddie took him out along the cliff paths, they'd be miles from anyone for most of the ride, and only a few short feet from the cliff's edge and a drop straight into the rocky sea.

"Miss Chase?"

I turned. Peter and Mary looked at me, their faces concerned.

"Are you all right?" Peter continued.

I swallowed and forced myself to smile. "Yes, Mr. Amherst. Thank you. I'm just"—I looked at the shelf before me—"in need of some new needles." I plucked a set from the basket and held them up. "And now I'm content."

Peter smiled. "Shall I add those to your account?"

"Oh, no. I'll pay for them now. My uncle will grumble at me, otherwise." I reached in my purse and pulled out the appropriate coin, which Peter accepted with a nod. "Are you getting anything, Mary?"

"Miss Hayworth has decided against the buttons today," Peter said, a playful look in his eye. Mary bit her lip to keep from grinning.

"She usually does." I looked at Mary. "Should we go, or do I need to examine the silver polish?"

"No, we should go." She seemed to wilt.

"Thank you for your help, Mr. Amherst," I said, pulling Mary toward me.

Peter nodded. "My pleasure, Miss Chase. Miss Hayworth." He brushed his hand against hers in such a way that no one else in the store could see.

"Mr. Amherst." Mary nodded, flashed him a quick smile, and then led me to the door, determined to get outside before her resolve failed.

We exited the store and paused at the edge of the street. Clouds had covered the sun, so we left our bonnets off, preferring to let the breeze play with our hair. Across the lane, a group of wide-eyed villagers were in passionate discussion, gesturing toward the inn at the end of the row.

"Shall we walk?" I asked.

We made our way toward the far end of the High Street, and I listened to passing conversations. Everyone we passed was talking about Mr. Reep and wondering what would become of the inn, and wasn't it a shame the poor man had no family? I imagined the quiet, kind man lying twisted in the middle of the road, his eyes wide and glassy, his skin pale. His face became Freddie's face, and I wrapped my arms around my body and quickened my pace. I needed to go home. I needed to find my cousin.

I turned down the first residential lane we came to, and with a surprised sound, Mary followed me.

"Catherine?"

"I need to go home," I said. "I think I am ill."

Mary caught up with me, and I could see her trying to angle her body enough to see my face without tripping. "You're worrying me, Catherine. Tell me what's wrong."

I shook my head. "I can't."

"That answer is not making me worry less."

"It's the only one I have."

"Is it Freddie?"

I stopped and looked wildly around, my movements jerky. "Where?"

Her eyes narrowed, but before she could say anything else, I resumed my frantic pace.

I turned a corner, Mary nearly trodding on my heels, and as if I had summoned him with my thoughts, Mr. Hale stood before us. I gasped.

"Mr. Hale," Mary said, her voice shifting quickly from surprise to warmth. "How delightful to see you. Are you heading to High Street for some shopping?"

"No," he said shortly, his eyes on me. Then he seemed to remember himself. "No shopping for me today. I have... other business."

Mary nodded and turned her head slightly toward me. It was my turn to make conversation, but I couldn't ask any of the questions fighting for dominance in my head. The way Mr. Hale looked at me, as if trying to read my mind, did not make it easier to think. A sudden stab of panic made my stomach lurch. If Mr. Hale was here, where was Freddie?

"I'm surprised to see you, Mr. Hale," I said, fighting to keep my tone in check. "I was under the impression you were riding with my cousin today." Mary gave me a sharp look, which I ignored.

"Ah, yes. I'm afraid I had to disappoint Mr. Martin this afternoon." His gaze somehow intensified, and I took a small step backward. "A personal matter came to my attention late last night that, when combined with Mr. Reep's death, places a certain urgency on my current situation."

"Oh, dear," Mary said as I tried to remember how to breathe. "I hope you're able to sort everything out to your satisfaction. I'm sure there are plenty of families in the village who would be honored to have you as their guest."

"I'm sure you're right, Miss Hayworth. And now, if you'll excuse me." He nodded to each of us and continued around the corner.

Mary and I both turned to watch him, and once he had gone from our sight, Mary tugged me into motion.

"Poor man," she said. "I hope the personal matter he alluded to is not something to do with his family. He looked distressed, don't you think? Tired. Understandable, though, as he no longer has a place to stay."

I wanted to point out that chasing women through the woods in the middle of the night would make anyone tired, but instead I said, "I'm sorry, Mary, but I have to go."

"I'll come with you."

"No, please."

"But I'm worried. I want to make sure you're okay."

I squeezed her hand. "I'm fine. I'll see you tomorrow, all right?"

She sent a sharp look in the direction Mr. Hale had just disappeared, then nodded and backed away. She turned toward her house without saying good-bye, but I could apologize later.

I lifted my skirts and ran.

I took the shortcut to Uncle Gerald's house. It required climbing two fences and shimmying beneath a hedge, but I didn't see anyone else in the ten minutes it took me to sprint across the village.

I burst through the back door and into the kitchen, ignoring Polly's protests and cries of dismay at my appearance as I dashed toward the front of the house. The front parlor was empty, but I found Uncle Gerald in his study.

"Where's Freddie?" I gasped.

Uncle Gerald started and looked up from his book, squinting at me through his bifocals. "Good heavens, Catherine, what happened? Were you attacked?"

I looked down at my grass-stained dress and pulled a leaf from my sleeve. "I tripped. It's nothing. Is Freddie here?"

Uncle Gerald sighed, a sound I remembered from my childhood, and waved a hand. "He's in the stable, grooming his horse. Can't imagine why, when we've got Daniel to do these things for us. He'll spoil that stallion of his, treating it like a pet. It's not a dog, it's a horse..."

The rest of Uncle Gerald's speech was lost to me as I retraced my steps through the house, startling Polly once again in my haste to get back outside. Her shouted admonition about ladies and manners was cut off as the door slammed shut behind me. A few seconds later I was in the stable, blinking at its dim interior. I could hear someone murmuring to my right, a few stalls down, the kind of gentle, constant sounds used to calm horses.

"Freddie?"

The murmurs paused, and then I heard him say, "Catherine?" Hay swished as he moved to the front of the stall, and my eyes adjusted enough to see him poke his head over the door.

Repeating his name, I rushed down the stable aisle and threw my arms around his neck—an awkward motion, as the stall door still stood between us.

Freddie pried me off. "What's happened this time?"

"I saw Mr. Hale in town, and you weren't with him, and I thought maybe he'd murdered you, and then he looked at me and I could tell he knew that I saw him last night, and oh, Freddie, what if he *does* try to murder you? Or me? Or someone else? What if he murdered Mr. Reep?"

Freddie pushed me gently backward until he had room to open the stall door. He stepped out, giving his horse a quick rub when it nudged him in the shoulder, then turned toward me.

"Mr. Reep died of natural causes."

"Yes," I snapped. "The same natural causes that killed Michael Smith *and* Ann Claybrook."

"Which, I concede, is a very suspicious coincidence," Freddie said evenly, "but I must again point out that Mr. Hale was not here when they died, so it's unlikely he's the cause of either death."

I crossed my arms and looked away, unable to argue with him. He was right.

"You're worried Mr. Hale might murder me?" he asked. I didn't need to see his grin. I could hear it in his words.

I was suddenly grateful for the dim interior of the stable. "Among other things," I said stiffly, "like him murdering *me* for witnessing...whatever I witnessed last night. With the knife and the chasing."

Freddie laughed, and I stomped toward the stable door, whirling to face him again after a few steps and nearly causing him to run into me.

"You were fine with the plan this morning," he said. "What changed?"

"Mr. Reep changed. And I was never fine with it." I straightened and glared at him. "Well, tell me what happened this afternoon, then. You were so excited about having a battle of wits with the man while you rode, and here you are, talking with a horse instead. Fat lot of good you are."

Freddie shrugged, his hands dropping away from me. "It's not my fault Mr. Reep's death puts him in something of a bind. He was very gracious about it, but I was firmly turned away, manners or no." He shrugged again, then ducked his head to see my face in the light from the door. "What's all this about him seeing you?"

I turned slightly away, my hands smoothing my skirt. "I could tell by the way he looked at me, as though he were trying to dissect me with his eyes. He knows I'm the one who saw him last night, and he didn't like it."

Freddie made a thoughtful noise and moved past me, out into the sunshine. I followed.

"You're sure he wasn't just looking at you oddly because you were having a nervous fit in the middle of the lane?"

"I was not having a fit!" I said loudly.

He shook his head. "You're overexcited, Catherine. Your imagination is running away with you. How certain were you, before you hurtled into the stable, that I was dead?"

I bit my lip instead of answering.

"Look at it objectively, Catherine. How do you see your encounter with him this afternoon in the cold, distant light of logic?"

I closed my eyes and relived the short conversation, remembering the strength of my shock at seeing him, and the surge of panic on Freddie's behalf.

"Fine," I grumbled. "It's possible his scrutiny was provoked by my odd behavior."

Freddie grinned. "There. See?"

"But Mr. Reep is still dead of mysterious causes, and I still saw what I saw last night. And that is far more odd—not to mention ominous—than anything I may have done today."

He paused, then nodded. "Very well. Compromise achieved. What now?"

I thought a moment, my gaze sweeping the woods behind our house. "I want to talk to the Claybrooks' servants."

six

Late afternoon of the next day, I entered the Amhersts' general store, Freddie close behind me. I'd tried to convince him to stay home, as it would be easier to talk to Peter without an audience. My friendship with Mary had long ago translated into a friendly acquaintance with Peter, but that was not something I could demonstrate in front of my cousin if I wanted to protect Mary's secret.

Freddie, however, brushed all my reasons and excuses aside, determined not to miss a moment of what he had started calling our Grand Mystery. I reminded him that four people were dead and Mr. Hale was prone to chasing people through the woods with a hunting knife, which knocked his jocularity down a notch or two but only made him more resolute in not allowing me to do anything related to the mystery on my own.

Peter came toward us, a polite smile on his face. "Miss Chase, Mr. Martin. What can I do for you today?" He looked at me. "Were the needles unsatisfactory?"

I shook my head. "They're fine, Mr. Amherst, thank you. I'm here on a personal errand, actually."

Peter rocked back on his heels and clasped his hands behind his back. His eyes had gone cautious, and they flicked quickly toward Freddie before returning to my face. "How can I help?"

I smiled reassuringly, hoping Freddie hadn't noticed the exchange. I felt him hovering at my elbow. "I found this prayer book in the lane." I lifted the slim volume I'd found in Uncle Gerald's study. "It was near the Claybrooks' place, and I think it must belong to one of their help."

Peter relaxed slightly and nodded.

"I don't want to disturb the Claybrooks for something so small," I said, "and I'm afraid that if I tried to go around to the kitchen in order to find the book's owner, whoever I met would feel obligated to notify Mrs. Claybrook of my presence, which just wouldn't do. They're still in mourning, you know. I don't want to be a bother."

"Shall I keep it here?" Peter asked. "Mrs. Boyd, their cook, comes in once or twice a week."

I blinked, and Freddie tugged at one of his cuffs, likely to cover a laugh. He was no help at all in situations like this and never had been.

"Oh, no," I said quickly, "I wouldn't want to burden you with it. Perhaps you know when Mrs. Boyd will next be doing her shopping? I'd prefer to meet her myself. That way I could discreetly inquire if there's anything I can do to help the Claybrooks through this terrible time."

Peter gave me a warm smile, and I saw again how easily Mary had fallen in love with him. "Of course, Miss Chase. We usually see her in the store on Tuesday and Saturday mornings, so I'd suggest coming back tomorrow. I'm sure she can see the prayer book back to its owner."

I dipped in a shallow curtsy. "Thank you, Mr. Amherst. You've been most kind."

Peter bowed his head and moved to assist a pair of women who'd just entered the store. I dragged Freddie through the door and out onto the street.

"You're amazing," he said, looking at me in wonder. "You were always a fabulous liar, of course, but you've gotten even better since I went to university. *I* believed you, and I knew better. The bit about discreet inquiries was especially brilliant. How could he disappoint such a kind, charitable, humble creature as you?"

I covered the flush of combined shame and pleasure by turning and heading toward home. "You're just impressed because you're such a terrible liar. You would have suffered three times the whippings as a boy if I hadn't been around to talk you out of trouble."

"For which I am eternally grateful, in case I've never mentioned it."

"You haven't, actually."

"Well, now I have." He adjusted his hat. "What does the rest of this plan of yours involve?"

∞∞∞

The next morning, we loitered on the outer edges of Harwick, waiting for Mrs. Boyd. We'd been there since dawn, and Freddie hadn't forgiven me yet for waking him up while it was still dark outside.

He leaned against a tree and yawned. The tree, a lovely young apple, stood at the far edge of the Claybrooks' small orchard, a few yards off the path. I could just see the corner of their house around the bend in the road.

"What if she doesn't come?" Freddie asked, the first part of his sentence muffled by his yawn.

I flattened a few blades of grass with the toe of my shoe. "Then we'll try again on Saturday."

He yawned again. "She'd better come. I can't remember the last time I saw this side of a sunrise. It doesn't agree with me."

I stared down the lane, willing Mrs. Boyd to appear. She didn't seem inclined to obey, as the lane remained empty.

Freddie pushed himself away from the tree and slouched over to stand next to me. He rubbed a hand over his hair, mussing it terribly. "So we're waylaying this poor woman in the road to ask her...what, exactly?"

"When the search party found Ann Claybrook and brought her body back to the house, Mrs. Boyd apparently took one look at her and started screaming in Gaelic. I want to know why."

He gave me an insolent look. "Because she was upset that Miss Claybrook had died, maybe?"

I shook my head. "It was more than that. The gossip reports say she was inconsolable and nearly walked out. Something frightened her, something more than the tragic but natural death of a young girl."

Freddie raised an eyebrow.

I sighed. "All right, *maybe*. But that's why we're going to ask. And you look just like your father when you do that."

He straightened. "Do what?"

"Sneer at me with your eyebrow. That's exactly what Uncle Gerald does whenever Mrs. Ellerby tries to get him to diagnose her terrier."

"You can't sneer with an eyebrow."

"*You* can." When he seemed pleased at this, I reached up to flatten his wild hair. "You also look like you just rolled out of bed."

"I did." He smirked. "Do I get to play with your hair, as well?"

"Only if you can put it back just as you found it."

He eyed the dozen or so pins holding my hair in place and raised his hands in surrender. I smiled in triumph, and turned to look down the lane once more.

Thirty minutes later, a solid-looking woman appeared, walking toward us from the direction of town, and I realized I didn't know what the Claybrooks' cook looked like.

"That her?" Freddie murmured.

"Um."

"You don't know, do you?" He sighed and turned a small circle in the grass. "So you only give the impression of having this perfectly planned. It's really a sham."

"You've caught me. Now shut up."

The woman drew near enough to dip her head and smile, and I stepped forward.

"Excuse me, are you Mrs. Boyd, the Claybrooks' cook?"

She stopped, and her gaze grew guarded. She gripped her shopping basket with both hands, as though we might try to rob her of her flour and oats. "Aye. You're Miss Chase, yes? What can I do for you?" Her Scots accent was thick, much thicker than Mr. Hale's.

"I wondered if I might be of service somehow to Mrs. Claybrook. I knew if I asked her directly she would never admit to needing anything, so I thought perhaps you might have some idea of a way I could..."

I wasn't sure how to end that sentence, but I didn't need to. Mrs. Boyd's face softened, and she released her basket with one hand so that she could brush her fingers across her cheek. "It's been right hard on her, it has, losing her youngest like that, and both her other children married and gone already. Just her and Mr. Claybrook, all alone in that house." She sniffed.

"Miss Claybrook's death was a shock," I said. From the corner of my eye, I saw Freddie nod, then sadly shake his head at his boots. "And so horrible, too. I can't imagine what you—the house as a whole, I mean—must have gone through when she was found as she was."

Mrs. Boyd looked toward the Claybrook home, her eyes widening. "'Twasn't natural, I can tell you that much, no matter what that doctor says. You southerners might call it naught but a bedtime story, but I know what fell things roam at night."

I bit my tongue to keep from smiling at Mrs. Boyd's reference to us "southerners." To most of England, Harwick sat in the northern wasteland, our dank and dreary lands good for little more than sheep grazing and the running of wool and cotton mills. I tilted my head to allow the bright June sun to warm the back of my neck and fought to keep a straight face.

"What, like highwaymen?" Freddie asked.

Mrs. Boyd shook her head. "Far worse than any mortal man could be, young sir. Mark my words, if the *baobhan sith* have come to Harwick, we'd all be best served by leaving."

I caught my breath.

"I'm sorry, the what?" Freddie asked.

The cook drew back, and her eyes darted to either side. "Nothing, Mr. Martin. I was just prattling about old faery stories, that's all. Nothing of import."

"No, please," I urged, reaching toward her sleeve. "Tell us, what are...*baavan shee*? Is that what you said?"

Mrs. Boyd shook her head and backed away. "I didn't say anything. You just—" She stopped and looked at me. "If you want to help Mrs. Claybrook, I reckon the best thing would be just to come and sit with her a while. Visit with her, give her someone to talk to."

I nodded. "I'll do that. Thank you for your help."

With one last look at both of us, she turned and hurried toward the house. I grabbed Freddie's arm.

"*Baavan shee*! What do you suppose she meant?"

He shrugged and pulled me deeper into the trees. Cutting through the orchard would lead us to the creek, which we could follow home. "She mentioned bedtime and fairy stories. Obviously she thinks some mythological creature killed Ann Claybrook."

I stopped and gaped at him.

Freddie rolled his eyes. "Oh, for heaven's sake, Catherine. She's not *right*."

He shifted his grip on my arm and propelled me forward. I hardly noticed, busy going over the details of the night scene between Mr. Hale and the strange woman for the twentieth time. I sighed. The woman had been strange, but she was a woman.

"I didn't *actually*—"

"Yes, you did." Freddie sent me an amused sideways glance. "For a second, you absolutely did."

I wrenched my arm out of his grasp and smoothed my hair. "It's a strange situation, and she was very...certain."

He smiled, then stumbled as a yawn seemed to take over his entire body. "We got up that early for a fairy tale."

I scuffed my feet through the grass, kicking a small green apple. It bounced off a nearby tree trunk. "Sorry," I muttered.

"That's all right. We've still got Mr. Hale to suspect of dastardly deeds."

I felt the expression on my face darken. We did indeed.

seven

Uncle Gerald sighed and handed me the letter he'd just finished reading. "Not another party. We just went to one."

"It's summer," I said, opening the letter. "Everyone wants to take advantage of the weather." I scanned the wording of the invitation.

"Who is it this time?" Freddie asked from his sprawled position across the parlor's sofa.

"The Laceys." I held the letter toward him, and he nearly fell off the couch stretching to take it from me.

"No doubt in honor of their guest," Uncle Gerald said. "They've given Mr. Hale the use of the empty cottage on their grounds."

Freddie's eyebrows rose. "That's unexpected."

"Not at all," Uncle Gerald said, settling himself deeper into his armchair. "A smart arrangement on both their parts. Mr. Hale gains a small amount of privacy for the duration of his stay, and Mr. Lacey puts his cottage to financial use." He sighed. "I'm not going. I can't keep up with you younger folk, and I won't try."

"I'm not going, either," I announced.

Freddie sat up, his waistcoat twisted around his torso. As he wrestled it back into place, he gave me a sharp look through his fringe. "Nonsense, Catherine. You know you'll regret missing it if the entire village shows up and you don't."

I shook my head. "Every unmarried woman in town will be doing their best to capture his attention. I have no desire to participate in such a display."

"Quite right," Uncle chimed in. "It'd be unseemly, you marrying Freddie and all."

Freddie and I exchanged the same look we'd been exchanging for the last ten years.

"Come on," he urged. "The Laceys are good people. You don't want them to feel snubbed, do you?"

I wavered, and he pounced.

"Besides, it'll be amusing, watching the women of the town at work." He paused, the look on his face growing mischievous. "I might start a bet."

As much as I wanted to stay as far away from Mr. Hale as possible—him and his unsettling stare, not to mention his knife—Freddie was right. There was a certain social obligation involved.

"Oh, I suppose," I said. "As long as you promise to keep me entertained."

Freddie grinned. "Of course. Maybe we'll even make headway in our Great Mystery."

I considered that a moment, then slowly smiled. "You can finally have your battle of wits."

"Precisely."

Uncle Gerald sighed. "I don't know what you two are talking about half the time."

∞∞∞

Freddie and I walked into the Laceys' front hall, arm in arm. A wiry servant stepped toward us and took my shawl and Freddie's hat. He gave us a short bow, then waved a hand toward an open set of double doors. Laughter and light spilled through them in equal measure.

"The drawing room's just through there, if you please."

"Thank you, Marsh," Freddie said, leading me toward the party.

I looked over my shoulder to see the servant disappear into a small cupboard with our items. "Did the Laceys get a new servant?" I whispered. "And how do you know his name?"

"I pay attention," Freddie whispered back. At my look, he continued. "I met him the day I didn't go on a ride with the mysterious Mr. Hale. He was kind enough to fetch Mr. Hale from his room for me, bring me some tea from the inn's kitchen, then kick me out once it was clear Mr. Hale didn't have time for me. Nice chap. I like him."

"But why is he manning the front door?"

Freddie shrugged. "Maybe he was bored."

We entered the drawing room and took stock of the persons assembled. Behind us, I heard the bell at the front door and the steps of Marsh as he went to answer. Mrs. Lacey greeted us, expressed her hope that Dr. Martin was well, then rushed off to meet the next guest to enter the room. Mary hadn't yet arrived, but Mr. Hale stood in the far corner, listening politely as Mr. Richardson regaled him on some subject.

"Well?" I tilted my head toward Mr. Hale's corner. "Now's your chance—go battle his wits."

"All right," Freddie said brightly, then latched onto my wrist and dragged me across the room with him.

I swatted at him twice before remembering where I was. With an odd skipping step, I increased my pace to match his instead of pulling against him.

"I'll get you back for this," I murmured out of the corner of my mouth. Freddie beamed at me, and then Mr. Hale had noticed our approach and all I could do was smile. Freddie released my wrist as we joined the conversation.

"Mr. Martin," Mr. Hale said with what seemed to be genuine warmth. "I'm sorry, again, that I had to cancel our ride."

"Completely understandable," Freddie replied. "I'm glad to hear you've found a new place to lodge until your business is complete."

"The Laceys have been very generous." He turned to me and dipped his head. "Miss Chase. A pleasure to see you again."

Freddie and I exchanged pleasantries with Mr. Richardson, who then excused himself to go speak with Mr. Brock. I turned to see that the Brocks had indeed arrived, Susannah wearing her most flattering gown and already eyeing our corner.

"So when do you anticipate your business being complete?" Freddie asked. He flashed a smile. "Not that we desire your departure."

Mr. Hale gave me a quick look before answering. "I'm not certain. At first, I thought I might only be in Harwick for a few days, but now I'm not sure when I'll be departing. It could be a day or two, it could be a few weeks."

"What sort of business is it that's so fickle?" I asked.

He blinked once, then said, "My father is interested in the abandoned estate outside of the village. He wishes to retire and thought, due to its condition, that it might come at a comparably small price for its size and serve as an adequate country house. I came down to examine it, to see if it could be adequately renovated, and sent him my report. Now I await his instructions, but first our solicitor must contact their solicitor, who must in turn contact the family..." He spread his hands.

"The Markham estate?" Freddie said. "It's been empty for years, perhaps decades. Is it really worth refurbishing?"

"Possibly. That's for my father to decide."

The Markham estate sat on a large chunk of land half a mile outside the village and was one of the larger houses in the area, though that wasn't saying much. By the standards of someone from a city like Edinburgh, it would seem no more than a dilapidated farmhouse. It had been empty my entire life, slowly giving way to the elements. We'd often played there as children, drawn by the inherent spookiness of any abandoned house.

"Why not go home while he negotiates?" I asked. "I'm fond of Harwick, but there can't be much of interest here after such a city as Edinburgh." Before he could answer, I added, "And aren't you a part of your family's business? Surely there's work to be done." I paused. "What exactly is your family's business?"

Mr. Hale studied me for a moment. "You're very inquisitive, Miss Chase."

"She's gotten worse with age," Freddie said.

Mr. Hale ignored him, still addressing me. "First of all, I see no point traveling back to Edinburgh when I would most likely simply have to turn around and come back to hire a staff and oversee the first stages of renovation. Second, I find myself more than occupied at present in Harwick. And third, I am a partner in my father's business and have dedicated the last few years of my life to helping him grow it to its present size. My mind is rather absorbed with other things lately, however, so I have made my report and opinion known on the estate but am leaving the daily business doings to my father, for the moment, while I focus on other matters."

"And that business?" I prompted.

"We're printers, Miss Chase."

"I see," I said simply to have some sort of response.

"A new family would be good for the town," Freddie added weakly.

Mr. Hale finally turned his attention back to my cousin. "Indeed. Now, if you'll excuse me, Miss Brock has been trying to catch my eye for several minutes. To avoid her any longer would be rude."

With a brief bow, he left me and Freddie to our corner. We turned as he left, our eyes following him as he stopped in front of Susannah Brock and bowed. I noted somewhat vaguely that Mary and her parents had arrived.

"Well, that was more or less useless," Freddie said.

"Useless?" I hissed, poking his arm. "Didn't you *hear* him? He all but admitted he's up to something nefarious."

Freddie turned to me. "Where on earth did you get that? He's a printer. He might buy a house. How is that nefarious?"

"All that nonsense about being 'more than occupied' and having other things on his mind. Plus, at the Hayworths' party last week, he said his business in town was personal. Now he claims it is business. What do you make of that?"

"Buying a house is a personal business."

I frowned. "Oh. I suppose that makes sense."

"Thank you."

We watched Mr. Hale talk with Miss Brock for a few seconds in silence. Susannah was at her most charming, but Mr. Hale's attention seemed focused elsewhere. After only a few minutes of conversation, he took his leave and crossed the room to greet Mr. Hayworth.

"Well," Freddie said, "I'm glad I didn't put my money on Miss Brock as the Harwick lady destined to win Mr. Hale's heart."

I covered a short laugh with my hand. "Who did you decide on, then?"

Freddie tugged at one of his cuffs and smirked sideways at me. "You, actually."

My laugh turned into a choke, but before I could protest, music filled the room. The Laceys' home wasn't quite large enough to have its own ballroom, but one of their front rooms, when cleared of furniture, was easily large enough for six couples to stand up together. Eight, if they did not mind being crowded. An excited murmur rose toward the ceiling, and the party quickly shifted into the other room. After a few minutes, one of Mrs. Witherpoole's favorite jigs began, and couples took the floor.

Mary moved against the flow of people, reaching out to take my hand when she neared us. We watched the crowd thin out. In the new, relative quiet, the jig covering much of the noise of conversation, Mary turned to me and smiled.

"It's a lovely evening, isn't it? I love the Laceys' house." She looked fondly around the room.

"Yours is much grander," I pointed out.

"Perhaps, but theirs is so...cozy." She looked at me. "Like yours."

"You're a disgrace to your station in life," I told her.

She grinned and turned to my cousin. "Freddie, are

you going to dance with me tonight?"

"Absolutely," he replied, then winced as the pianoforte missed a chord. "But let's give Mrs. Witherpoole a few songs to warm up, shall we?"

Mary laughed. "As you wish." She turned toward the front room, then stopped. "Are you coming?"

I gestured toward the refreshment table. "In a moment. I haven't had a chance to try the punch yet."

"Me either," Freddie chimed in, so quickly his sentence nearly ran over mine.

Mary shook her head. "I'm not sure how the two of you manage to be separated long enough for Freddie to go to sleep, much less spend months on end at Guy's."

She moved toward the door, and Freddie bodily dragged me toward the refreshment table.

"Do you think he's really here about the house?" he asked, carefully filling a cup with punch.

I glared at him and refused, for a long moment, to take the cup he held toward me. "Oh, *now* you're suspicious?"

He filled a second cup. "Of course I'm suspicious. You saw him running about in the middle of the night with a knife. I just like to point out the flaws in your irrational accusations." I spluttered, but he talked over me. "So—the Markham estate. Real or a fabrication?"

I thought a moment, taking a sip of punch. It was quite good, light and fruity without being overly sweet. "I don't know," I admitted. "It could be either, though I can't imagine anyone of supposed wealth actually wanting to live there."

"Maybe they're not that wealthy. Maybe the Markham place is just right for them."

I shrugged.

He knocked his punch back as though it were something much stronger and made a humming noise. "We're very bad at solving mysteries."

I smiled and opened my mouth to tease him in return, but a voice stopped me.

"Miss Chase?"

Freddie's eyes widened, and I turned, my stomach shrinking against my spine. Mr. Hale walked toward us, stopping a few feet from me. He looked normal, if slightly nervous. It was hard to believe he was somehow connected to the recent deaths.

On my first attempt to speak, no words came out. I closed my mouth, coughed delicately—I hoped—into a fist, and tried again. "Yes, Mr. Hale?"

"I wondered if I might have the next dance."

Freddie made a small noise in the back of his throat. I stared at Mr. Hale for a few long seconds before realizing he required an answer.

"I—suppose."

Mr. Hale held out a hand and looked at me expectantly, and I panicked. I glanced over my shoulder at Freddie, but he seemed stunned beyond speech for the first time in my memory.

Having no other choice I could see, I placed my hand in Mr. Hale's and allowed him to lead me to the dance floor.

We took our place at the end of the row of couples. He bowed and I curtsied, and then we began the dance, stepping toward each other and then away. We spun, our hands came together for a brief moment, and then we returned to our original positions.

After completing a cycle of the dance, I felt recovered enough to scrounge up a few shards of courage. As I tried to come up with a way to casually bring up his late-night adventure, Mr. Hale spoke.

"I must thank you, Miss Chase, for saving my life the other night."

He pitched his voice so low I could hardly hear him, but his look was so sincere, I missed my footing and stumbled through the next few steps of the dance.

I knew I was gaping in a very unladylike manner, but I couldn't help myself. "Wh-what?"

"The other night, when I was in your back garden. You must remember." He seemed almost amused by my discomfort, and indignation restored my composure.

"Oh, you mean the night you chased a woman through the woods with a knife?" I hissed. "I do remember."

He looked away for a moment, a strange emotion flickering across his face, and then returned his attention to me. We spun around each other, our backs whispering inches apart, and then stepped away. As we closed again, he leaned forward and asked, "Why did you shout like that? Did you know I was in danger?"

My hand slipped from his as I remembered the dread of that evening. "No," I said automatically, but even as I did, I knew it was a lie.

Mr. Hale seemed to sense this, as well. He gave me a sharp look. "No? Then why?"

"I...I was..." I was suddenly very aware of the couple beside us, of the many eyes throughout the room watching our every move. Any words I could have used to describe what I felt that night dried up inside me, and I was aware only that I was dancing with Mr. Hale and half the village was watching.

"Enthralled," Mr. Hale said.

I blinked and pulled my gaze away from the shocked face of Mrs. Ellerby. "Pardon?"

"You were enthralled. By the...woman. She was trying

to lure you out of the house, wasn't she? If I hadn't shown up, she probably would have done it."

I remembered my hands grappling against the door latch, frantic to get it open. "No," I whispered.

"It seems I saved your life as well. That will save me a spot of obligation." Mr. Hale's eyes were sharp, but there was something familiar in them. Something that reminded me of Freddie.

He was teasing me.

Ire replaced my dismay. I yanked my hand from his grasp and ceased dancing. He looked at me in surprise. So did half the room, but I could spare them none of my attention. I was fully focused on the man before me, the man who seemed to know what I experienced that night, who was obviously involved in this whole situation somehow, and had the nerve to make light of it.

"How dare you?"

Mr. Hale blinked. "What?"

The dance ended, the couples dispersing toward the refreshment table or card room. Under the cover of the noise of dozens of conversations striking up around us, I took a step closer to Mr. Hale and spoke so that only he could hear me.

"How *dare* you? People have *died,* and you're a part of it. You may feel you can joke about it to me, thinking you're safe, but you're *not.* I know your purpose in Harwick is of the darkest sort, and I will not stand by and let you commit any more of these crimes. I will *not.*"

I said all this in a frenzied whisper, my hands in fists at my sides. I couldn't imagine the image we must have made.

Mr. Hale looked at me, his eyebrows lifted slightly. "Are you finished?"

I tried to ease my breathing, but I felt as winded as if I'd just raced Freddie to the swimming pond. "Yes."

"Good. I want to explain something to you."

I stepped back. "I have no wish to hear your explanation or to ever speak with you again."

"Miss Chase—"

I turned and walked as quickly as I could toward the exit. I could feel my hands start to shake and pressed them into my hips. Every person in the room watched me leave, and their whispers followed me into the foyer.

"To make such a scene in front of everyone—"

"—and engaged to Mr. Martin! The shame—"

"—obviously a lover's tiff. Have you ever seen anything so horrid?"

It took all my self-control not to break into a run, but somehow I made it into the foyer and out the front door. When I was halfway down the drive, I heard Freddie call my name. I kept walking.

Gravel crunched behind me, and Freddie's voice called again, much closer. I lengthened my stride but only managed three more steps before he caught my arm and spun me around.

"What on earth are you doing?" he asked. "Are you trying to get yourself killed?"

I tried to yank my arm out of his grasp, but he was either worried or angry—or both—and too strong for me.

"Let go. He's horrid, and I won't be in the same room with him."

"Who, Mr. Hale?" Freddie pulled me closer. I couldn't help meeting his eyes, and what I saw there stopped my struggles. "He dashed right into the middle of a conversation to insist I come after you immediately before you did some damn fool thing like walk home by yourself."

My indignation returned. "And what is it to him if I do? I'm perfectly capable of getting myself home. Are you afraid I'd get lost?"

"Catherine." Freddie's voice was low, the voice he used to soothe his horse. I bristled at the implication, but his next words sent my heart into my throat. "What happened to the last young woman who went walking alone at night?"

I stared at him, suddenly flooded by images of Ann Claybrook lying pale and translucent in her coffin, horrified by what I had almost done.

By what Mr. Hale had almost made me do.

"Freddie!" I pulled him down the drive to the street. "Mr. Hale!"

"Yes, I know. You made quite a spectacle of yourself, apparently. He looked upset."

"*He* looked—? Freddie, he's *behind it all*. He admitted as much!"

His eyes widened and he rocked back on his heels. "What, he *told* you?"

"He knew all about the strange woman I saw that night. He knew..." I swallowed. "He *knew*. They're connected."

He looked at me for a moment, then started walking, his hand still firmly clamped around my wrist.

"Freddie?"

"We're going home, and then you're going to tell me what happened between you and Mr. Hale before I hear it from someone in the street."

I caught a glimpse of the fierce look on his face and decided not to speak until we were safely indoors. Instead, I tried to make myself useful by peering into the hedges and trees we passed as we walked. Once I saw a dark shape that made my steps falter and my breath hitch, but it was only Mrs. Harker's wash, which she'd left outside again.

eight

We reached home without incident, and Freddie pulled me inside and bolted the door behind us. The parlor was dark, which meant Uncle Gerald had already gone to bed. Freddie lit a candle. Once the flame caught, he set it on the mantel, then settled himself on the sofa and looked at me expectantly. I gingerly lowered myself onto the edge of an armchair, as if it would swallow me if I rested the entirety of my weight upon it.

Freddie didn't speak. He just looked at me and waited.

I relayed my conversation with Mr. Hale as faithfully as I could. In retelling, it took on a somewhat different light. "And then I...well, I told him I never wanted to speak to or see him again and stormed out."

I shifted, suddenly feeling embarrassed under Freddie's steady gaze.

"And how does this fit into your theory?" he asked.

I looked at the candle, watching the small flame twitch. "I don't know."

"It certainly puts a different spin on things, what with you saving his life."

"He could still be dangerous," I said, giving him a sharp look. "Have you considered that it could all be a trick on his part? He knows I saw him and is trying to cast his involvement in the best possible light."

"Perhaps," Freddie responded evenly, "but we also can't dismiss the fact he may have been telling the truth."

"Either way, he's admitted his involvement. I was right on that count."

He held up his hands in a conciliatory gesture. "I never said you weren't." At my look, he added, "Tonight, at any rate."

I stood and began to pace. "What now? We know for certain Mr. Hale is wrapped up in this somehow, but in what way? Did he cause these deaths?" I stopped, looking at my cousin without really seeing him. Instead, I saw Mr. Hale's sincere face before me as he thanked me for saving his life. My frown deepened. "Is it possible the events aren't related at all?"

"While we're asking questions," Freddie said, moving to stand in front of me, "what about this woman? Where is she?"

I blinked at him, sure my mouth hung open. "Freddie! You're brilliant!" Grinning, I lunged forward to hug him. My enthusiasm caused him to stumble backward to keep his balance, but before he regained it, I'd already let go of him and resumed my pacing. "Of *course!* Why haven't we seen her in the village? Who is she? There aren't many places to hide. Can she have moved on already? If so, why the short, clandestine stop? To meet Mr. Hale?"

I was still pacing and excitedly running through idea after idea twenty minutes later when Freddie gave up on me and went to bed.

∞∞∞

I woke late the next morning, my mind still tired from its feverish speculation the night before. I rolled onto my side and pulled the quilt over my head, stifling a groan. Judging by the amount of light streaming through my window, I'd missed breakfast.

After a lengthy internal debate with myself, my complaining stomach won, and I threw off the covers and went in search of clothing.

When I reached the main floor, I could hear Uncle Gerald and Freddie discussing something in the study, but I turned and instead went to the kitchen, where I convinced Polly to let me have a slice of the bread she'd baked for lunch. I slathered it with jam, smiling at childhood memories of sticky fingers, and took it back to the foyer. I paused outside the study door, but after catching a sentence of two of the clinical conversation occurring inside, I decided to take my breakfast outside.

I opened the front door to find a day quickly being overcome by clouds and Mr. Hale standing on our doorstep.

For a second, we stared at each other, he with one hand raised, preparing to knock, and me with a jam-covered thumb in my mouth.

"Miss Chase." He lowered his hand and cleared his throat. "Good. I was hoping to speak with you."

I stared at him, slowly becoming aware I still held my thumb between my lips. His eyes flicked toward it, and I pulled it from my mouth and lowered my hand to my side, trying to ignore the warmth shooting up my neck into my face. Across the street, Mrs. Ellerby's curtains twitched.

"Mr. Hale," I said. "How—" My instinctively polite

greeting dried up in my throat.

He shifted his weight. "May I come in?"

"No." I straightened, reclaiming the dignity my jam and bread had stolen from me. "I don't think that's a good idea."

"Please." That damn sincerity was back, filling his eyes, and I wavered. He saw my weakness and pressed forward. "*Please*. I wish to explain."

I shook my head and took a step backward, preparing to shut the door, but Freddie bounded up behind me.

"Hello, who's here?" Though I couldn't see him, I felt his surprise through the fingertips that suddenly pressed against my back. There was a miniscule pause, and then Freddie collected himself. "Mr. Hale, what brings you here today?"

My cousin gently pushed me aside and ushered Mr. Hale into our house.

"Mr. Martin," Mr. Hale said with a nod. "I trust you are well?"

"Oh, very. Very. Please, come into the parlor." Freddie led Mr. Hale toward the parlor door, halting on its threshold to look back at me. Mr. Hale did the same.

"I'm just going to…" I lifted my half-eaten breakfast in explanation, then fled toward the kitchen. Once safely ensconced in the warmth and smells of Polly's domain, I tossed my bread onto the counter and collapsed into a chair at the small table where Polly and her son, Daniel, took their meals. I leaned over and buried my face in my arms.

"Whatever's the matter with you, dear?" Polly asked, patting me on the head as though I were eleven. "You haven't got that stomach ailment going around, have you?"

I shook my head without lifting it. Polly hovered for another few seconds, then went back to her lunch preparations, mumbling about how I used to come sit with her for ages, I did, back when I was little, and how I'd ask all sorts of silly questions like who invented bread, but now I was grown up I didn't have time for old Polly anymore...

Mr. Hale was in my house. Mr. Hale currently stood or sat in our parlor, talking with Freddie and probably Uncle Gerald too about the weather or politics or whatever men talked about when they were alone.

He'd come to see me.

I groaned, not ready to relive the conversation from the night before. There was still too much to think about, too much to figure out. I'd felt myself drawing closer to an answer of some sort, to a reason behind all the strange things that had happened in this town, but Mr. Hale had snatched it out of reach, twisting everything I thought I'd understood until it no longer fit in the puzzle the way I expected.

It didn't help that Freddie seemed to believe him.

Polly slammed a cup of tea on the table in front of me, and I jumped, lifting my head and sitting back in my chair. She gave me one of her looks, jabbed her chin at the tea, and said, "Go on, then."

"Thank you, Polly."

She turned back to the fire, and I decided to take her advice. Instead of drinking the tea, however, I stood and smoothed my dress. There was only one way to figure out what Mr. Hale was up to, and that was to ask him.

I turned toward the kitchen door, only to be nearly smacked in the face when it flew open.

"There you are!" Freddie pulled me into the hallway. Still recovering from nearly having my nose bashed in, it took me a second to regain myself and yank my wrist from his hand.

"What are you on about?" I demanded.

"Mr. Hale wishes to speak with you, and you're hiding in the kitchen."

"I was just on my way back."

He shot me a disbelieving look. "Not soon enough. Father's currently setting him straight regarding our supposed engagement. Wouldn't want him to get any ideas, after all."

I closed my eyes. "Wonderful." I followed Freddie down the hallway. "What does he want?"

He shrugged. "Probably to tell you whatever he wanted to tell you last night before you stormed off in a strop."

"I was not in a strop!" I hissed. We were nearly to the parlor.

"You were, and you know it. Now get in there." Freddie opened the door and shoved me inside, following close behind so I couldn't escape.

I had no intention of escaping, however. I walked confidently into the middle of the room to greet Mr. Hale, who stood at my presence. I gave him a small curtsy. "Mr. Hale. Forgive my behavior earlier. I'm afraid your visit took me by surprise."

He bowed his head. "Only if you'll forgive me in turn, Miss Chase. I did not mean to interrupt your snack."

I felt my cheeks warm but refused to acknowledge either my flush or the small cough Freddie gave behind me.

"Mr. Hale wishes to speak to you, Catherine," Uncle Gerald said, pushing himself out of his armchair and moving toward the door. "He says it is a matter of some importance and confidence." He gave me a long, hard look as he walked past me, as though if I were not properly warned, I might fling myself into Mr. Hale's arms as soon as the door was closed.

"Shall I have Polly bring in some tea?" Freddie asked, being pulled toward the exit by his father.

I looked briefly at Mr. Hale, then shook my head. "We don't want to take up any more of Mr. Hale's morning than necessary."

Uncle Gerald looked slightly mollified by this, and Freddie tossed me a small salute before shutting the door.

I turned to Mr. Hale. "You wanted to speak with me?"

"Yes. I..." He seemed to fumble for words for a moment, then waved his hat toward the chair to my left. "Won't you sit down?"

I lifted my chin a fraction higher. I didn't think the muscles in my back could tighten any more, but I refused to add a false sense of comfort to a decidedly uncomfortable situation. "No, thank you."

He nodded, studying me, and leaned over to set his hat on a nearby table. "Very well." After a few more seconds of silence and staring into my face, he said, "I'm glad to see you made it home all right."

My fingers twitched, and I clasped my hands in front of me, hoping to hide the movement. Mr. Hale's eyes never left mine, and I sensed he knew he'd surprised me. "I would have thought you'd be glad to see me come to harm, considering what I've seen."

I'd surprised him in turn but felt no triumph in it. Hurt quickly replaced the shock in his face. "Is that truly what you think of me? No wonder your words were so hard last night."

"Imagine the scene from my view, sir, and tell me how you would react."

He looked away and raked one hand through his hair,

causing it to stand up in licks.

"You had a knife," I reminded him, "and you chased after that woman. How could I misinterpret your intent?"

"That *creature*," he spat, moving quickly toward me, "is no woman. Once, perhaps, but now she merely wears the shape of a woman the way you wear that dress."

I retreated before his anger. The almost tangible quality of his hatred took my breath away, and I backed into a bookshelf. A copy of Jenner fell to the floor.

Mr. Hale stopped, his eyes widening, and stumbled backward across the room. When we stood against opposite walls, as much space between us as was possible, he said, "Miss Chase, forgive me. Please. This...black passion of mine is not directed at you." He closed his eyes and shook his head. "I've just destroyed any hope of making you believe me."

I didn't trust myself to speak. My hands gripped the shelves behind me, and I watched Mr. Hale where he stood, sagged against the wall. His hair, still mussed, made him look young, which only enhanced his helpless expression. Somewhere in the midst of the fear still dominating my body, I felt a tiny spark of something else, something softer. My fingers released their hold on the shelf.

He straightened slowly, as though tired, and raised his face to meet my eyes. "I should go."

"Yes," I whispered.

Mr. Hale moved toward the door, then paused, his hand on the doorknob. "I have no right to ask, but please, Miss Chase—don't go anywhere alone after dark. I don't want..."

I kept my gaze trained on the lamp between us.

He hovered near the door a moment longer, then left.

His hat lay forgotten on the table.

∞∞∞

I couldn't sleep.

Having told Uncle Gerald that Mr. Hale wished to inquire as to his chances with another young lady of the village—hoping Mary would forgive me when the rumour spread, as Uncle Gerald's mind would naturally turn to her first—and having told Freddie nothing at all, I retired to my bedroom immediately after lunch, pleading a headache. Freddie knocked a couple of times, but I ignored him.

I needed to think. Mr. Hale's passionate outburst was alarming, both in its intensity and because I had no idea what it meant. I suspected Freddie had been right all along and Mr. Hale had nothing to do with the death of Ann Claybrook and the others, but that still left the puzzle of the mysterious woman to be solved.

Remembering the pull she'd had on me that night, I shivered. Mr. Hale had called her a creature, and I imagined, had Mrs. Boyd heard him, she'd have agreed. Lying in my dark bedroom, listening to the wind outside my window, it was not at all hard to entertain otherworldly possibilities.

But it was ridiculous. The strange creatures that populated myths didn't actually exist. Faeries and giants could no more walk down High Street than a unicorn or a sphinx.

I crawled out of bed and moved to my window, peering through the darkness toward the tree-lined creek. Clouds covered the waning moon, and I could make out little more than the darker mass of the woods against the sky. There could be a battle happening beneath my window, and I wouldn't be able to see it.

I turned back to my bed but then pulled on my dressing gown and moved to the door instead. Uncle Gerald had gone to bed a while ago, but I hadn't heard Freddie come upstairs. Knowing I'd find him in the study, either finishing some horrid gothic novel or sleeping beneath one, I crept down the stairs.

A warm, low light emanated from beneath the study door. Freddie looked up from his book when I entered. He sat up, tossing the book aside, and tried to stand, but the motion had to wait while he was overtaken by a yawn. He stretched, then sagged back against the chair.

"What wretched manners," I said, moving toward the bookshelves. My fingers trailed along the leather spines. "Don't you know you're supposed to stand when a lady enters the room?"

Freddie yawned again. "As you couldn't be bothered to dress like a lady, I can't be bothered to treat you like one. You'll have to settle for being treated like Catherine."

I felt one corner of my mouth lift in a smirk. "Good. I much prefer being Catherine, anyway." I scanned the shelves in front of me, hoping for a mythological title hidden among Uncle Gerald's medical and scientific texts.

His clothes rustled as he flopped sideways in the armchair, limbs sprawling off in various directions. "Headache gone, I take it?"

I sighed at the sarcasm in his voice. "I needed to think."

"Did it work?"

"Not even a little."

He rolled out of the chair and came toward me, waistcoat unbuttoned and hands in his pockets. "What are you looking for?" He nodded toward the shelves.

I shrugged. "Nothing in particular. Just...couldn't sleep. Thought one of Uncle's more boring books would do the trick."

He didn't challenge me, and I felt a stab of guilt. Lying had become too natural for me since Ann Claybrook died.

Giving up on the shelves, I moved around the desk and toward the window, looking across the front lawn to the lane that separated our house from Mrs. Ellerby's. The light from Freddie's lamp reflected off the glass, restricting my view, so I used one of the tricks of our childhood and pulled the curtain around me, shutting out the rest of the room. The lamp's beams thus blocked, I could see into the night, the light streaming out the room's other window falling on the grass and the hedge that marked our property line. My eyes moved distractedly over the familiar scene, barely taking in the tree trunks or the front gate. I could hear Freddie moving behind me, chuckling softly at my behavior and flipping the pages of a book.

I leaned against the glass, my mind replaying the scene between Mr. Hale and the strange woman yet again, and wondered for the first time if I truly wanted to know the truth.

Then something moved in the darkness. I stiffened as a form took shape just beyond our hedge. It was too small for Mr. Hale, and long hair hung loose around its shoulders. My breath caught as I realized it must be the mysterious woman.

"Freddie," I hissed. He joined me almost instantly, pulling the other curtain around him in identical fashion to mine.

"Oh," he said, more a startled exhalation than a word.

His sudden movement and the change in light did not

go unnoticed. The figure turned, looking directly at us. The weak lamplight touched her face, and I gasped and stumbled away from the window, tripping on my dressing gown and falling.

Freddie helped me to my feet, his face white, and hauled me out of the room into the relative safety of the unlit foyer. We clung to each other's arms, breathing hard, for several seconds.

"Was that..." he started, then swallowed and shook his head.

"Yes." I could feel my hands shaking where they gripped his forearms. "Ann Claybrook."

nine

Freddie and I stood in front of the Laceys' house and stared at the cottage just visible behind it, Mr. Hale's new lodgings.

"How do you know this will even work?" Freddie asked. "You did throw him out of our home yesterday."

"I didn't throw him out," I said testily, trying not to wring my hands. "He left of his own accord."

"He didn't act like a man leaving of his own accord. He looked devastated."

Instead of responding to that statement and the shrewd look that accompanied it, I said, "He called that woman—the other woman, the original one, not..." We exchanged a look. "Right. He called her a 'creature.' He said she wore the shape of a woman the way you or I wear clothing." I took a deep breath and looked back toward the imposing house. "He'll be able to explain what we saw last night."

"I certainly hope you're right," Freddie muttered. "I'm not sure anything can explain it. Nothing *should* be able to explain it." He closed his eyes and rubbed his forehead. "I've spent the whole of the night and morning wishing you hadn't seen it too, so I could tell myself it was simply a hallucination brought on by the fancies of novel-reading."

"Now you know how I've felt for the last week and a half," I said.

I took a deep breath and a step forward, but someone called my name. I turned to see Mary hurrying down the lane toward me.

"Catherine! I've been looking everywhere for you!" A few wayward strands of hair stuck to her neck, and her face lacked color. She gripped my wrist and tugged, barely sparing Freddie an acknowledging glance. "I need you."

Tossing a helpless look at Freddie over my shoulder, I allowed her to drag me a few yards away. "What's wrong? What's happened? You look—"

"It's Peter," she said in a frantic whisper.

Dread took the strength from my legs. "Oh, no," I breathed. "Is he..."

Mary shook her head, near tears. "He wants to elope. Now."

Relief finished the job dread started, and my knees buckled. Mary steadied me, her distress instantly transforming into concern for me. I waved her away. "I'm fine. I just...didn't eat breakfast this morning."

Mary paced a few steps away, then turned back. Her fingers tangled together, wrenching at each other. "What do I do? I can't elope. I just can't. But he says he can't bear being separated from me any longer, and if we're not married by the end of the summer, he's enlisting in the army." She stopped before me, crying in earnest. "He'll *leave*, Catherine. What do I do?"

I pulled her into my arms and held her, letting her cry into my shoulder while I thought. Turning my head, I caught Freddie's eye. He lifted his hands, then gestured toward Mr. Hale's cottage. I gave him a minute shake of my head and closed my eyes. Mary meant more to me than almost anyone else in the world—Freddie and Uncle Gerald excepted—but Ann Claybrook was walking the streets of Harwick at night when she should be lying in her grave, and I feared more would join her if we didn't do something about it.

I pushed Mary gently away from me and looked at her. "There's nothing to be done this instant, and I have something I need to do this morning. Go home. I'll come see you this afternoon, and we can figure this out."

Mary wiped her cheeks and looked over her shoulder at the Laceys' house. "Something you need to do at the Laceys'?" Her gaze shifted. "Or is it Mr. Hale?" She looked at me, her brows pulled down over her nose. "You don't even like him."

"I need to apologize for my behavior at the party. There was no excuse for it."

"Then write him a note or come back tomorrow. Please. I don't think I can—" Her voice broke.

Smoothing my hands over her shoulders, I leaned a little closer. "Go home, drink some tea, and have a lie-down. I'll be along shortly, I promise."

She stepped back, hurt. "It's that important, seeing Mr. Hale?"

I bit my lip and nodded.

Her face seemed to close down. She pushed back a lock of hair and lifted her chin. "Fine." She turned and walked quickly away, not looking back, though one hand snuck up to wipe her eyes again before she turned off the road and cut through the field toward her house.

I bent my head and scrubbed furiously at my face with my hands, then marched toward Freddie.

He looked slightly alarmed, though whether at Mary's

distress or the look I wore, I couldn't tell. "Is she all right? Are *you* all right?"

"Yes, and yes. Or at least, she will be, one way or another." The look of mystification on Freddie's face increased. I exhaled and swiped at a piece of hair that kept blowing in my eye. "Let's just get this over with."

I strode up the gravel path that led around the main house. It took Freddie a couple of seconds to follow, and he trotted up to my side.

"Who are you angry with?" he asked.

"Myself." I paused. "Mary, Ann Claybrook, Mr. Hale, that other woman. Everyone."

"Ah. Right. Not me?"

I gave him a sideways look and knocked on Mr. Hale's door. We waited quietly for a few breaths before the door opened and Mr. Hale's man, Marsh, greeted us.

"I reckon you've come to see Mr. Hale, seeing as he's the only one here worth seeing." Marsh chuckled as he ushered us inside, then showed us into the cottage's main room. "I'll let him know you're here."

I planted myself in the center of the room, running through my words in my head and fighting the strange nervousness that threatened to take over my stomach. Freddie wandered the perimeter of the room, examining its furnishings, obviously provided by the Laceys. The room was fairly bare. Two armchairs and a small table sat grouped in the center of the room, while two bookshelves and a writing desk did their best to fill the walls. The furniture was comfortable but not expensive, and none of it matched. A single candlestick sat on the mantel. There was no fire.

We didn't wait long. Mr. Hale arrived only a few minutes after Marsh left, without jacket or cravat, hurriedly buttoning the last of his waistcoat's buttons. He ran a quick hand through his hair, which looked as though he had spent most of the morning doing just that, and looked at me with a combination of curiosity and wariness.

"Miss Chase." His eyes flicked to Freddie, who leaned against the wall and waved. "Mr. Martin. To what—" He shook his head. "I'm surprised to see you here."

I opened my mouth, intending to tell him about Ann Claybrook, but instead said, "I'm sorry for my behavior yesterday. It was inexcusable."

Mr. Hale's eyes widened, and he took two quick steps toward me before halting in a jerky stop. "No! I must apologize to you. I had no right to lose my temper that way. Please understand it was not directed at you. I've been able to do nothing since I left your home but be ashamed of myself."

I shook my head. "You wished to tell me something, and I wouldn't let you."

He smiled, small and rueful. "Perhaps neither of us was at our best."

A flush crept up my neck, and more words poured from my mouth. "And the other night, at the party, I—"

He lifted a hand to hover in the air between us, just at the level of my lips, stopping my words. "Let's forget both incidents ever happened and move forward with clean slates. I'm sure you can find other things to accuse me of."

His smile was full this time and bright, and it took me by surprise. I nodded, unable to find the words I wished to speak.

"Is that why you came?" he asked, the curiosity returning to his gaze.

"No, actually," Freddie said behind me. I jumped, having forgotten he was there, and the sharp turn of Mr. Hale's head made me think he'd forgotten, too. I turned to look at my cousin, and the sharp interest of his gaze made my fading blush intensify. "Tell him about Ann, Catherine."

"Ann?" Mr. Hale looked from Freddie to me.

I nodded, squaring myself. "Last night I saw Ann Claybrook in the lane in front of our house." I paused to gauge Mr. Hale's reaction, to see if he knew the name. He did. "Ann died almost two weeks ago."

For a long moment, he didn't move. Then, slowly, he drifted past me to one of the chairs and sank into it, waving me into the other and gesturing for Freddie to bring the desk chair over to join our circle.

"I know," Mr. Hale said. "She's why I stopped here. I saw the obituary in the Scarborough paper."

Freddie and I looked at each other.

"Are you sure?" Mr. Hale asked. "Absolutely sure?"

"I saw her, too," Freddie said. "Makes me sorry I ever doubted Catherine about what she saw that night you—well." He stopped and swallowed, but Mr. Hale hadn't noticed.

"So there are two of them now," the Scot said quietly, almost to himself. He gazed at the rug, his face dark.

"Two what?" I asked, my fingers clutching at my skirt. "Two of…whatever that woman is?"

Mr. Hale nodded and lifted his head. "Yes. I've been tracking her for months, following her down the coast, trying to find her, trap her, figure out her weakness." His voice, though quiet, thrummed with the hatred I'd seen unleashed in our library yesterday afternoon. "Kill her."

I stared at him, stunned, and it was Freddie who asked, "Why?"

Mr. Hale stood and looked down at us. "She murdered my sister."

I gasped, and my perception of recent events swung wildly toward a new angle, making me dizzy. I gripped my chair with both hands and tried to swallow past the knot in my throat. Beside me, Freddie seemed to have frozen.

"Oh, God," I whispered.

Mr. Hale moved quickly to a bookcase and pulled a slim volume from the few books stacked on one shelf. It seemed to fall open where he wanted, as he didn't turn any pages before handing it to me. I accepted it mutely and stared down at it for several seconds before my eyes focused on the text. Freddie leaned toward me, peering at the words.

It was a children's book, a collection of fables. *Bedtime stories*, Mrs. Boyd's voice said in my head. *Faery stories.*

The Pale Women, the chapter heading said. Below it was a small woodcutting of a woman, one arm outstretched toward a man who stood, his arms at his sides. Her nails reached toward his throat.

I forced my eyes past the drawing and read the first few lines, quickly tripping up on a Gaelic phrase. *Baobhan Sith*. It seemed familiar, but I couldn't wrap my tongue around it.

I looked up at Mr. Hale. "What is this—?"

"*Baavan shee*," he said.

I straightened. "Mrs. Boyd used the same phrase when we talked to her about Ann's death."

Mr. Hale frowned. "Who's Mrs. Boyd?"

"The Claybrooks' cook. We didn't believe her, of course, but she was right." I smacked Freddie on the knee in some sort of triumph. "What does it mean?"

"A somewhat inaccurate translation is 'banshee.' They're not the same as traditional banshees—no screaming—but the basic concept is the same: otherworldly women who prey upon people."

Freddie gave a strangled laugh. "Banshees. You can't be serious."

Mr. Hale turned his intense gaze on my cousin, giving me a short respite from its force. Freddie swallowed. "You said you saw Ann Claybrook up and walking last night, Mr. Martin. Do you have another explanation?"

"No," Freddie admitted. "But I'm going to need a few moments to get used to this one, if you don't mind."

Mr. Hale softened and resumed his seat. "Of course. I'm sorry. I've lived with this for several months now. I can't expect you to embrace it as completely as I have in just a few minutes. It took me days to reconcile myself to their existence, and I came face to face with one." He gestured toward the scar that ran across his cheek.

I looked down at the book's illustration, at the woman's nails, then went back to the story. It told of four men traveling through the Scottish highlands. When they stopped for the night, one of the men produced a flute. The music drew three ethereal women from the darkness, and they beckoned the men into a dance. They danced for hours, until finally the spell dropped away from the flute player and he realized his companions were dead, their bodies covered in cuts and the women crouched over them, drinking the blood from their wounds. The man ran for his horse and galloped into the dawn. He reached his home the next day and never traveled more than a half day's journey from home again.

I slowly lifted my head to look at Mr. Hale, feeling the twisting emotions of the discovery playing across my face. He slowly took the book from my slack fingers and smiled sadly.

"I see you, Miss Chase, believe."

I remembered Dr. Haviland's explanation that Ann's body was cut from falling into a hedge. I remembered the pull of the strange woman, the desire to go to her, seeing that same thrall fall over Mr. Hale before I broke it with my shout. I closed my eyes against the onslaught of memories and pieces falling into place, and nodded.

"Banshees," Freddie said, his elbows on his knees and his head in his hands. His fingers tangled in his curls as he shook his head and laughed.

I didn't find it at all funny.

Mr. Hale stood and moved toward the sitting room door.

"Where are you going?" I asked, standing as well.

He looked at me over his shoulder as he opened the door. Sticking his head into the hall, he bellowed, "Marsh! Fetch my jacket!" Turning back to me, he said, "Are you up for a walk, Miss Chase?"

I nodded, suddenly wary.

"Good." Mr. Hale smiled. "We're going to the cemetery."

ten

"You're taking this very well," Freddie said, dipping his head to see my face. We walked toward the village church, nodding at neighbors and acquaintances as we went, hoping no one would stop us. The dark, determined look on Mr. Hale's face seemed to have deterred conversation so far, and I hoped its power lasted.

I wrapped my arms around myself and wished my heart would slow down. "You didn't feel her. I did. It makes it easier to believe something is supernatural once it's cast its spell over you."

"That makes a...strange sort of sense." He turned to Mr. Hale. "So you've actually been in a brawl with one of these things? Seen them in action?"

"I'm not sure *brawl* is the right word. She gave me this"—Mr. Hale indicated the scar on his face—"and a few others, then threw me into a wall. By the time I could get back on my feet, my sister was dead." He said this flatly, without emotion, and I looked at him from beneath the brim of my bonnet. The corner of his jaw came into sharp relief as he clenched and unclenched it.

Freddie, who stood between us, caught my eye. The sympathy in his face surprised me, and we walked in silence for several minutes. I wondered what Mr. Hale's sister was called, if she was pretty. How old she was when she was killed.

"Uh oh," Freddie said. I looked up to see Mrs. Ellerby walking toward us on the other side of the lane.

I groaned.

Mrs. Ellerby spotted us, waved, and hurried across the street. "Catherine! Freddie! Oh, I'm so glad to have caught you." She paused, her eyes moving quickly between us and our companion. "And Mr. Hale! No doubt you'll find my news most interesting, as well. You won't *believe* what has happened!"

I felt Freddie stiffen beside me. I tried to answer Mrs. Ellerby, but my tongue stuck to the roof of my mouth. I couldn't handle another tragedy today. Not after Mary's crisis and discovering that mythical creatures existed and were slowly killing off my village.

Fortunately, she didn't require encouragement from me to share her news. "Mr. Thompson's cow returned! Just showed up in his barn this morning as if she'd never left." She beamed at each of us in turn and nodded. "You should look so relieved. He never could have afforded to buy another, and I don't know what I'd do without the milk he provides me. Sells me a half-quart whenever I want it for half what I'd pay at Mr. Jenkins' farm. Now that's friendship."

Once all the dread had drained out of my body, leaving my fingers tingling, I straightened and smiled at Mrs. Ellerby. "How lucky for Mr. Thompson. She was a good cow, and I know our Polly's bought cheese off him more than once."

She placed a hand on my arm. "Do come to tea this afternoon. All of you." She beamed at Mr. Hale, who seemed to be struggling to keep a pleasant look on his face. Freddie didn't bother hiding his alarm.

He'd had an irrational fear of Mrs. Ellerby's house ever since we were children. She used to keep a pair of lovebirds, and the birds got out once while Uncle Gerald, Freddie, his two brothers, and I were there, taking our tea. They decided Freddie's unruly curls would make a good roosting place. Freddie had never liked birds—an abhorrence born from being forced to care for two dozen hens; stupid, vicious creatures that attacked him whenever he brought them their feed. The lovebirds, though not malicious, still bore claws and beaks, both of which inadvertently tore at his scalp. It was several minutes before Mrs. Ellerby was able to coax them back into their cage, and by that point, poor young Freddie had curled into a tense ball in his chair, trying not to cry while thin streams of blood trickled through his hair and down the side of his face.

He'd never set foot in her house again, even after the birds died.

"You're so kind," I said quickly, patting Mrs. Ellerby's hand, "but I'm afraid Freddie and I have already committed to taking Mr. Hale up to Slattery Hill for a picnic luncheon. He's informed us he's a great walker, and I'm sure we'll spend most of the afternoon exploring the area."

Mrs. Ellerby looked up at the sky. The clouds, light and harmless when Freddie and I had left the house an hour earlier, had started to darken and build around each other. "You didn't pick a very good day for it, I'm afraid. You'll be rained out before you even reach your pudding."

"We're tough," Freddie said. "A little rain won't put us off our purpose."

Her eyes widened. "Oh no, you can't! You'll catch your death!"

He exchanged a look with Mr. Hale, then turned back to our neighbor. "We're quite resolved."

She clutched at my arm and straightened her back. "Well, you can't take Catherine. I won't have her gallivanting about the countryside in a rainstorm." She looked at me. "These men have no consideration for your delicate constitution."

Freddie snorted. "Catherine's tougher than an ox. No mere illness can take her down."

Mrs. Ellerby ignored him, a haughty tilt to her nose. "You shall have tea with me this afternoon, Catherine. I can't prevent these young men from carrying through this foolish idea of theirs, but I won't let them drag you into it." She sighed, as though already mourning their inevitable deaths from pneumonia. "Besides, there's something particular I want to discuss with you."

I closed my eyes, knowing exactly what she meant. My behavior at the Laceys' party only two nights before. No doubt she wished to correct my obviously lax concept of propriety and ladylike behavior.

I could have argued, tried to come up with another excuse to postpone our conversation, but I could feel Mr. Hale's anxiousness. Completing our errand, discovering what we could about these women—these banshees—was more important than anything else. I'd already slighted Mary today. My independence and pride were a small sacrifice in comparison.

"Yes, Mrs. Ellerby," I said meekly. "I'll call on you this afternoon."

Satisfied, she nodded, patted my arm with sincere affection, and said her good-byes to the gentlemen. "I look forward to our discussion, Catherine. I think it will serve you well."

"I'm sure," I murmured, dipping my head in an abbreviated curtsy.

Mrs. Ellerby bustled back across the lane, and Mr. Hale immediately resumed our course for the church, though at a much brisker pace than before.

"Finally," Freddie said. "I was afraid we'd never get rid of her."

"Yes. That was a good idea about the picnic and hiking," Mr. Hale added, looking at me.

"Catherine's a stunning liar," Freddie announced cheerfully. Mr. Hale's eyebrows lifted.

Embarrassed, I quickened my pace and left them behind. When I reached the churchyard, I pushed open the gate, which creakily protested as it always had, and walked along the winding, flagstone path toward the back of the church, where the cemetery began. I stopped in the shade of the bell tower and waited for the two men to catch up.

I'd always thought of our cemetery as a peaceful place, despite its purpose. The thick, ancient trees that marked out the cemetery's perimeter stretched their arms over the tidy rows of headstones, some crumbling with age, others sharp and fresh. Two such new graves, their stones small and unassuming, lay in the farthest row. The soldier's body had been sent to his family. Ann Claybrook's monument, larger and topped with a small stone maiden, lay to my right. The grass which dotted the grave of Michael Smith had yet to touch hers or Joseph Reep's.

Two rows closer to me lay the graves of my parents and Freddie's mother. The flowers I'd planted had been devoured by rabbits before they'd even bloomed. They always were, but I still planted them every spring.

"Now what?" I asked when Freddie and Mr. Hale joined

me, the amusement gone from their faces.

"The girl you saw last night, the one who died." Mr. Hale paused to take a breath. "I want to see her grave."

He held my gaze for a moment while Freddie ran through a string of swear words under his breath, and I nodded and led the way. I already knew, somehow, what we would find; as, I suspected, did Mr. Hale. Winding through the weathered headstones, I made my way to Ann's grave and stood over it, frowning.

"Should it be lumpy like that?" Freddie asked.

"I don't think so." Mr. Hale crossed his arms and glowered at the headstone.

"Not a particularly good thing, I reckon," Freddie continued.

"No," I agreed.

We stood around Ann Claybrook's grave, staring morosely down at it. It wasn't obviously disturbed, not in a way that would attract attention. If we hadn't been looking for something out of place, we might not have noticed the uneven way the soil seemed to be settling or the remains of a few small handprints, a woman's hand, left from smoothing the dirt back into place.

"I suppose we should have brought a shovel," Freddie said.

Mr. Hale shook his head. "I doubt we'd learn much more if we dug it up. And I'd rather not be caught doing so."

"This must have taken a lot of work," I said, waving a hand over the recovered grave. "A lot of time. Moving that much dirt with their bare hands."

"They're strong." Mr. Hale looked at me. "Where are the others?"

I pointed to the opposite side of the cemetery.

Mr. Hale strode off, and Freddie dropped his arms to his sides. "Good God. Are you saying there are *four* of them?"

I followed Mr. Hale down the row, Freddie behind me. The graves of the men who had died looked untouched. We spent several minutes circling them, bent over, looking for similar signs to those we'd found at Ann's, but the grave was pristine. Young grass grew upon the shallow mound of Michael Smith's resting place. The dirt covering Joseph Reep's grave was still dark and fresh.

Giving up, I straightened, rubbing the kinks from my lower back.

"I take it we won't be seeing them wandering around town anytime soon." Freddie leaned on Joseph Reep's headstone, then seemed to realize what he was doing and straightened, wiping his hand guiltily on his trousers.

Mr. Hale stared down at the graves, chewing on his bottom lip. "Why not them? Why just the girl?"

He spoke so quietly, I wasn't sure he wanted an answer, but then he raised his head to look at me. I turned my face away and focused on the dates beneath Michael Smith's name. He was eighteen when he died.

"I don't know the myth as well as you," I said, my eyes drifting to the trees at the edge of the cemetery, "but that book you showed me, that story—they were called the 'pale women.' And you've called them banshees several times now." I turned and saw the realization in Mr. Hale's eyes. "Aren't banshees women?"

He turned and looked back toward Ann Claybrook's grave. "Yes. Of course."

Shaking his head, he looked up at the sky. The clouds had thickened since we'd entered the cemetery, and the tree branches above us cut most of what weak light remained. It felt like dusk rather than noon, and I shivered suddenly, seeing the cemetery around us in a foreboding, sinister way I never had before.

"We're done here," Mr. Hale said, moving toward the gate.

Freddie moved to my side, and I took his offered arm, feeling a need for warmth and comfort. We silently followed Mr. Hale out of the cemetery, and back toward his house. Most of the town had gone indoors for their meal and to avoid the approaching storm, and I barely heard the called greetings of the few people we passed. Information clogged my brain. Ann's face in the moonlight, a handprint in the soil, the imagined image of travelers seduced and killed in the highlands of Scotland, Mr. Hale confronting the first banshee near the woods behind our house, his scar, and his first encounter with the *baobhan sith*, of which he'd spoken so little.

A few yards from Mr. Hale's cottage, I stopped with a cry. My hand dropped from Freddie's arm, and I stared in horror at Mr. Hale, who turned at my outburst. The concern on his face fell into unease when he took in my expression.

Freddie's hands fell, warm and heavy, on my shoulders. "Catherine? What is it?"

I shook my head, still staring at Mr. Hale. He took a step toward me. "Miss Chase?"

Freddie shook me lightly, and words spilled out of my mouth in a whisper.

"Your sister."

Mr. Hale froze, and the blood drained from his face. He closed his eyes and swayed, and I feared he would faint. I slipped from beneath Freddie's hands and crossed the small distance between us, wrapping Mr. Hale's fingers in mine. His eyes flew open, and the intensity of his pain and grief and horror froze my breath in my chest.

He took a step backward, pulling his hands free, and muttered, "Excuse me." Then he turned and stumbled into the cottage, slamming the door behind him.

eleven

"Well, bollocks," Freddie said darkly, kicking at the gravel beneath our feet.

I sank my fingers into my hair, tugging at it, pulling it from its pins. It unwound slowly, pieces drifting down my neck, past my shoulders.

Freddie took my wrists in his hands and gently lowered my arms. "Come on, Catherine. Let's go home."

"His *sister*." I couldn't get the look on Mr. Hale's face out of my mind. "Do you think she's.... If *you* were—"

"I know. Come on."

Freddie urged me toward home. A drop of rain hit my arm. We cut through the woods, jumping easily across the creek, and came up on our house from behind. Mr. Hale must have taken a similar path the night he tried to kill the woman—the banshee, vampire, monster—that killed his sister.

Freddie opened the back door and ushered me into the kitchen. Polly must have been elsewhere, cleaning. The light sprinkle of precipitation had turned into a steady mist. In another fifteen minutes it would be a summer rainstorm that would turn the roads into strips of mud, give the creek a trifle more life, and drip through the corner of the stable roof and turn our straw musty.

In the kitchen, I turned when I realized Freddie still stood outside, the door open. He pulled his hat down to keep the rain from his eyes.

"Where are you going?" I asked.

"For my walk up Slattery Hill. Mrs. Ellerby will know if I don't go, and the last thing you'll need, as you'll be in her living room drinking her tea, is to have her think we lied because we don't like her."

I made a small, frustrated noise and waved him into the house. He didn't move. "I couldn't possibly sit with Mrs. Ellerby right now and be pleasant. And you can't go walking. That storm is going to hit any minute."

"I can, and I will. And the same goes for you." He took a step backward. "Go put your hair back up, put on a smile, and spend an hour with Mrs. Ellerby. I'll be home before you; I promise."

He turned and jogged through the thickening rain toward the stable, and a few minutes later he led his horse out, mounted it, and urged it toward the woods. When I could no longer see him, I shut the door and slowly climbed the stairs to my room.

∞∞∞

I ate more of Mrs. Ellerby's cakes than I should have, but it was the only thing that kept me from snapping at her when she started to chastise me for my outburst at the Laceys' party. As she lectured, I nodded, having no trouble looking serious, and tried to keep my mind away from the Laceys' cottage and what Mr. Hale must be going through, burdened with the possibility that his sister had become one of those creatures.

Eventually the tea grew cold and I stood, thanking Mrs. Ellerby for her time and advice. She nodded, pleased she had saved my reputation, and walked me to the door.

"I do hope your cousin and Mr. Hale don't catch cold from their walk," she said, squinting out her door at the steady downpour that had served as background music for our afternoon. "I can't believe they went through with it."

"I tried to talk them out of it," I said, "but they were determined." I lifted my parasol above my head with one hand, gathered as much of my skirts as I could in the other, and prepared to run. "Thank you, Mrs. Ellerby. It's been a pleasure, as always."

She smiled warmly, and I bolted out the door and across the street, through the gate I had left open so I wouldn't have to fight it on my way back, and up the path to our small porch. Polly met me at the door. She must have finished her cleaning and set herself the task of watching for me.

"Thank you, Polly." I let her take the dripping parasol and my bonnet. "Is Freddie home?"

She shook her head and frowned at my shoes. Even in that short dash, I had mud nearly to my ankles. I bent and worked at the laces, leaving my shoes in a pile by the door as Polly instructed. My skirts hadn't fared too badly, but I'd still have to change. I could feel the moisture creeping up my petticoat.

Before climbing the stairs to my room, I stuck my head in Uncle Gerald's study. He paused in writing a letter to smile at me.

"Catherine! I haven't seen you since breakfast. Having a good day?"

I hesitated, the damp of my skirts cold against my

stocking feet. "Yes. Lovely. I just had tea with Mrs. Ellerby."

He nodded. "She dotes on you. It's good of you to keep her company." He turned in his seat to look out the window. "Still raining?"

"Yes. So much so that I need to change before I catch a cold."

He waved me away, returning to his letter, and I shut the door. Hefting the sodden fabric of my dress, I took the stairs two at a time, anxious for dry clothes and Freddie's return in equal measure.

I had just pulled a new frock over my head when I heard someone knock on the door below. I smiled, glad Freddie had returned, before realizing he wouldn't have knocked. I hurried to close the last few fastenings, already halfway down the stairs when Polly came to fetch me.

"It's Miss Hayworth," she whispered, looking over her shoulder. "Right frightful, she looks. I put her in the drawing room." She paused, then leaned toward me. "Don't let her sit on the furniture."

"Thank you, Polly." I squeezed the housekeeper's hand, smiled at her, and moved past her and into the parlor.

Mary stood at the window, wringing her hands. Polly was right—she looked dreadful. She had run out of the house without a parasol, bonnet, or shawl, and her wet hair clung to the sides of her face and neck. Mud had splashed past her knees, and she'd left the floor a mess.

She turned to me, her face pale, her eyes and nose red and swollen. Without a word she flung herself toward me, and I just had time to close the door as she crossed the room before catching her. She shivered against me.

"Mary! You're freezing! What were you thinking, coming all this way in the rain?"

I herded her toward the fire, glad Polly had remembered to light one this morning, and eased her down to sit on the hearth.

"You didn't come," she said. "I waited, but I couldn't be by myself anymore. I didn't dare go down to sit with Mother and Father." She smiled wanly. "So I snuck out, just like we did as children in order to swim in Farmer Hodges' pond or pretend we were faeries, dancing in the moonlight."

"Mary." I smoothed a wet lock of hair off her forehead to hide a rush of guilt. I'd forgotten her. In the excitement of discovery and the horror of that discovery's true nature, I'd forgotten that my friend needed me. I'd been sitting in Mrs. Ellerby's parlor, eating her cakes and ignoring a lecture on manners while Mary paced her room, alone and conflicted. "I'm so sorry."

She shook her head. "It doesn't matter. I just don't know what to do." She looked up at me, her eyes wide and pleading. "What would you do in my position? If Peter demanded you elope or he would leave."

I paused a moment, hoping she was ready to hear my answer. "I'd pack a bag—a couple of dresses, some toiletries, nothing more—and I'd ride the half day to Hull, and there I'd meet Peter at the inn and board the coach to Scotland."

She closed her eyes and drooped. "I want to. Oh, I want to. But how can I? Louie married so well, and Mother and Father expect the same from me. They'd never forgive me." She lifted her head. "I'm not sure I could bear that."

"Not even for Peter?"

For a long moment, she didn't answer. "I don't know."

We sat quietly, the heat of the fire at our backs. Mary's hair began to curl as it dried, surrounding her in a delicate, golden halo. I frowned at my bare feet. I loved Mary like a sister, but I found it hard to understand her hesitation.

Mary sniffed, and something in her countenance seemed to shift. "How could he ask this of me? It's—it's—he knows how I feel about him! About us!" She turned to me, color rising to her cheeks. "Is this a test? How can he force me to choose between my family and him?"

I stood and paced a few steps away, trying to quell my irritation. It didn't work, and I turned back to my friend, unable to stop the words from coming, not sure I wanted to. "Frankly, I'm surprised he's waited this long. You've been engaged for two years already, Mary, with no end in sight, no hope. He loves you, and how could he not, but he can't wait forever. And he shouldn't have to."

Mary stared at me for half a second, mouth open in shock, then rose to meet me, anger replacing the strength despair had stolen from her.

"So I'm to just give up everything that matters to me in order to be with him?" she demanded. "I'm to cut myself off from my family, my home? Any hope of an inheritance with which to support myself?"

"And he'd be sacrificing nothing?" I asked in return. "His reputation will be just as damaged as yours. He'll lose his right to the store, his livelihood. Possibly his family too. He'll lose everything—except you. Apparently he thinks that a worthy trade."

Mary stepped back as if I'd slapped her.

I continued. "To him, you don't appear to value him as he values you. You're stalling, Mary. Waiting for something to change, something to open the door so you can be married as you want to be married." I paused, taking a breath. "For all intents and purposes, you're waiting for your parents to die, to settle their money on you now so you can marry whom you please."

Mary's face reddened, and she clenched her fists. "How dare y—"

"No." I sank onto the edge of the sofa, suddenly tired. My head fell into my hands. "I know you're not doing it on purpose, but it's what you're doing all the same. But it doesn't matter. What matters now is that you can't do it any longer. Peter is forcing a choice, and I say good for him for doing so." In what felt like a feat worthy of Greek mythology, I lifted my head and looked at Mary, at the anger and shock and guilt on her face. "You have to marry him—now, elope—or you'll lose him. That's it, Mary. Two options. You have to choose."

She stared at me for a long moment as though seeing me for the first time, the clock on the mantel behind her ticking loudly in the sudden silence. Then, without saying a word, she moved to the door, quietly opened it, and slipped out. A few moments later I heard the front door open and close.

I dropped my head back into my hands, smiling ruefully at my new ability to chase people from my home with my words. The clock chimed the hour. Four o'clock and Freddie still wasn't home.

The clock ticked on, seeming to grow louder and louder, until finally it forced me to my feet and out into the hallway, desperate to escape. Without thinking, I walked quickly to the kitchen and out the back door, hardly noticing the rain. My bare feet slipped on the wet grass, and I broke my fall with my hands, coating them in wet debris. I scrambled down the slick incline toward the creek, reaching the Bulbous Tree. My hands gripped the rough bark, dark from the rain, as I picked my way around its trunk and settled into a gap amidst the gnarled roots that seemed to boil out of the ground. Rivulets of water ran past them, heading for the creek, and the rain on the leaves above me sounded like laughter. I pulled my knees into my chest, wrapping my arms around them, and buried my face in the small, dark shelter of my skirts.

And I cried.

I cried for Mary, whose friendship I had injured, if not destroyed. I cried for Mr. Hale and his sister, for Ann Claybrook, for Joseph Reep.

Freddie found me an hour later, when my tears had run out. The rain had let up, returning to a gentle mist that drifted past me in translucent curtains. I didn't lift my head as his boots appeared in my vision. He stood above me for a long moment, then slowly lowered himself into the mud next to me. I leaned into his warmth.

"You're soaked," he said.

I sniffed. "So are you."

He wrapped an arm around my shoulders and pulled me into his side. "Polly said you had an argument with Mary."

I gave half a laugh. "Sweeping the hall just outside the door, was she?"

"Something like that, yes."

I could feel the tears begin again and wiped them away, trying to find something to distract myself. "Did you have a good walk?"

"A little wet."

I laughed.

"And I almost fell in the ocean three times but somehow managed to return home unscathed."

"You always were talented."

He didn't answer, just pulled me closer. I curled into

him, letting his warmth dull the ache inside me. I focused on the burble of the creek, the movement of Freddie's breathing, the water droplets that fell on us from the tree above.

"Some day, eh?" he said quietly.

I nodded, rubbing my cheek against the fabric of his coat.

We stayed that way, the leaves whispering around us, until the last of the light faded from the sky.

twelve

Freddie sneezed all through breakfast the next day, and Uncle Gerald spent the morning mixing him a tonic. Freddie drank it down, then pouted and grumbled for half an hour afterward, most of it directed at me, as I'd woken in perfect health.

He went to sleep off his medicine, and I helped Uncle Gerald pack for his yearly trip to Brighton. His oldest friend, a colleague from school and a fellow doctor, lived there, and Uncle Gerald spent every July with him, arguing the finer points of medicine and walking the shore. When we were younger, the whole family had gone, but in recent years we'd convinced Uncle Gerald to go by himself. He looked forward to the trip all year, and I smiled as he bustled about his bedchamber, trying to decide which of his new volumes to take.

"Worth won't have this one, I wager," he said, holding up a treatise on the cause of various mental afflictions.

"Perhaps you should swipe some of Freddie's textbooks," I suggested, joking.

Uncle Gerald's face lit up at the idea. "Do you think so?"

I laughed. "I doubt he brought any home with him."

Uncle Gerald drooped slightly, then leveled a serious look at me. "Take care of him while I'm gone. Make sure he takes his tonic and gets plenty of rest. I know it's just a cold, but he thinks the rules of convalescence don't apply to him."

"I'll make sure he behaves," I said. "Polly will help, since she'll be staying here as well. All we have to do is threaten to withhold food, and he'll do whatever we ask."

He cupped my cheek and kissed my hairline, an unusual display of affection. "You are good for him, Catherine. And for me."

I blushed and fussed with the apron I'd put over my dress. "I need to sweep the parlor," I said, backing toward the door. "Polly's missed it four days running, now."

"Wait."

I stopped in the doorway.

Uncle Gerald tilted his head down and looked at me over his spectacles. "What should I bring back for you?"

A smile burst across my face, and I felt years younger. Uncle Gerald always brought back presents from his trip, fancy sweets or the latest bonnet from London, seashells from the Brighton shore. I was about to say he could bring whatever struck his fancy when another idea came to me. "A book on mythology," I said. "Specifically the legends of Ireland and Scotland."

His eyebrows rose. "A new hobby?"

"I can't keep reading those dry old medical tomes of yours," I teased. "The London booksellers are bound to have dozens of volumes to choose from on the subject. I'm sure you can find me one that looks interesting." Mr. Hale likely would have loaned me the copy of fairy tales he'd shown me the day before, but we might find some small nugget of useful information in a new source.

Uncle Gerald gave me an exasperated, sideways look, turning back to his packing, and I bounded forward to kiss his cheek.

"Thank you, Uncle."

He nodded, his attention focused on two anatomy books, which he weighed in either hand like a scale. Smiling, I left to see to my chores.

∞∞∞

Freddie managed to make it downstairs to see Uncle Gerald off later that afternoon. Uncle planned to take our small carriage to Hull and then the coach to York. From there he would catch the southbound coach. Freddie would ride over to Hull once he was well to fetch the carriage back again. He looked so pale and drawn, however, that my uncle almost changed his mind and gave up his trip altogether. It took several minutes of convincing on Freddie's part and mine to get him out the door and into the carriage.

"You mixed enough tonic to last me a month," Freddie said. "Catherine will make sure I take it." He made a face at me. "Probably she'll have me drinking nothing but it and chicken broth for days. Starve this cold right out of me."

I made a face back at him. "At last, I shall have you completely at my mercy."

He grinned, though it seemed to take more effort than normal. "Your deepest desire."

Uncle Gerald squinted at us and tapped his walking stick against his boots. "If you're sure you'll be all right, my boy…"

Freddie waved his concern away. "I'll be good as new tomorrow."

I nodded in agreement.

"Very well," Uncle Gerald said. "Take care of him, Catherine. Take care of her, Freddie."

Freddie slung his arm across my shoulders. Uncle Gerald clucked his tongue, and our old horse, Belle, started forward. We waved until the carriage turned onto the lane. Once it was out of sight, Freddie sagged against me.

"I thought he'd never go," he said. "I'm not sure I'd have been able to stand here much longer. I need a lie down."

"You're useless," I said, helping him back into the house.

We opted for the parlor sofa instead of tackling the stairs, and Freddie was asleep two minutes after he lay down. I sighed and went to fetch a blanket. When I came back, he'd curled onto his side, his mouth slightly open. I tugged off his boots, tucked the blanket around him, and went to help Polly with the silver polishing.

Freddie frowned at me from beneath his small mound of blankets. He'd propped himself up against his pillows in order to read, and I sat on the edge of his bed, an invitation in my hand.

"You're not going," he said. "Not by yourself."

I rolled my eyes. "It's a party, Freddie. The only danger will be tripping on my gown and embarrassing myself in front of several prominent town gossips."

His frown deepened. "It's at night."

"Most parties are."

"With those *things* out there. You can't go alone."

"Of course not." I folded the invitation and slipped it into my apron pocket. "I'm going with Mrs. Ellerby. I can't very well traipse about unaccompanied."

Freddie blinked at me. "Mrs. Ellerby? Why on earth are you going with her? I'd have thought you'd go with the Hayworths."

I smoothed my skirt. "I haven't spoken to Mary for a few days."

"Ah." He sank back into his pillows.

After a few seconds of silence, I stood. "So that's settled, then."

Freddie opened his eyes. He still looked pale and exhausted but was finally on the mend. I'd worried his cold had taken a deeper hold on him and turned into pneumonia, but in another day or two, he'd be on his feet and entertaining himself by making me crazy, as usual.

"Maybe I should come," he said.

"Don't be ridiculous. You'd pass out before we even got through the door."

He frowned. "Would not."

I raised my eyebrows.

He huffed. "Stop maligning my masculinity."

"Masculinity has nothing to do with it. You can be manly and still too sick to go to the Brocks' party." I gestured toward his nightstand with my chin. "Drink your tea."

He made a face. "I've drunk more tea in the past three days than in the entire previous year."

"Once you're better, you never have to drink it again if you don't want to. I'll bring you some more broth."

I moved toward the door, and as I walked down the hall, Freddie called after me.

"Has Polly got any of those sticky buns left?"

∞∞∞

"I told him," Mrs. Ellerby said, adjusting her reticule on her wrist the next evening. "I told him not to go on that walk, and now look what's happened."

I hummed in agreement and waited patiently for Mrs. Ellerby to finish the final touches to her appearance. I only half listened as she continued scolding my absent cousin, more worried about whether Mary would attend the party and what I would say when I saw her. Or Mr. Hale.

This had the potential to be an extremely awkward evening.

At last Mrs. Ellerby was ready to go, and we walked the short distance to the Brock residence. The door stood open to the warmth of the summer night, golden light streaming out to greet us.

We were some of the last guests to arrive, and Mrs. Brock swooped down upon us as we entered the drawing room. "Mrs. Ellerby! Miss Chase! How good of you both to come." She kissed the air near Mrs. Ellerby's cheek and ushered us toward a small, low bench, saying she'd send her son Matthew over with drinks for us in just a moment.

I sat, looking over the gathering. Mary stood in a small circle that included Susannah Brock and two other young girls from the village, Elizabeth Johnson and Jane MacGregor. She didn't look at me, though she must have noticed my entrance. My stomach dropped slightly.

Matthew Brock, a good-natured, eager boy of seventeen, brought Mrs. Ellerby and I each a cup of punch. His brow furrowed in concentration as he walked so as not to spill on his mother's expensive rugs.

"Thank you, Matthew," I said, accepting my cup. I smiled and he blushed, then scurried back toward his father. Mr. Hale, I noticed, stood near Mr. Brock, nodding at something the older gentleman said. I quickly bent my head and took a sip of my punch.

"Oh!" Mrs. Ellerby shook my arm, nearly causing me to dump punch all over my best muslin. "There's Miss Hayworth! Let's go say hello."

I found myself dragged toward Mary's circle. She turned toward us, and I smiled, though it felt wobbly. Mary nodded, then smiled at Mrs. Ellerby and took her hand.

"Mrs. Ellerby! Just the woman we need. Please, do give us your opinion on the latest style of bonnet. I think them perfectly dreadful, but Susannah is determined to embrace them. What do you think?"

Mrs. Ellerby, thrilled at the attention, forgot all about me and moved to close the circle at Mary's gentle tug, leaving me outside.

I stared at Mary. I'd expected her to be hurt, but I had not expected her to be cold. I noticed the amused, triumphant smirks of Susannah Brock and Elizabeth Johnson and the pitying look of Jane MacGregor and straightened, wiping my expression clean of any emotion and turning abruptly toward the refreshment table.

Mrs. Brock had provided a small plate of biscuits as well as some cucumber sandwiches, and I picked up one of the small china plates and slapped two of each onto it. Crumbs burst off the biscuits and skittered across the surface of the china. I moved toward the punch bowl, set my plate down with a solid *thunk*, and picked up a glass.

The glass Matthew had given me was only a few feet away, next to the bench where Mrs. Ellerby and I had taken stock of the gathering, but I would have to pass Mary again to retrieve it, and I was afraid what I might say if faced with more visual proof of her snub.

"Are you all right?" a voice at my elbow asked.

I whirled, sloshing punch over the edge of my new cup. Mr. Hale took half a step back, watching the pink liquid drip onto the rug, then gave me an amused half smile.

"Oh!" I stared at him, trying to come up with something to say. "Hello."

His smile grew. "Hello." He nodded toward my cup. "Can I get you a napkin?"

"What?" I looked down. Punch dripped down my fingers. "Oh! No, thank you. I can manage." I turned back toward the table, set my cup down, and picked up a napkin. Fingers dry, I faced Mr. Hale. "You asked me a question, I think."

"You were scowling. I thought I should make sure you were all right." He dipped his head, and his smile faded into a look of genuine concern. "Are you?"

A sudden rush of gratitude made my arms fall slack to my sides. "Yes. Mostly. I just...my friend Miss Hayworth is upset with me and..." I turned my head, looking toward the window. The brightness of the room reflected against the night, and I could see my own fuzzy face and the shape of Mr. Hale standing next to me. "I'm afraid I lost my temper and said some things I shouldn't have."

"You seem to do that often."

I lifted a hand to my forehead and closed my eyes. "Yes. I'm starting to notice a pattern."

When I opened my eyes, he was smiling softly at me. I smiled back.

"Where is Mr. Martin?" His forehead creased momentarily, then smoothed back into a pleasant expression. "It's rare to see you apart."

I laughed. "Freddie is ill, poor thing. Laid up with a nasty cold he got wandering around the cliffs during a torrential downpour."

Mr. Hale's eyes widened. "He actually went? I forgot all about it after..." He looked away for a moment, and I remembered his tortured retreat after realizing his sister might have become one of the banshees.

One of my hands stretched across the distance between us, but before it could touch his arm, I pulled it back. "And you?" I asked quietly. "Are you all right?"

"Sometimes." His eyes searched my face, his own expression suddenly intense. "Can I speak to you privately?"

I blinked and gestured toward the party. "I'm not sure how we could manage that without causing a small scandal."

He gave the other guests a look of vague surprise, as if he'd forgotten they were there. "Right. Of course. Your engagement. Could we perhaps—"

"Engagement?" I asked, my tone sharp.

He rocked back on his heels and gave me the same look of surprise. "Yes, your engagement." His forehead creased again. "You are engaged to Mr. Martin, yes? I was told..."

I sighed and closed my eyes. "Yes, I'm sure you were told. That doesn't make it true."

"But you—" Mr. Hale closed his mouth and watched me for a moment in confusion. "I'm not sure I understand."

I shook my head. "Sometimes neither do I." I looked up at him. "Since Freddie and I were young, everyone around us has assumed we would marry once we were older, but neither Freddie nor I have any desire to fulfill this prophecy. We think of each other as brother and sister and are most certainly not engaged, whatever the entire village may think."

Mr. Hale blinked several times before saying, "I...I see." He shifted his weight and looked again at the other guests, seeming to struggle with some internal debate. In a voice so low I had to strain to hear it, he asked, "Could you—would you be willing to meet me later tonight?"

If I had still been holding my punch, I'd have dropped it.

"Perhaps near the trees behind your house," he continued, "where this all began."

There was no flirtation or passion in his gaze, just a fierce determination, but as I gaped at him, a tiny flash of amusement sparked in his eyes. I finally recovered my voice. "You—this is..." I glanced quickly around, but no one stood within earshot of our low conversation. "This is for the same purpose as our conversation the other day? Regarding the—"

"Yes. I know it's more than I have the right to ask, to risk your reputation, but you were able to break her hold on me that night behind your house. I might need that help again." His eyes flicked toward the center of the room, and his face darkened slightly. I risked a glance and saw Susannah Brock heading our direction, all traces of the amusement she'd worn earlier gone. "Will you? Tonight?"

I barely had time to nod before Susannah was upon us.

"Miss Chase! Mr. Hale! Stop sequestering yourselves. It's not neighborly." She aimed her brightest smile at Mr. Hale. "We have need of you, sir. Perhaps you'd be good enough to solve a dilemma for us?"

Mr. Hale gave her a small bow of his head. "May I ask who is included in your 'we'?"

Boldly, as though she'd been doing it all her life, Susannah wrapped her hands around the crook of Mr. Hale's arm and steered him toward the middle of room. "Mother, Miss Hayworth, Mrs. Ellerby, and myself, of course. Who else?"

She led him away, her shining black hair gleaming in the lamplight. I watched, frowning, trying to sort out the strange twinge I felt at her forward behavior.

Mr. Hale looked at me over his shoulder and raised his eyebrows, though whether he was amused or requesting a rescue, I couldn't tell. Either way, his look made me feel better, and a few seconds later, I was pulled into a passionate discussion with Mr. Haviland and Mrs. Witherpoole on the benefits of eating beef on a regular basis.

After two hours of moving from conversational group to conversational group—though never the same one as Mary—Mrs. Ellerby declared a headache and insisted we leave at once. I knew her real cause of distress was that Mrs. Witherpoole had once again refused to share the recipe for her apple tarts, the only dish at which anyone in the village was capable of out-baking Mrs. Ellerby, but I could not refuse her.

As we left the parlor, I caught Mr. Hale's eye. He held up three fingers, and I nodded, feeling my breath quicken.

At least my silence on our walk home did not strike Mrs. Ellerby as unusual, as one rarely had a chance to speak in her presence.

thirteen

I snuck down the stairs of the house, holding my skirts off the floor with one hand and my sturdiest pair of walking boots in the other. Praying the creaking of the stairs wouldn't wake Freddie, I moved down them and into the foyer, then passed through the dining room to the kitchen.

I stopped by the back door and bent to put on my boots. As I worked the laces around the final hooks, the clock in the study struck three.

Pulling my shawl closer around me, I eased the door open and slipped into the cool air of night. The rain that had sent Freddie to his bed had also banished the summer heat, and I shivered.

There was no moon, and the light from the stars was barely enough to make out the darker masses of the woods and the barn against the rest of the night. I tried to remember what part of the moon's cycle we were in, or if I had seen it earlier that night while walking to or from the Brocks' party, but my memory failed me on both counts.

I moved slowly down the slope of the lawn, placing my feet with care and hoping I didn't meet Ann Claybrook or any other mythical monster. At least the dark would hide me as well as it hid them.

When the whisper of leaves seemed to come from directly above my head, I stopped. Beneath the trees, the faint light of the stars was extinguished altogether, and I grew more unnerved with every moment that I couldn't see anything but the black of night before me.

"Mr. Hale?" I whispered.

I heard nothing, but then came the soft crunch of a footfall. My breath froze in my chest, and I fought the urge to run, though I couldn't stop myself from taking two quick steps back.

"Miss Chase," a voice said, and I relaxed.

"Mr. Hale. You're here." I frowned. "I think, at least. I can't see you."

Somehow, he managed to infuse amusement into his whisper. "I assure you, I'm here. I'm glad you came. I've a lantern several yards away, but in order to reach it, I'm afraid you'll have to forgive that I must—"

I heard two more soft footsteps, and then something touched my shoulder. I jumped but managed not to shriek. Mr. Hale's fingertips drifted lightly down my arm until they reached my hand. The sensation made me shiver—he stood right next to me, so close I could hear him breathe, but I couldn't see him.

He took my hand firmly in his, and I felt him turn away. I ignored the warming of my face and focused on following his slow, steady movement through the woods. I moved as quietly as I could, marveling that he could make his way through such impenetrable darkness with such certainty.

We covered ground slowly, and it was long minutes before I noticed a soft glow in front of us and slightly to our left. Mr. Hale altered his course and led me toward it, moving faster now that his destination was in sight, and in a few steps we stood over the small tin lantern he had tucked beneath a bush.

Mr. Hale released my hand and crouched beside the shrub. I saw his hand reach toward the lantern, heard the tiny squeak of metal, and the light went out.

I gasped.

I heard the rustle of cloth and felt Mr. Hale's arm brush mine as he stood.

"It's all right," he whispered. Metal squeaked again, and light appeared, shining in a thin beam on my skirt. "The less light we use, the less likely we are to be seen." He adjusted the lantern and aimed the beam at the ground. "Follow me."

"Wait." I grabbed his arm with both hands. "What are we doing?"

"We're going to keep watch, see if they hunt tonight."

I shivered again. "And if they do?"

"Then we'll watch and learn and hopefully prevent them from harming anyone else."

He took two steps and paused, and I hurried to catch up. We moved in this way, Mr. Hale picking his way across the ground with the help of the lantern, me following his partial silhouette as closely as I could.

We skirted the edge of Uncle Gerald's property, crossed the Fitzgeralds' field, carefully navigated the Claybrooks' orchard, and so circled the outer edge of the village until we came to the back of the cemetery.

Mr. Hale helped me over the low, wrought-iron fence and led me through the headstones.

"Do you expect them to come back here?" I asked as quietly as I could.

We reached the hedge that lined one side of the cemetery, and he stopped where it met the churchyard fence.

He shone the lantern at the base of the hedge, where I could see a hollow in the branches. At his gentle push, I sank to my knees on the ground and tucked myself into this gap in the hedge. Mr. Hale closed the lantern, extinguishing our light, and eased himself down beside me, between me and the street.

If it had been daylight, we would have been able to see the whole of the village square as well as a good portion of two of the main village streets. In the dark, I could see little more than the silhouette of the church steeple, outlined against the stars.

Without being told, I understood that from this point until Mr. Hale called an end to our effort, there could be no talking. I crossed my arms against my belly and bent my legs, wincing at the loud rustle of fabric the movement caused. I sensed the turn of Mr. Hale's head and resolved not to move again if I could help it. The grass was damp against my skirts, and I couldn't stop myself from leaning into Mr. Hale's warmth, pressing my shoulder against his, thankful when he didn't react.

I tried to keep watch, tried to spy some movement or light in the village, but the darkness seemed to swell and deepen so that staring through it began to make me dizzy. I closed my eyes and focused instead on listening. Mr. Hale breathed beside me, soft and even, and I felt the rhythm of my own breath aligning with his. Leaves whispered around us, a soft, soothing sound. My head drooped, sinking toward my chest.

A crunch of gravel, and Mr. Hale stiffened against me. I snapped awake, straightening from where I had fallen against him, my body half-curled into his. I held my breath and could hear Mr. Hale do the same.

The sound came again, a soft footstep on the lane to

our left, on the other side of the hedge. I tried to turn my head to peer through the bush's leaves, but my neck protested before I could glimpse little more than a soft light.

The footsteps continued, and the light grew, brushing against the shops and houses that lined the square. The footsteps came quickly, too quickly for one person, and I realized it must be two, or perhaps even three. My fingers curled into the fabric of Mr. Hale's sleeve, and we watched the figures come into view.

The lantern was held low and only touched the lower legs of the two people who crept across the square—a man and a woman. My grip on Mr. Hale's sleeve tightened.

One of the banshees had found her prey.

Mr. Hale slowly rose to his feet, nearly silent, and I followed as quietly as I could, swallowing a gasp when my cold, stiff legs protested the change of position. The figures stopped at the junction of Shepherd's Lane with the square, and the light shone on their shoes as they faced each other and moved close.

I gasped as Mr. Hale burst through the hedge and sprinted toward the figures. I would have been just behind him had my skirt not caught on a branch as I tried to scramble through. By the time I jerked myself free, barely noting the sound of ripping fabric, Mr. Hale had opened his lantern completely, and the light illuminated the square as though it were daylight. It flashed against the blade of the knife he had drawn and on the startled faces of the couple who stood in the lane.

I chased after Mr. Hale, one fear replaced by another as I recognized Mary and Peter.

Mr. Hale skidded to a halt, realizing his error, and I reached him a second later, positioning myself slightly in front of his right side, hoping to hide his knife.

"Mary!" I cried. "You can't be out here! It's dangerous!"

Peter lifted his lantern, adding its light to Mr. Hale's. He stood with his body turned half away from us, shielding Mary, who gaped at me from where he held her pressed against his chest.

"Catherine? I—what are you doing here?" Her eyes shifted to my left. "Mr. Hale?"

Realizing that my situation looked no better than hers, I froze for a moment, uncertain what to say.

Mr. Hale cleared his throat. "We're—"

"Hunting a rabid dog!" I blurted.

Mary's eyes widened, and Mr. Hale turned toward me, his eyebrows raised. Peter's lantern swung as he tightened his grip on it, making gravel and bushes and tree trunks flash in and out of visibility.

"I saw it behind our house this afternoon and mentioned it to Mr. Hale at the party." The words rolled off my tongue with little or no forethought, and I silently prayed my story made sense. "They're dangerous, you know, and neither of us liked the thought of it prowling the village." I stopped for breath.

"But why not wait until morning?" Peter asked.

"Catherine, you shouldn't be—it's dangerous!" Mary slipped out from under Peter's arm and ran toward me, hands outstretched to take my own. "What if it had attacked?"

"Mr. Hale will protect me," I said brightly. "He wanted to come alone, but he doesn't know the village as well as I do, and with Freddie laid up for the moment, who else could go with him?"

"Plenty of people," Mr. Hale grumbled, and I wasn't sure if he was serious or playing the part. I thought a trace of amusement hid behind the annoyance in his eyes, but it might have been a trick of the lantern. Either way, he seemed to be going along with my tale.

"I know it's not the most appropriate behavior, but I was very insistent. Poor Mr. Hale never had a chance. As for why we're doing it *tonight*," I said, addressing Peter, "we thought the dog might be more likely to prowl around in the dark, once the town had gone to sleep."

I stopped, waiting for more questions, but everyone seemed satisfied.

"I wish you'd stopped and actually *thought* about this for a moment," Mary chastised, shaking my hands in hers. "You haven't acted this recklessly since we were girls, and then only under Freddie's influence."

"Who says it was *Freddie's* influence over *me*?" I asked.

Mary rolled her eyes, but her smile was warm and affectionate, and I was so glad that she didn't seem angry with me anymore that I hugged her. She returned my embrace with a strong grip of her own, then pulled away.

"You'd better get home," I said. "That dog could be anywhere."

"We were heading that direction," Peter said. "I'll keep an eye out as I walk her home."

That would leave Peter on his own until he reached his own home. I exchanged looks with Mr. Hale, and he stepped toward Peter.

"Look, I don't want to intrude on your evening"—he glanced at Mary, who blushed—"but I'd feel a lot better if you let us come with you. A sort of armed escort, if you will." He indicated the knife, now safely sheathed at his hip.

Peter wavered for a moment, his look at Mary equal parts longing and protectiveness. "Very well. Let's go."

We moved quickly down the lane toward Mary's

house. Apparently feeling there was no longer any need to pretend in front of Mr. Hale, Mary and Peter held hands. I walked on Mary's other side, Mr. Hale next to me, his eyes roving in every direction.

"You mustn't meet Peter at night anymore," I said quietly to Mary. "I know it's trickier during the day, but it's not safe."

"Catherine, what are you—"

"Please," I said, my voice so quiet I could barely hear myself.

Mary must have heard the depth of emotion behind my plea, because she nodded. "All right. If you insist. Is it just because of the dog?"

I didn't have an answer to that question, suddenly sick at the thought of telling another lie.

We didn't speak until we arrived at the Hayworth house's back door, at which point I pulled Mr. Hale a little distance away so Mary and Peter could say their goodbye properly.

"Fast thinking," he murmured.

I was glad for the low light of the lantern, as it hid my flush of shame. Twice in this man's presence I had lied to a close friend. I would not be surprised if, after tonight, he never wished to see me again.

I didn't have time to wonder why this bothered me, because Peter joined us.

"Thank you," he said, the words sounding stiff. "I won't detain you from your purpose any longer." He turned to go.

"Wait!" I cried, forgetting for a moment my proximity to the Hayworth household. Both men shushed me, and we scurried for the cover of the trees that lined the drive. "Let us come with you," I whispered after a few tense moments watching the house for any signs of waking.

"I don't need an armed escort," Peter hissed.

I groped for his arm in the darkness. "Peter, I'm sorry. We didn't mean to interrupt you; we just wanted to warn you. And I'm sorry I made Mary promise not to meet you again. It's nothing personal; I think you're marvelous, and she's an idiot for not running away with you months ago. I just...I couldn't bear it if either of you were hurt. So please, for my sake, though I don't deserve it—let us walk you back to your house?"

For a long moment he didn't speak, and I desperately wished I could see his face. Then he covered my hand with his and said, "Very well. To please you."

We crept down the Hayworths' drive and back into the lane. None of us spoke as we walked briskly toward the center of the village until we reached the back of the Amherst store.

Peter held out his hand, and Mr. Hale shook it. He turned to me, and I placed my hand in his. "Thank you, Miss Chase. It's good to know you're on my side, as far as Mary's concerned."

I grinned. "I'll keep working on her until she finally realizes what needs to be done."

He nodded, gave my hand a final squeeze, and slipped through the back door.

Mr. Hale and I looked at each other.

"I suppose," he said, "that we should call an end to the night and try again another time."

I nodded, and we turned toward my house.

After a few minutes of walking, the lantern light a narrow beam illuminating the road just before our feet, a thought struck me.

"Once I'm home, you'll be alone."

"Yes," Mr. Hale agreed, his voice indicating what he thought about this obvious statement.

"But what if you run into one of *them?* The whole point of walking Mary and Peter home was to prevent that exact occurrence."

"I arrived safely at your house earlier this evening." His voice had stiffened. "I can make the return trip just as easily."

"Maybe you were just lucky," I insisted, unable to shed my fear at his leaving himself open to such danger. My step hitched. "You haven't been coming out alone all this time, have you?"

"Of course not. Not since that first night, when you saw me and I realized the spells they could cast. Marsh and I hunt together, but he's gone to York on an errand."

I felt slightly better at that, but it didn't solve our current problem. "You'll still be alone once I go home. Your cottage is on the other side of the village."

He sighed. "What do you suggest?"

"There's nothing for it. You'll just have to—"

The thin beam of lantern light, which had been skipping lightly over rock and gravel, suddenly illuminated a pair of bare feet peeking out from beneath the hem of a dress.

Mr. Hale grabbed my arm and swung me behind him, then opened the lantern to its full brightness.

The illuminated figure before us smiled.

"Hello," Ann Claybrook said.

fourteen

Before I could gasp, Mr. Hale had removed his knife from its sheath and slashed at Ann's chest. I saw the blade slice through fabric and skin, but the wound healed almost instantly, leaving a narrow gash in her bodice as the only evidence of his attack.

The smile still playing on her lips, she casually blocked his next thrust, wrenching the knife from his grasp and knocking him backward into me. Our legs tangled, and we fell to the ground. The lantern rolled a few feet away, the flame guttering but continuing to burn. We tried to scramble away from the banshee, but Mr. Hale's weight held my skirt to the ground, preventing me from rolling off his left arm.

Ann Claybrook loomed over us, Mr. Hale's knife in her hand. She looked at it for a moment, then mimicked his attack, slashing down at him. He raised his arm to shield himself and cried out as the blade bit through skin and muscle.

The creature that had once been a bright young girl began to speak, her voice a low, comforting murmur, the words indistinguishable. I felt Mr. Hale still beside me, and his bleeding arm slowly lowered to his side.

Panic coursed down to my toes and back up in waves,

drowning out Ann Claybrook's words and making my limbs shake. I stretched out my arm, reaching for the lantern, which lay on its side just out of reach. My fingers clawed uselessly at gravel. Ann bent over Mr. Hale, one hand extended toward his face, and with a small scream, I wrenched my skirt from beneath him. I lunged the last few inches, and my fingers closed around the ring at the top of the lantern. Sitting up, I swung the lantern into the side of Ann Claybrook's head.

The thin metal bent and burst at the impact, spraying her with hot oil and flame. She screamed and staggered backward, dropping the knife as she lifted her hands to her burning face.

Mr. Hale jerked and came back to himself, then noticed the knife lying at his feet. In one motion he leapt up, scooped the knife off the ground, and threw himself at Ann Claybrook, burying the blade as deeply as he could in her chest. She fell to the ground, screaming and writhing in a way that made my stomach twist in upon itself.

Mr. Hale pulled me to my feet, and we ran.

We threw ourselves toward the nearest building, navigating more by memory and instinct than sight. We slammed into the door in unison, and it creaked in protest. Behind us, the banshee howled. My hands found the handle, but it held firm beneath my desperate tugs.

"It's locked!" I gasped.

Mr. Hale shoved me aside, and over the roar of my own breathing, I heard the whisper of his hands over the wood of the door, then a soft crunch as he took a step backward. He flung himself against the door with shattering force, breaking the latch and tumbling into the building as the door flew back on its hinges. My cry of surprise and horror mingled with his shout of pain.

I stood frozen for a moment in the blackness, the sounds of the injured banshee behind me, the creaking door before me, until a moan from Mr. Hale brought me back to myself and I hurried into the building.

He lay on the floor just inside the door. Trying not to step on him and not entirely succeeding, I fumbled for the door and pushed it closed, but it drifted open again, the latch torn from the wood. A few seconds of frantic groping brought a low, heavy trunk beneath my fingers, and I threw my weight against it, dragging it in front of the door with a strength that would probably have surprised me in the light of day.

The door more or less barricaded, I knelt next to Mr. Hale, my hands slowly moving toward the sounds of his shallow breaths until they rested against his chest.

"Mr. Hale?" I whispered, my voice trembling. "Mr. Hale, we can't—"

"My shoulder," he hissed. "I think it's broken."

I closed my eyes against the darkness and tried to think past the panic. Standing, I crept to the window just visible next to the door. My eyes had adjusted to the night, and the light of the stars was enough for me to see the shape of Ann Claybrook as she staggered to her feet. Starlight glinted off her bared teeth as she turned to face the building where Mr. Hale and I had taken shelter—the blacksmith's workshop, a distant, logical part of my brain told me, based on the smell and its location in the village.

She raised one of her hands to her chest and then lowered it. It now carried the dull sheen of Mr. Hale's knife, and she seemed to stare straight into me. I tried to duck but couldn't. A soft warmth flooded my body, and though my mind fought against it, I couldn't move.

The banshee rushed forward, knife raised and mouth

open, and I stopped breathing.

A few yards from the blacksmith's door, so close that I could see her eyes shining in the blackness, she stopped, her face twisting. The warmth left my body as quickly as it had come, and my legs nearly buckled. I gripped the windowsill to keep myself from falling. For a long moment Ann stood, shaking and glaring at me through the whorled glass of the window, and then she took a long, slow step backward, turned, and ran into the night.

Mr. Hale moaned again. I heard a rustle of cloth and a sharp gasp. My eyes frantically searched the darkness on the other side of the window, but I could see nothing but the stars shining softly off the remnants of the lantern in the lane.

"I think she's gone," I whispered. My fingers explored the windowsill while I silently prayed that Mr. Potter, the blacksmith, kept a candle near the door. He did. A book of matches lay next to it.

The light of the match flared bright, searing my eyes and making me turn my head with a gasp. Squinting, I lit the candle, and by the time I knelt again at Mr. Hale's side, my eyes had greedily adjusted to the light.

He shook his head and tried to sit up. Sweat shone on his face. "No, it'll see. The light—"

"Shh. She's gone." I pressed him back to the floor. "Try not to move."

He obeyed, sinking back to the packed dirt floor, and I held the candle up so that the light fell on his injured shoulder. I could feel the fear and panic starting to fade, making it easier to think. I swept the candle down his arm, nearly dropping it when I reached the blood-soaked lower sleeve. I'd forgotten about the banshee's return strike with the knife.

"Let's get you bandaged up," I said, looking for someplace to set the candle. I dragged a footstool to Mr. Hale's side, wedged the candle into the wax-clogged holder I found on the windowsill, and set it atop the stool.

Repositioning myself next to him, I gently lifted Mr. Hale's forearm, trying to jostle his shoulder as little as possible, and turned it so that I could see the cut through the shredded fabric of his sleeve. It was deep and long and bled heavily. Already a small puddle of blood crept across the floor, soaking into Mr. Hale's waistcoat and my skirt at the knees.

"You're lucky you're with me," I said briskly, trying for the kind, professional tone Uncle Gerald had always used with his patients. I set Mr. Hale's arm back on the floor. "My uncle used to be the village doctor, and I've learned everything from him I possibly could."

With a quick glance at Mr. Hale, who faced the ceiling, his eyes closed tight against the pain, I wrestled my outer skirt up over my knees and ripped mercilessly at the seam of my chemise. I spent a moment pining for Mr. Hale's lost knife, but then the stitches gave and the fabric split. Convincing the fabric to rip across my body to the other seam took more work, but eventually a large panel of cotton tore itself loose. I quickly yanked my dress back over my legs. Mr. Hale didn't move, except for a quivering that seemed to start in his jaw and spread down the length of his body.

"So this kind of thing," I continued, holding the partial chemise into the light to find the cleanest and driest part, "is old hat for me. I'll bandage this arm up first to stop you bleeding all over Mr. Potter's floor, and then we'll take a look at that shoulder."

I ripped the chemise until I had three long strips of

fabric I could use for bandages. Mr. Hale started to groan as I lifted his arm again, but bit it off, his eyebrows drawing down toward his nose as he clenched his teeth. His eyes opened slightly, just enough to watch me.

I ripped his sleeve down through the cuff, then up toward his elbow so that it fell completely away from the wound, trying to ignore the blood on my fingers. "You'll want to go see Mr. Haviland tomorrow, make up some story about catching your arm on a tree while riding or something. You need stitches."

I wrapped the bandages tightly around the cut, doing my best to press the sides of the wound together so it could mend. As I worked, he frowned ferociously at the ceiling. I didn't want to know how much I was hurting his shoulder, no matter how careful I was.

"There," I said after a few minutes. "Done."

He turned his head slightly to look at his arm and seemed surprised by the neat, snug bandage. Blood started to peek through the fabric in the center of the cut, but I hoped the bleeding would slow soon. I'd check it in a few minutes, after I'd examined his shoulder, and see if I needed to add another layer of bandage.

"You're right," he said, looking back toward the ceiling. "I am lucky to have you here. It seems you've saved my life again."

I stood, wiping my hands on my skirt—it was already ruined, so why not—and moved a step up his body so that I could kneel next to his shoulder. Lightly, so lightly I could hardly feel him, I touched his shoulder with my fingertips. His body stiffened. "No more than you saved mine," I said, hoping to take his mind off what I had to do.

He shook his head, wincing as I pressed my fingers into the flesh around his joint, feeling for the bones. "That bit with the lantern—if you hadn't done that, we'd both be as dead as that monster."

I shuddered, seeing again the way the flame crawled across Ann Claybrook's face as the oil splattered over her. "Well, if you hadn't broken yourself in rather spectacular ways getting us through that door, we'd be dead as well."

He smiled wanly, his eyes closing again. "We're even, then."

"Yes." I pressed again, my fingers drifting over the joint. Something wasn't right. It didn't feel broken, it just felt....

I remembered the summer Freddie fell off the stable roof, how I had to help Uncle Gerald by kneeling on my cousin, holding him in place while my uncle yanked his leg back into its socket and Freddie screamed—

I sat back, and Mr. Hale relaxed slightly as the pressure from my exploring hand disappeared. "Not so spectacularly broken after all," I said. "Just dislocated. I'll have to put it back in."

Mr. Hale looked at me. "You can do that?"

I nodded and stood again, hoping I looked calmer than I felt. "It's going to hurt like hell. You'd be best off passing out now, if you think you can manage it."

He seemed to grow paler, but it might have been a flicker of the candle. "I know it's bad if a lady is swearing at me."

A smile tugged at my mouth but didn't make it all the way to my lips. "You forget who I live with."

He turned his head back to the ceiling. "No. I don't."

When he didn't say anything else, I went in search of something for him to hold between his teeth. A wooden spoon would have been ideal, but I had to settle for a thin wooden dowel on which Mr. Potter had hung some tools whose purpose I couldn't fathom.

"Here," I said, holding it above Mr. Hale's face. "You're going to want this."

He obediently opened his mouth and lifted his good hand to help me position the rod between his back teeth.

"Ready?"

He nodded and took a deep breath, and so did I. The impact with the door had knocked the ball of his joint down and back, out of its socket, which meant I'd need to pull it nearly straight up from Mr. Hale's current position in order to put it back in.

I stood and moved to his side, easing both feet between his arm and his body. We looked at each other for a second, and then I pressed one foot onto the hollow between his shoulder and his chest. He groaned and closed his eyes, his teeth tightening on the dowel. Bending down, I wrapped both hands around his arm just above his elbow, took two fast breaths, and then straightened. As smoothly and quickly as I could, I pulled his arm up until it pointed nearly straight up in the air, wishing there was some way to block Mr. Hale's cries from my ears, and then pulled as hard as I could in one swift jerk.

I felt something give, and Mr. Hale screamed, his back arching off the floor. He yanked his arm from my grasp and rolled onto his side, curling in on himself and hugging his injured arm to his chest.

I took half a step backward and fell to the floor, landing hard on my hip and the heels of my hands. For a few long seconds, we both lay there, panting.

"Did it work?" I asked, my voice hoarse. I placed a hand against his back. I could feel him trembling, feel how tight his muscles were, even through his waistcoat, but slowly the trembling faded, and he relaxed.

He rolled onto his back and turned his head toward me, his arm still cradled against his chest. "Yes, actually." He managed a small smile. "I'm impressed." He relaxed even more as I watched, and his smile grew. "It hardly hurts at all, now. Just a dull ache."

I pushed myself to my knees and picked up the remainder of my chemise. "Tomorrow you won't feel so kindly toward me, when it stiffens up. You'll be lucky if you can move."

"What are you doing?" he asked, watching me turn the fabric in the light.

"Making you a sling, or at least attempting one."

He sat up, wincing, and gave his bandage a more thorough examination. "Harwick seems to be missing out on the attentions of a very skilled physician." He looked up at me. "What else can you do?"

I shrugged, adjusting my grip on the fabric before carefully tearing it parallel to the seam. "Diagnose several dozen illnesses, advise medicines for several dozen more. I've read all the medical texts in Uncle Gerald's library. There's not much else in the house to read, so one makes do." Laying the main body of the sling aside, I started tearing strips in order to tie it around his shoulder. "You, however, are my first patient."

"Well, so far, I'm very satisfied with my care." He turned his head, taking in our surroundings, then scooted toward the hearth, which he leaned against. Though he was putting up a good front, I could still see the tightness in his face. Shoulder and forearm, despite being as patched as I could manage in the circumstances, must have still throbbed and ached to a wretched degree.

I followed him to the hearth, holding the chemise and half-assembled sling in one hand and dragging the stool and our candle with the other. Mr. Hale chuckled, watching me awkwardly shuffle across the floor on my knees, but I found I didn't mind.

Another few minutes saw the sling snugly holding the injured arm in place against his chest, and Mr. Hale seemed to relax a bit more. His eyes closed, and he rested his head on the bricks of the large fire pit. Deciding it couldn't hurt to try, I stood and lifted the candle.

A line of low cabinets ran along one wall. I had the first one open, my head stuck inside, when Mr. Hale spoke.

"Again I must ask, what are you doing?" A glance over my shoulder showed that he'd half-opened one eye.

"I just thought that, since we've already broken down Mr. Potter's door and bled all over his floor—"

"I'm fairly certain I did both of those things all by myself," Mr. Hale protested.

"—we might as well see if there are any other ways we can impose upon his hospitality." My voice echoed dully around my head as I pushed tools, bottles of polish, cleaning rags, and spare candles around on the shelf. Giving up on that cabinet, I moved to the next.

"Did you have anything specific in mind?"

"Yes, actually," I said, emerging triumphantly from the second cabinet with a bottle of whisky in hand. Mr. Potter was a fine blacksmith, but the entire village knew he was never more than thirty feet from a drink at any time, if he could help it. I moved back to Mr. Hale's side and handed him the bottle. "To take the edge off. No glasses, I'm afraid."

"You," he said emphatically, "are an absolute angel." He took the liquor almost greedily, pulled the cork out with his teeth, and took two large swigs. After a short pause and a quick breath, he took another long pull, then handed it back to me.

"Well," I said, impressed despite myself. "I guess what they say about Scots and their drink is true."

He laughed and leaned his head back against the hearth again. "Mm. Not really. But I suppose that will actually work in my favor, in this case." He lifted his head just enough to give the bottle an appreciative glance. "That's marvelous."

I took a tentative sip of the whisky and gasped. Mr. Hale smiled, and I recognized more than a little challenge in the expression. Lifting my chin, I took a decent-sized swig of the liquor, swallowed it without making a face, and shoved the cork back into the neck.

"Bravo," he said.

I felt the whisky travel down to my stomach and from there radiate out along my limbs. Once the burning in my throat stopped, it was a rather pleasant sensation.

I set the bottle on the ground between us and stretched my legs alongside Mr. Hale's. We sat for a while, listening to the breeze move through the trees outside and creak through the shingles of the blacksmith's roof.

"I suppose we're stuck here until daylight." I turned my head toward him. "They are purely nocturnal, right? I mean, they're monsters. Monsters should only come out at night." I chewed on my bottom lip. "Are they? Nocturnal?"

He shrugged, then winced and rubbed his injured shoulder with his other hand. "I have no idea. The legends say so, and I've only ever seen them at night, but that doesn't mean anything."

"Great." I chewed my lip for a moment. "How many times have you seen them?"

"Counting tonight, three."

"Ha! Then we're even."

He laughed again, and I smiled. "Is it a competition, then?"

"Growing up with Freddie Martin, everything is a competition. Even finding the newest competition is a competition."

His laughter faded into the silence, and I reached for the liquor bottle again, my mind drifting back to the attack. I took another small sip of whisky and passed him the bottle.

"Mr. Hale—"

"I think, after tonight—considering I've bled all over your dress and you had to stand on me—that you have the right to call me James." He paused. "If you want."

My hands lay in my lap, and I laced my fingers together and studied them, unable to look at him. Out of the corner of my eye, I saw him take another long pull from the bottle, then hold it out toward me. When I didn't move, he set it back on the ground.

"I'm sorry," he started. "I shouldn't have presumed. With your permission, I'll blame the extraordinary events of tonight and the combined effects of blood loss and spirits. Please know I won't—"

"No," I said quietly, pressing my hands into my lap and lifting my head. He stopped immediately and watched me, the candlelight flickering across his features. "I appreciate—I mean, I'd be honored—" I sighed, wondering when it had suddenly become so hard to meet his eyes. "And you can call me Catherine," I said finally.

I risked a glance at him and just caught the boyish grin that flashed across his face before he turned away for a moment. I bit my lip to quell my own smile, crossed my arms, and stared determinedly at the candle flame. I wasn't sure I could blame the giddy feeling that flipped twice in my stomach entirely on the whisky. To even the odds, I plucked the bottle from the floor and took my longest drink yet.

"Perhaps," James said, "for the sake of appearances, we should restrict our use of Christian names to our new secret lives as hunters of mythical beasts."

A giggle burst from me before I could stop it, and I clapped a hand over my mouth. "It's like one of those horrid gothic novels Freddie's always reading."

"Yes!" He took the bottle from my hand. I noted with warm detachment that it was a third empty already. "What shall we call it?"

I hummed for a moment while I thought, wiggling my toes inside my boots. "How about *The Pale Women of Harwick*?"

"Dull, dull, dull," he scolded, passing the bottle back to me. "Where's the mystery? The danger?"

I sat up, pulling my back away from the hearth, and rounded on him. "Fine. What do you suggest?"

"Watch where you're waving that bottle," he said, ducking. I sheepishly set it back on the ground. "I'd call it —I don't know, *Terror on the Moors* or something equally sensational."

I snorted without a thought to Mrs. Ellerby's hypothetical horror. "We haven't got any moors around Harwick. They're miles away."

"Yes, but London doesn't know that. They assume the entire island north of Cambridge is nothing but moors and sheep."

"And banshees."

"And banshees," he agreed.

I leaned back, my shoulder brushing up against his

uninjured one. His warmth was pleasant and matched the warmth that coursed from my middle up to my head. I didn't move. "It's a funny word, banshee. Oh! The banshee!"

I struggled a little more upright so I could see his face. His look of amused affection reminded me of Freddie, and for a moment I lost my train of thought. Freddie was at home, sleeping off the last of his cold, with no idea what I was up to. He'd be furious tomorrow when I told him Mr. Hale and I had nearly gotten ourselves killed, as well as jealous that he'd missed everything.

"What is it, Catherine?" James asked, and my thoughts, on their way back toward my intended topic, got stuck on the sound of my name coming from his mouth. His accent had become a little stronger with every drink of whisky he took; I'd never heard my name said that way before. I wanted to hear it again.

The bottle seemed to leap into my hand; I took another drink.

"The banshee," I said, trying to focus through the whirl of thoughts in my head. "Ann. She tried to come after us. She knew where we were, could see me through the window. I—I felt her, holding me in place. But within a few steps of the door, she suddenly turned and ran away."

We were silent for a few minutes. James gently took the bottle from my hand and set it on his far side, out of my reach.

"I'm not drunk," I protested. "That's what happened."

"You *are* drunk," he replied, "and I believe you."

"Oh."

"I think we're both drunk."

"But just a little," I said. This was very important for

some reason. "A very little."

He chuckled. "Fine. Barely drunk."

"Barely," I said with satisfaction, sitting back against the hearth. "Very barely."

After another few minutes, I found myself listing sideways until Mr. Hale's shoulder kindly volunteered to hold me up. I peeked up at him through my eyelashes to see if he minded, but he had closed his eyes and sat with a small smile on his face.

"Tell me about Scotland," I said.

He turned his head to look at me without lifting it from its resting place, and our faces seemed very close together. "What about it?"

"Everything," I said instantly, and he laughed. "I've never been there. What does it look like where you grew up?"

He took a breath and turned his face back to the candle. Over the next hour he told me about his childhood, then demanded I do the same in order to determine the vast and foreign differences between a Scottish upbringing and an English one. In the end, we decided there really weren't any, not of the vast and foreign variety, and Mr. Hale laughed at my disappointment.

"The sky," he said.

"Hm?" I lifted my head from his shoulder with some effort. The warmth from the whisky had cooled into a delicious sleepiness that made it hard to move.

"It's getting lighter." He looked down at me. "We should go before Mr. Potter wakes up and finds us here."

For a moment, neither of us moved, but then I straightened and stood, stretching. He was right—the silhouettes of the trees that lined the lane were visible against the dark blue of the sky, a blue that seemed to lighten and fade even as I watched.

Mr. Hale pushed himself to his feet, wincing as the movement jostled his arm. "You're right. Abominably stiff."

I snuffed the candle and put it back on the windowsill, and Mr. Hale helped me drag the heavy chest away from the door, which listed drunkenly on its hinges.

We hurried across the lane onto a smaller road, ducking off of that as soon as we came to some wooded cover. A bird started to chirp in anticipation of dawn, and another joined it. The sky slowly leached itself of night's color as the sun prepared to make its appearance.

"Oh," I said, suddenly remembering. "About Mary and Peter. Please—"

"Not a word," Mr. Hale promised. "How long have they...?"

"A couple of years." I plucked a leaf off a low-hanging branch as I ducked under it. "Peter wants to elope, of course, but Mary can't bring herself to do it. I've been trying to convince her it's her only option for months." I glanced at him, noting the slight surprise on his face. "It's what we quarreled about, actually."

He didn't say anything in response, and we passed the rest of the walk to my house in silence.

In the trees behind the house, we paused at the creek to clean ourselves as best we could. It was getting hard to look at him again, as the alcohol faded from my system and I washed his blood off my hands.

"I'm sorry about your dress," he said.

I looked down at myself, at the rust-brown smears and stains marring most of my skirt. "It's all right. I never liked this dress anyway. Horrid, drab thing."

His fingertips touched my chin, lifting my face, and I

stopped breathing. I hadn't realized he'd moved so close. He pushed a lock of hair off my forehead. His fingers were still damp.

"I'm glad you're not engaged to Mr. Martin, Catherine," he said.

I stared at him, unable to pull a single coherent thought from my mind.

He dropped his hand and took a long step back, smiling. He gestured toward the house with his chin. "Go on, then."

I turned obediently and walked toward the house but stopped at the edge of the trees. "Change those bandages before you go to sleep. And wash that cut. You don't want it to get infected."

"I will," he said, amusement clear in his voice.

I crossed the lawn toward the house, trying not to think. When I reached the kitchen door, I looked back toward the woods. White flashed through the trees as Mr. Hale raised his uninjured arm in farewell, and then his form turned and made its way toward his cottage.

As I closed the kitchen door behind me, the first rays of sunlight spilled over the horizon and turned the sky orange.

fifteen

I peeked in on Freddie before going to my room. He stirred sleepily when I pressed my hand against his forehead. His skin was cool.

He made a muffled, moaning sound, yawned, and opened his eyes just long enough to ascertain my identity. "Cathy," he breathed.

He hadn't called me Cathy in years. I'd thrown such a fit about the nickname at age fifteen that eventually even Freddie gave it up.

"You're healed, I think," I whispered.

He nodded, his eyes still closed. "How was the party?"

I hesitated. "Interesting. I'll tell you after breakfast. Or lunch, rather."

Even half asleep, he could smirk. "Stayed up past your bedtime, did you?"

"Yes," I said simply. A lump of lingering dread and fear in my throat kept me from saying any more.

His breathing deepened, and he didn't wake as I left.

∞∞∞

"Miss Chase!"

Polly's voice cut through the oblivion of sleep into which I'd fallen as soon as I found my bed. I lifted my head from the mound of blankets and pillows under which I'd burrowed to glare at the door.

"Mrs. Ellerby is here to see you," Polly said.

Groaning, I looked at the small clock on the table beside my bed. I'd only been asleep for three hours. "Ask her to come back after we've had a chance to eat breakfast."

"I told her you weren't up yet, miss, but she said it was important. Said she'd wait, as she had urgent news to tell you."

I sat up, suddenly awake. "Tell her I'll be right down."

Polly nodded and closed the door.

I hurled myself out of bed and out of my nightgown, my mind already moving from one horrible possibility to another until it landed on a vision of Mr. Hale—it felt odd to think of him as James in the light of day—murdered in the woods near his cottage.

My hands shook as I pulled on the first dress I saw. Without bothering with shoes or my hair, I raced down the stairs, stubbing my little toe on the corner of the hallway.

Mrs. Ellerby stood in the foyer, wringing her hands. "Catherine!" she cried as soon as she saw me, rushing forward to take my hands. "You won't believe what's happened. It's just too strange!"

"What?" I gasped. My legs could barely hold me up.

Mrs. Ellerby pulled back and looked me up and down. "My dear, you're a bit disheveled. Are you feeling all right?"

It took everything I had not to shake her until she told me what had happened.

Before I could give an answer, the gleam returned to

her eye, and she leaned forward. "You'll never guess! The whole town's in an uproar."

"Please," I said, near tears. "What—?"

"Mr. Potter's blacksmith shop was broken into last night!"

Mrs. Ellerby waited for my gasp of shock and was thus baffled when I nearly collapsed in relief.

"Is that all?" I asked, holding onto her arms for support.

"What do you mean, 'is that all'? Didn't you hear me? Someone has broken into the blacksmith! Who knows which of us will be next?"

My strength surged back and burst out of my mouth in a laugh. He hadn't been killed. He was alive. "What'd they take?"

Still uncertain at my response, Mrs. Ellerby said, "That's the strangest part. They broke down the door to get in but then didn't take anything. They drank half a bottle of whisky, and one of them must have been injured, because Mr. Potter found blood on the floor, but that's it."

"How mystifying," I said. "I hope Mr. Potter is able to fix his door."

She waved a hand, dismissing this practical thought. "Oh, yes, I'm sure. He'll have it back together by the end of the day. But who do you think it could have been? Passing ruffians?"

"I'm sure."

"I can't think what they were after," she said, frowning into the space just past my shoulder.

"Perhaps they were thirsty," I hazarded.

She gave me one of her looks. "I think you should have some tea, dear, and breakfast. You're obviously not awake yet."

∞∞∞

Two hours later, I'd managed to put up my hair and find some shoes, as well as eat the toast Polly forced on me.

I lay dozing on the sofa in the parlor, one arm flung across my eyes, a cup of long-cold tea on the floor beside me. I'd been there for an hour and a half and kept jerking awake in sudden bursts of panic.

"Miss Catherine?"

Polly's voice startled me, and I sat up abruptly, nearly knocking over the teacup on the floor and cursing under my breath.

"Language, Miss Catherine," Polly scolded, and I froze.

"Sorry, Polly." My face reddened, and I set the teacup on the small table next to the sofa, feeling ten years old again.

Polly sniffed. "Miss Hayworth is here. Shall I show her in?"

I scrambled to my feet. "Yes. Yes, of course."

Mary entered the room, and Polly shut the door behind her. We looked at each other for a moment, and I felt the distance that had crept into our friendship since our quarrel.

Then Mary flung herself across it.

"Oh, Catherine! Can you forgive me?" she cried, wrapping her arms around me.

I returned her embrace, feeling some of the darkness and confusion that marred my world lift. "Don't be silly. Can you forgive *me?*"

"Of course! Of course!" She let me go and took a step back, capturing my hands in hers. "I was awful, I'm sorry.

And you were right—if I want to be with Peter, I only have one option."

I felt my jaw drop, and I sank onto the sofa. Mary followed. "You're going to elope?"

She nodded and squeezed my hands. "Not tonight, mind you, but soon. Next week, perhaps, or the next. Before the month is out."

I grinned and hugged her again. "I know this isn't easy for you, but I'm so glad to hear it."

She shook her head, laughing softly. "Now that I've finally found the courage to make the decision, it feels like the easiest thing in the world. There's just one thing. Last night—"

"Mr. Hale won't tell anyone," I said. "He gave me his word."

Mary relaxed back into the sofa, her gaze shifting to mischievous suspicion. "And how did your hunt for the rabid dog go?"

I flushed but managed to answer evenly. "We didn't find it. Mr. Hale sent me home as soon as we'd seen you and Peter safely indoors. He says he and Freddie can continue the hunt today, though he suspects the dog has already moved on."

Mary made a thoughtful humming noise.

"What?" I asked, feeling my back stiffen.

"Nothing." She smiled.

I glared at her. "That's right. Nothing."

She stood, still smiling, and put on her bonnet. "One of these days, Catherine, we're going to sit down for a chat, and I'm not leaving until you tell me everything that's happened to you lately." She tied the ribbon beneath her chin and pinned me with a look that made me fidget. "I'm sure it will be the most fascinating story I've heard in ages."

"Oh, yes," I said softly, giving her a sheepish smile. "Thank you, Mary."

She moved toward the door and paused. "Please thank Mr. Hale for me next time you see him." She flashed a mischievous look over her shoulder. "I'm sure it will be long before I do."

Before I could muster a response, she was gone.

∞∞∞

Freddie found me an hour later, lying on my stomach on the sofa, my head buried beneath the only two throw pillows Uncle Gerald possessed. I heard him pause in the doorway to yawn.

"What on earth's the matter with you?" He shuffled over and shoved my legs to the back of the sofa so he could sit by my feet.

"Not all of us had the luxury of actually sleeping last night," I said without removing the pillows.

He poked the back of my knee, making my leg twitch. "I told you not to go to that party. You should have stayed home and seen to your duty of nursing me back to health."

I swung one of the pillows blindly behind me, knowing I couldn't miss at this range. Freddie *oof*ed as it bounced off his chest. "You're not sick anymore, apparently."

"No thanks to you."

"*Very* thanks to me." I twisted until I could prop myself up on one elbow and glare at him, the pillows tumbling to the floor. "Don't you want to know *why* I didn't get any sleep last night? I guarantee a party of Susannah Brock's was not entertainment enough to keep me out until morning, especially with Mrs. Ellerby as my escort."

He leaned against the sofa back, trapping my legs and pressing them down into the cushion. I tried to kick him off, but he was too heavy. "Tossing and turning, fretting over my condition, were you?"

I snorted. "More like creeping through the woods, hunting banshees, and nearly getting eaten in the process."

That got his attention, and for the next half hour he sat, wide-eyed, while I told him about my night's adventures. I had to leave out certain elements, of course—our encounter with Mary and Peter turned into stumbling across Peter alone, trying to cure his insomnia with a walk. And then there was me, Mr. Hale, and the whisky. I hoped Freddie didn't notice the color creeping up my neck as I glossed over that part of the evening.

"You really put his shoulder back in place?" Freddie asked, his face a mix of pride and awe.

I bit my lip, trying not to look too pleased with myself. "The best part is that Mrs. Ellerby stopped by first thing this morning—I'd only been home three hours—to tell me all about how some passing ruffians broke into the blacksmith."

I expected him to be amused, but instead his expression slowly darkened. "You shouldn't have gone, Catherine. It was too dangerous. What would have happened if Ann Claybrook hadn't just run off like that? You weren't exactly winning that fight, from the sound of it."

My stomach clenched with remembered terror, but before I could say anything, I heard someone knock on the front door, and I rolled my eyes, grateful for the reprieve.

"I suppose Mrs. Ellerby is back to give me the latest update on the state of Mr. Potter's broken door." Freddie was still sitting on my legs, and I shoved at him again as I heard Polly's footsteps in the foyer. "Get off. She'll be appalled if she catches us like this; I'll get lectured for months."

Grumbling, Freddie leaned forward enough for me to extract my legs. He looked me over as I stood, his eyes lingering on my hair. The seriousness in his eyes faded, and he smirked. "Your burrowing behavior has not, I'm afraid, done wonders for your appearance."

My hands flew to my hair, flattened and mussed into a disaster only half-held in place by hairpins. There was no time to fix it, however, because Polly was knocking on the parlor door, opening it, and announcing the guest.

"A Mr. Marsh to see you, miss." She bobbed a short curtsy, gave my rumpled hair and dress a disapproving look, and left.

"Marsh?" Freddie repeated quietly behind me. I stopped fussing with my hair, trying to remember where I'd met a Mr. Marsh.

My mind placed the name just before Mr. Hale's man entered the room, giving us a brief but courteous bow.

"Oh!" I was suddenly aware of my heartbeat.

Marsh looked up at my exclamation and didn't blink twice at my state, though I must have looked as though I'd just wrestled an entire herd of sheep into submission. "Mr. Hale sent me, Miss Chase. He wanted to come see you"—his eyes flicked toward Freddie—"and Mr. Martin himself, but he was thrown off his horse this morning and is under strict orders from Mr. Haviland not to move if he can help it."

There was a twinkle in his eyes, and I relaxed slightly. "I'm sorry to hear that. I hope he wasn't injured too badly?"

Marsh seemed pleased at my response, and I felt certain he knew everything that had passed the night before. "Dislocated his shoulder and took a nasty cut on his arm," he said, "but he'll heal up quick. He had good care after the accident."

I blushed. "I'm sure he's in even better hands now."

Marsh's smile widened. "That he is, miss. He'll be pleased to hear you're in good health. And you, Mr. Martin." He nodded. "Shall I tell him you're back on your feet?"

Freddie stood and moved to my side. "Please do."

Marsh bowed his head. "Miss Chase."

I curtsied. "Mr. Marsh. Give Mr. Hale my—our regards."

Freddie showed him to the door, giving me a moment to myself. When he came back, I was ready for the odd look he wore.

"That was kind of Mr. Hale," he said, "being so concerned for your welfare. And assuming you would worry for his."

"We were nearly killed last night. I think concern on both our parts is perfectly natural."

"Perfectly natural," he repeated.

I pulled a few pins from my hair and tried to smooth it back into a semblance of order before replacing them.

"Cathy," he said quietly, and I stopped fussing with my hair to look at him, struck by the gravity of his voice. "This banshee thing started as a lark, but promise me you won't go out hunting like that again."

I could feel the mulish expression forming on my face, and Freddie noticed.

"Or at least take me with you next time," he amended. "I couldn't bear it if something happened to you and I wasn't there to prevent it."

My defensiveness faded at his genuine concern. Touched, I reached out a hand and caught his fingers in my own. "I promise."

∞∞∞

After church the next day, as the village milled about the churchyard, enjoying what little sun was able to slip weakly through the clouds, I returned greetings automatically, hardly hearing the questions put to me or the answers I gave, my entire being aware of Mr. Hale's presence a few yards away. My hand rested in the crook of Freddie's elbow, and he steered us toward the gate, as eager as I was to escape the interminable small talk.

Mr. Hale appeared in front of us, and my world came sharply into focus. We stopped, and he smiled first at Freddie, then me. His right arm hung in a linen sling, but his eyes were bright, his color good. He must have been healing well, as his man Marsh had said.

"I'm glad to see you've recovered, Mr. Martin." Mr. Hale turned to me and nodded. "Miss Chase." His eyes smiled at me, and I remembered his words about our secret lives and blushed.

"Heard about your fall," Freddie said. "I'm sorry to see you injured. Perhaps you'll consider the possible consequences before you make a similar attempt."

Mr. Hale rocked back on his heels as though he'd been slapped, and his face flickered from open amiability to a closed, tight expression. Freddie took an aggressive step toward him.

"Freddie," I hissed, tugging on his arm. He ignored me.

"Believe me," Mr. Hale said, "harm was never my intention."

I looked quickly around. No one seemed to be paying any attention to us, but that wouldn't last, not with Freddie posturing like a drunken boxer.

"Intention or not," he said, "it could hardly be avoided in the circumstances."

"Freddie!" I turned to Mr. Hale. "Excuse us, Mr. Hale. I hope to see you well and whole soon."

Neither man acknowledged me, but when I pulled Freddie toward the gate, he followed. Mr. Hale caught his arm as we passed, stopping him. They stood nearly nose to nose for a long moment, giving each other the same measuring look.

"I would never let any harm come to her, not if it was within my power to prevent it," Mr. Hale said in a voice so low I could barely hear him.

After another endless moment, Freddie replied, "Good." He took a small step back. Mr. Hale dropped his arm. "But it's those things outside your power that frighten me."

Mr. Hale's shoulders relaxed, and his face opened again. "Me too."

With a nod, Freddie turned, and we walked out the gate and down the lane. When I looked back, Mr. Hale was watching us and ignoring Susannah Brock, who stood chatting at his shoulder.

The walk back to the house was silent and tense, and as soon as we passed through the door, I rounded on Freddie. "What was *that* all about? I do not appreciate being talked about as though I'm not present."

He jammed his hat onto the foyer table and slammed his walking stick next to it. "Did he take any liberties with you?"

I blinked, my annoyance shaken by his question. "Liberties?"

He glared at me, his eyes fierce. "You spent the night alone with him in a smithy. By all rights I should either be forcing him to propose to you or challenging him to a duel."

The mention of marriage caused a swirl of conflicting emotions to burst to life in my stomach, but I couldn't worry about that right now. I hadn't realized Freddie was still this upset about my encounter with Ann Claybrook. He had seemed fine yesterday and this morning, and it hurt to know that he could hide his emotions from me this well.

"I know that's not what you're really upset about, but he was a perfect gentleman," I said quietly. When he relaxed slightly, I brightened my voice. "Other than asking me to hunt banshees with him in the first place, but I'm not sure society has rules about that."

The anger and energy seemed to flow out of him at the same time, and he lowered himself onto the stairs and rested his elbows on his knees. "It's not funny. Father would kill me if he came home to find your reputation ruined." He peered up at me through his bangs. "Or, you know, if you died."

I snorted and sat next to him on the step. "I promise to let you protect me and my reputation from here on out. Deal?"

"Deal." Freddie's expression turned mischievous. "You like him, don't you?"

I flushed again, something I was getting tired of doing so often. "I think so. It's all a bit overwhelming. It wasn't that long ago I thought he was a murderer, after all. But...

yes, I like him."

"I think Mr. Hale feels the same about you, for what it's worth. I'm not sure you noticed the way he looked at you after church, but I did."

I couldn't look at Freddie, but I also couldn't stop the smile spreading across my face.

He hooted and knocked against me with his shoulder. "If you marry Mr. Hale, I'll finally be free to pursue the lady of my choosing without shocking the entire village. Thank you, by the way, for being the shocking one. Makes my life much easier. Perhaps I'll run away with Susannah Brock."

Through my laughter I managed to say, "You'd get what you deserved if you did. Besides, don't you think it's a bit early for all that?"

Freddie grinned. "Trust me, it won't be long before I can run off with whomever I please. Unless we all get murdered by banshees, that is." He slapped his thighs. "I'm hungry. Are you hungry?"

"Famished."

We went in to lunch.

sixteen

The creak of my bedroom door woke me, and I sat up with a gasp.

"Catherine!" Freddie hissed. He crossed the room in three steps and pulled me out of bed. I struggled to free my legs from the tangled blankets and nearly fell, catching myself against his chest. He lifted me away from the mess and set me on my feet, holding me by the shoulders.

"What—"

"Someone's here. In the house."

A rush of heat flooded my body, followed by cold. What little moon there was hid behind a thick layer of clouds, and the darkness in my room was complete. I couldn't see Freddie, but his voice and the tension of his fingers told me everything I needed to know.

He took my hand and moved toward the door, and I followed as closely as I dared. We glided down the hallway, our feet moving with the surety of familiarity, our hands trembling together. I listened to his shallow breaths, the whisper of his shirt and trousers as he moved.

We crept down the staircase, and I gripped the back of his shirt with my free hand to keep myself from bolting out of panic. When we reached the bottom of the stairs,

Freddie paused and I huddled against him, listening. For a long moment I heard nothing but our two ragged sets of breathing, but then came the slightest whisper of fabric.

I knew that sound. A dress brushing against the floor.

Freddie stiffened. We squeezed each other's hands so tightly I could feel my pulse throb in my fingers.

He moved forward, and I nearly trod on his heels in my fright. It was no brighter on the main floor. Anyone could have been standing a foot away from us, and we wouldn't have seen them. We crossed the foyer as silently as possible, feeling our way toward the dining room door, and paused. Freddie's head turned, listening, and I held my breath and did the same. I heard nothing, and we eased into the room.

We skirted the table, heading for the narrow door that led to the kitchen and the back door. Halfway there, the floor creaked behind us. Freddie jumped and spun, throwing his arms back to keep me sheltered behind him. I stumbled at the sudden movement and caught hold of his shirt to keep myself upright. He took a step back, and I could feel him shaking.

A match struck, and light flared in the room. Freddie's breath stopped. I didn't want to look, but I forced my head from behind the shelter of his back.

Two women stood in the dining room doorway. Ann Claybrook held a candle in one hand, and the yellow light reflected off their skin. Except for her uneven hair, she looked unscathed from our encounter just two nights before. The other woman was taller than Ann but more delicate and wore a fashionable silk gown.

My eyes were drawn back to Ann, and she smiled, her teeth flashing in the candlelight.

Freddie moved backward, his arms still shielding me.

He pushed me steadily back, but I was unable to tear my eyes from Ann until my heels hit the hearth stone of the fireplace and I nearly fell. Freddie pressed against me, trapping me between his body and the mantel. The door to kitchen was to our left, just a few strides away.

Ann and the other woman moved forward, one on each side of the table. Ann's gaze never wavered from my face, and I dared not meet it. Freddie turned his head toward the other woman, and his body suddenly relaxed against me. The woman smiled, and his body shifted forward, as though preparing to go to her.

My fear tripled as Freddie took a step toward the woman, clogging my throat. I tried to say his name, to get his attention, but my voice failed, so I desperately grasped his shoulders and pulled him back toward me. He tilted and wavered but threw me off and took another step. The banshee beckoned him forward, and there was something familiar in her smile, in the shape of her nose and eyes.

Ann set the candle on the table and moved toward me, checking my frantic attempt to grab Freddie's wrist. I backed into the fireplace, and Freddie crossed the floor toward the dark-haired banshee. As I hit the wall, something jostled against my hip, clanging metallically. I groped with my hand and found the stand of iron fireplace implements, cold and sooty against my fingers. Ann glided closer, her smile as sweet and innocent as the last time I saw her alive, her hand raised in invitation. Freddie stood before the other woman. I couldn't see his face, but the banshee lifted a hand and stroked his cheek, her fingers trailing down his neck. He leaned into the caress.

"Freddie!" I shouted, fumbling at the stand until the poker came loose. I brandished it at Ann, and she hopped backward, her smile twisting into something malignant. "*Freddie! Please!*"

He jerked, shuddered, and turned to me. The light from the candle reflected in his eyes, wider than I had ever seen them.

He took a deep breath, as though waking up. "Cath—"

The banshee's hand flashed, and a dark line appeared across Freddie's throat. His voice stopped as though someone had snuffed it, and black spots materialized on the banshee's silk dress. Freddie lifted a hand to his neck, touching the spreading darkness, and staggered back into the wall.

I froze, the poker held before me in a two-handed grip. Ann laughed with delight and clapped her hands. The other woman smiled at Freddie as his feet slipped from under him, the darkness covering most of his chest. She licked his blood from her fingertips.

"Hurry, Sarah, before the best of it is wasted," cried Ann.

"No," the other replied. "I've ruined him. I can't drink that fast."

Her voice carried a touch of Scottish brogue, and I realized why she looked familiar. This creature had once been Mr. Hale's sister.

The spell of horror that had frozen me snapped. My arms shook, and Freddie's name spilled out of my mouth in a babbling stream. The wall I leaned against was the only thing keeping me upright.

Sarah Hale knelt next to my cousin, who gaped up at her, his mouth working silently, one hand vainly trying to staunch the flow of blood. With his other hand, he pushed feebly at her shoulder, but she leaned into him and ran her tongue along the length of his collarbone. She moved her mouth to his neck and sucked on the wound in his throat, her fingers entangled in his hair.

Freddie turned his head toward me, and his eyes locked on my face. I sobbed his name, and he mouthed a word: *Run.*

Then his hand fell away from his neck, landing limply in his lap, and his gaze grew vacant and drifted away from me. His head rocked as Sarah Hale adjusted her grip, drinking from his open throat, but I knew he was gone.

I made a sound like a wounded animal, and Ann turned to me and took a step forward.

"Don't worry," she said. "We'll keep you. We'll be sisters."

My fingers tightened around the poker, and I swung it at her head like a cricket bat. She dodged me easily, leaping several feet away and eyeing me from her half-crouch. I backed toward the kitchen door, my legs barely holding me, my breath coming in sobs. Ann matched my steps but didn't close the distance between us. I glanced at the other banshee, but she paid me no mind, focused on Freddie's blood-soaked skin. The wet sounds of her mouth made my stomach lurch, and I tore my eyes away.

Ann watched me as a cat would watch a bird, and I watched her just as intently as I backed away. I could feel the pull of her power, the longing to join her, but I could also see Freddie's hand out of the corner of my eye, lying pale and limp against the dark wood of the dining room floor, and the horror of it kept my mind clear

My back hit the kitchen door, and I pried one hand from the poker and fumbled behind me for the latch. When the door gave way, I stumbled, nearly falling, and Ann took two quick steps forward before stopping suddenly. I didn't waste her hesitation. I slammed the kitchen door, throwing the bolt.

As I turned and ran for the back door, I heard the impact of Ann's body and the sound of splintering wood. Then I was outside, racing through the darkness toward the stable. I groped for the large handle and heaved the stable door open, glancing over my shoulder. I could barely make out the dark shape of the house against the night sky, but I felt the banshee's pull. My breath came out in a whimper as I staggered into the stable.

My knee connected with something solid, and I heard Freddie's stallion, Bishop, snort and stomp a hoof a few yards to my right. I groped my way to his stall and swung open the door. The stallion snorted again, pawing at his hay, and I heard him back away from me. He sensed my terror, but I had no time to be careful, no words with which to soothe him. I lunged in the direction of his breathing, and my fingers found his muzzle, his cheek, the leather strap of his halter.

I pulled him toward the stall exit, but he balked and shook his head, trying to dislodge me. I dropped the poker, but my grip on his halter didn't weaken. I pulled again, and he changed tactics, bolting for the stable exit. I lost my footing and was half dragged beneath him. A hoof clipped my calf, my thigh. I held onto the halter with more strength than I knew I possessed, and some small part of my brain marveled that it hadn't broken, that it could bear my weight as the horse charged for escape.

Then the charge stopped. Bishop reared up halfway and took a few quick steps backward. I got my feet underneath me and peered past the stallion's head, though I already knew what I would see.

A figure stood in the stable doorway.

Bishop quivered against me and let out a whinny of

alarm. Before either he or I could think about it, I grabbed a fistful of mane and swung myself up onto his back. It'd been years since I'd ridden bareback, but instinct and childhood memories returned, and I squeezed Bishop's sides with my knees and knotted my fingers into the hair of his mane.

I heard Ann move forward, the whisper of hay brushing the ground, and Bishop rose up on his hind legs again, lashing out with his front. A hand reached for my leg, but Bishop, cornered in the narrow passageway of the stable, walls on both sides, channeled his panic into fight.

He slammed his body sideways, crushing Ann and my leg against the stable wall. Ann's hands scrambled against me, shoving at Bishop's flank and pulling my leg, my hip, the fabric of my nightgown. Bishop shifted, moving away, and my nightgown ripped. Hooves struck out, Bishop's frantic movements nearly knocking me from his back. I leaned forward as far as I could, hugging his neck, as he reared again and again, screaming as I had never heard a horse do.

I heard Ann cry out in pain, heard her stumble back. Bishop pursued her, striking again and again. Ann fell, and Bishop's hooves came down on her twice more.

Then the stallion leapt forward, racing for the stable door, and I clung to him as he galloped into the night.

seventeen

My world narrowed to the rhythm of Bishop's gallop, the grip of my knees and hands, and the image of Freddie's life pooling on the dining room floor. My leg ached, bruised from the fight in the stable, and I could feel the sticky dampness of lather coating the horse's skin.

Eventually Bishop slowed. The change in pace widened my awareness, and I stared into the night. A tiny light pricked the darkness, and I guided Bishop toward it. We cantered through fields, the stallion veering off course on occasion to circle around trees, walls, and other obstacles I couldn't see. The light seemed to fill my vision, and as we got closer, I realized it was a candle in a window.

Bishop weaved through a stand of trees, moving at a slow trot. Without further guidance from me, he continued until his nose nearly touched the wall of the small, familiar building that housed the candle. I slipped from his back, falling to my knees on the ground. It was growing hard to breathe, and I limped toward the cottage, my hands groping against the stone until they met the rough wood of a door.

I pounded my fist against it and tried to call out, but my voice choked and turned into a sob. I pounded and pounded, my sobs growing in strength until I felt as though the very air around me had died.

The door opened, taking my support with it, and I fell into a soft yellow light. Someone caught me, and a voice thick with brogue said, "Christ Almighty! What the bloody—Miss Chase?"

My legs could no longer hold me up, and Marsh lowered me gently to the floor. The light shifted as he held a candle near my face. He gave me a quick, searching look, then turned and yelled across the kitchen toward an open door.

"Lad! Quick!"

I took several deep, gulping breaths and tried to push myself up from where I lay on the floor, but my arms shook too badly, and my legs wouldn't do what I told them. Something heavy and warm draped across my shoulders, and I looked up into Marsh's kind, weather-hardened face. He'd given me his jacket.

"Here, lass," he said, helping me sit up. "We've got you now. We've got you."

The pounding of running footsteps pulled my head up in time to see James burst into the kitchen. He stopped when he saw me, his face contorting in surprise and a surge of fear, and then he was kneeling by my side, holding me up, his hands brushing my hair and tears from my face. My fingers fisted in his shirt.

"Catherine! What's wrong? Are you hurt? What's happened?"

"They—" I choked on the words, the images they carried, and my grip on Mr. Hale's shirt tightened. "They came for us. Freddie—"

James looked up, exchanging a look with Marsh, and the older man quietly slipped out of the room.

James gently pried my fingers from his shirt and then

ran his hands over my arms and shoulders. "Are you hurt?"

I shook my head, then shut my eyes. I couldn't stop shaking my head.

He caught my face in his hands, stilling my frantic movement. I opened my eyes and looked at him, but he suddenly seemed very far away.

"Catherine," he whispered.

"They laughed," I said, distantly aware that my voice sounded far too calm and flat. "I watched him die, and then I ran away. They killed him, and I ran away."

"They?" I could feel his hands shaking against my shoulders.

"Ann Claybrook and another. Ann called her Sarah. She looked like you."

James shut his eyes, and his fingers dug into the flesh of my arms. I hardly felt it.

Marsh returned and set a pair of boots next to James. Then he jammed a worn hat on his head, used the candle to light a lantern, and jogged into the night. I watched him go. I'd stopped shaking. I felt like I'd stopped everything.

After a long, shaky breath, James released me and pulled on his boots. He picked me up off the floor, and my arms instinctively wrapped around his neck as he carried me outside. I heard the snort of a horse and lifted my head to see Marsh leading two horses out of the Laceys' stable. Bishop stood nearby, watching us, his head low.

As James lifted me onto one of the horses, Marsh's coat nearly slipped off my shoulders. I caught it and shoved my arms into the sleeves. The horse's mane felt rough and real beneath my fingers, and I clutched it as James mounted behind me.

My mind seemed to be having trouble keeping up with what was happening around me, because suddenly we were galloping across a field, the bobbing glow of Marsh's lantern lighting the way. James had wrapped one arm around my waist to hold me in place, and I saw the edge of a bandage peeking out of his open cuff. I touched it gently with my fingers, marveling that only two nights ago I had wrapped this wound, praying the bleeding would stop, that it would not become infected. His arm tightened at my touch.

Then we were splashing through the creek, weaving through familiar woods, and the light of the lantern fell on Uncle's stable and the back of the house. The doors to both stood open, gaping and black.

A coldness started in my stomach and spread to my limbs. I didn't move as James slid from the horse and then lifted me from its back and set me on the ground. My hurt leg gave out, and I nearly fell. He caught me.

"You *are* hurt," he said, one arm around my waist, the other gripping my arm.

"My leg," I mumbled. I couldn't take my eyes off the stable door. "It'll be fine."

"Come on." He guided me toward the kitchen door, Marsh a step ahead.

"No."

They stopped and looked at me, and I pointed toward the stable.

"She's—could you check? Ann Claybrook was in there when I left."

"I'm sure she's not there now, Catherine," James said.

I shook my head. "She was hurt, maybe even— The horse. Please."

After exchanging another of those silent looks with

James, Marsh nodded and moved cautiously toward the stable door, holding the lantern out before him. James and I followed at a safe distance. The circle of light drifted into the stable, and all three of us gasped as it fell on a pale hand lying in the dirt.

Marsh took two more steps into the stable. He raised his arm to widen the spread of light and looked down at the ground for several long moments. James moved toward him, but Marsh shook his head. "The lady shouldn't see this, lad. You can have a look if you want, but I wouldn't bring Miss Chase any closer."

James hesitated, looking from me to the stable.

"Is she dead?" I asked.

Marsh looked at me for a moment. "Aye."

I nodded and limped toward the stable. After three steps, James caught my arm.

"Catherine, you shouldn't—"

"I want to see her. I want to be sure." I looked toward the house. "It can't be any worse than..."

James didn't respond, but his hand slowly released its hold on me. I walked to Marsh's side, James following.

"She's a bit of a mess," Marsh said apologetically.

I looked down at the body of Ann Claybrook, waiting for the nausea or horror to find me, but it didn't. I couldn't even feel surprise at this.

Her body lay in the stable aisle, battered and broken. Thick black blood oozed from her wounds. One arm was broken in several places, and a rib had stabbed through skin and fabric to gleam darkly in the lantern light. One side of her head and face had been smashed in, and were it not for her hair and dress, I wouldn't have recognized her.

"Catherine, come away." James pulled me gently toward the door. His voice sounded strained. "Marsh?"

The older man shook himself and turned away from Ann's body. We walked silently toward the back door, which hung open, creaking gently as it shifted on its hinges.

I stopped a few feet away, panic managing to break through the numbness and close off my throat. I wrapped my arms around myself and shook my head. "I'm not sure I can go back in there," I panted.

James moved in front of me, standing so close that my nose nearly brushed his chin. He placed his hands on my upper arms and squeezed lightly. When I didn't look at him, my gaze locked on the black entry to the house visible over his shoulder, he used one hand to tilt my chin up until my eyes met his. "I'm here," he said in a low tone. "You're not alone."

I stared at him until the panic receded and my breathing slowed, then nodded once. He pulled me into his side, his arm heavy against my waist, and we followed Marsh into the house.

The candle still burned on the dining room table where Ann Claybrook had set it. Its light flickered over Freddie's body, trying to warm the pallor of his skin.

I couldn't move. Several seconds passed before I realized James was calling my name.

"Catherine, is there anyone else in the house?"

My focus sharpened to a painful stab of awareness, and my eyes widened. "Oh, God. Polly. I didn't even think about—" I couldn't finish my sentence.

"Where?" Marsh asked gently. I pointed toward the room Polly used when she stayed overnight, and he disappeared down the short hallway.

I closed my eyes and felt myself sway. James's hands

settled on my waist, and for one hysterical moment I thought he meant to dance with me. Then I heard Marsh's footsteps returning. I opened my eyes and saw him sadly shake his head.

James's hands tightened on my waist. "How?"

"Neck's broken."

I covered my face with my hands. Polly lived with her son on a small farm outside the village and walked into town every morning to cook and clean for us. She was only staying in the house while Uncle Gerald was gone. And now she was dead. Simply because Freddie and I couldn't stay in the house alone.

Because Freddie and I…

Freddie.

James turned and spoke to Marsh, releasing me, but his words didn't penetrate past the image of my cousin lying pale and empty on the floor. I moved to his side and fell to my knees, my hands fluttering over his hair, his face, his chest. Except where it stained his shirt and the wooden floor, the blood was gone. His skin had been wiped clean. The wound in his neck lay ragged and bare, more monstrous, somehow, without the blood that should have covered it.

My fingertips brushed his cheek, and the vague shelter of shock within me shattered. Sobs poured out of me as I ran my hands over his face and tried to lift him into my lap. I needed to hold him, needed to keep him with me, but even in death he was too heavy. I buried my fingers in his hair and pressed my cheek to his, my forehead resting against the floor. I stayed like this, in a kneeling fetal position, prostrate, begging, until James's hands gently pulled me away.

I fought him, reaching for Freddie, the sobs coming

so hard and fast that I could hardly catch enough breath to produce them, but James simply pulled me into his lap and wrapped his arms around me, holding me as one would a child, until I gave in and curled into him and cried.

My strength left me after a while and the sobs quieted. Exhausted, my body relaxed into his, eager for the warmth and comfort he provided. His fingers gently drifted through my hair in a soothing, rhythmic motion, and his chin rested atop my head. His shirt collar hung open, and my cheek rested against the skin of his collar bone. I could feel his heart beating beneath my hand and the fabric of his breeches against my leg where my nightgown had ripped away during the struggle with Ann Claybrook in the stable.

Suddenly self-conscious, I pulled away and moved back to Freddie's body. I stroked his curls, pushing them back from his forehead, not bothering to wipe away the tears that ran down my face and neck. I could hear James shift positions behind me, but he neither spoke nor touched me.

At the sound of footsteps at the dining room entrance, I looked up. Marsh stood in the doorway. He still held the lantern in one hand and an empty burlap bag in the other.

"The rest of the house is empty," he said. "Front door was open, so I reckon the other one left the same way it came in." He lifted the bag. "With your permission, miss, I need to swipe your silver."

I looked from Marsh to James, struggling to understand, my fingers still tangled in Freddie's curls. "Our silver?"

James stood and held a hand toward me. Reluctantly, I let him pull me to my feet. I could feel the grain of the wooden floor against my bare feet, and when I looked down, I realized my left leg was visible from the knee down.

James's voice pulled my gaze up again. "Catherine, I need you to listen to me very carefully." He paused a moment, looking into my face, then continued. "Marsh is going to rifle through the house, taking your silver and maybe some candlesticks. As soon as we're gone, you need to run to Mrs. Ellerby and tell her that you heard a great crash, and when you came downstairs, you saw men fleeing through the back door. And you found Freddie. Then you ran to get Polly and discovered her dead, as well. Can you do that?"

As James spoke, Marsh set down his lantern and moved to the china cabinet. He pulled open drawer after drawer, stuffing some objects into his bag and throwing others on the floor. He didn't close any of the drawers, and in only a minute or two, the room had been ransacked.

I swallowed and nodded. "Yes. I can do that. What will you do with it all?"

James gave me an apologetic look. "Throw it over the cliffs, most likely."

Marsh looked the room over, gave a satisfied nod, and strode into the kitchen. I heard his boots bump over the doorjamb as he went outside.

"Will you be all right?" James's hands moved toward me, but he seemed to catch himself and instead clasped them behind his back.

I looked down at Freddie. "No. But there's nothing you can do about that."

"No," he quietly agreed. After a long moment, he said, "I'm so sorry."

I felt another surge of tears rise, tightening my throat,

and without pausing to examine the impulse, I turned and stepped into him, wrapping my arms around his waist and burying my face in his chest.

He had barely returned the embrace when Marsh burst into the room, lantern swinging and eyes wild. I took a guilty step backward and pulled the jacket closer around my body.

"She's gone!" Marsh cried. "The one in the stable, she's gone."

James stiffened. "Then she wasn't dead."

Marsh shook his head. "There's a whole other mess of footprints where she used to be, scuffing up the dust and dirt in ways it wasn't before. Someone carried her off, and I can guess who."

I covered my mouth with one hand. They'd come back.

And then I was being propelled out of the dining room and into the foyer. James strode quickly down the hall, pulling me behind him by the hand. At the front door, he paused and opened it slowly, peering carefully outside. He turned to me.

"Go now. Run. Don't stop for anything. Not until you've reached Mrs. Ellerby's porch, and then you pound on the door until she hears you. Scream. Wake the whole village."

My grip on his hand tightened. The fear had returned. "What about you?"

"I'll stay here, watch you. As soon as Mrs. Ellerby opens her door, Marsh and I will gallop home along the creek. We'll be long gone before anyone comes to investigate."

I looked across the wide expanse of pitch-black lane that separated me from Mrs. Ellerby's house.

"You can do it, Catherine."

I took a step forward, then realized I still wore Marsh's

jacket. I pulled it off and held it out. "Will you thank him for me?"

"Of course." James took the jacket and stepped back, tilting his head toward the door. "Go."

I nodded, took a deep breath, and ran.

eighteen

I woke the next afternoon in a narrow bed. The wallpaper of Mrs. Ellerby's spare bedroom consisted of faded morning glories marching in rows toward the ceiling. Each bloom was the size of my face, which made me feel as though I were lost in a giant garden.

I'd done exactly as James asked the night before. By the time Mrs. Ellerby opened her door to my frantic fists and screams for help, half the street was awake. Five minutes later, after I'd gasped the words "thieves" and "murderers," five of our neighboring men had armed themselves and entered the house. After that, little was required of me but to allow myself to be comforted. Mrs. Ellerby refused to let me tell my story more than once, and as the men formed a search party to look for the thieves, she led me inside and put me to bed.

I slept in fits and starts, my body desperate for sleep but my mind too afraid of what it would see when I closed my eyes. My right leg throbbed where it had been caught between Bishop and the stable wall.

"Oh! I'm sorry, dear."

I rolled to face the door, the click of the latch the noise that had woken me this time. Mrs. Ellerby moved into the room, carrying a tray that held a cup of tea and a plate of toast.

"I thought you might want something to nibble on." She set the tray on the small table next to the bed and hovered for a moment.

"Thank you, Mrs. Ellerby. That's very kind of you."

Her eyes filled with tears. "Oh, my dear girl. What you must be going through. To have found him like that—"

I closed my eyes and turned my head away, all too able to see how I'd found Freddie.

"Oh, forgive me. Of course you're not ready to talk about it." I heard a soft scrape as she straightened the tray. "When you're ready, if you'd like, I do know a bit about this sort of thing. I mean, my poor Joseph just dropped dead in front of the fireplace one evening. The picture of health, he was—but listen to me, prattling on when you'd probably rather just be left alone to have a good cry." She moved toward the door, then stopped. "Your uncle will need to be written."

My face still turned to the morning glories, I said, "Can you do it, please?" The wallpaper seam a few inches from my nose had started to peel away from the wall.

After a brief pause, Mrs. Ellerby quietly replied, "Of course, dear. I'll do it this morning."

A few seconds later, the door closed behind her as she left.

∞∞∞

Time passed. Two days, maybe three. I wasn't sure. I didn't move from the bed. Occasionally I ate a little of whatever food Mrs. Ellerby brought, but mostly I slept and stared at the wall, reliving memory after memory of

Freddie, afraid I might lose them if I didn't keep them constantly in mind.

One morning, as I stared at the ceiling, Mary entered the room in a swirl of skirts, ribbons, and the smell of spring. She eyed me as she removed her bonnet, then held one hand out toward me.

"It's time to get up, Catherine."

I rolled toward the morning glories.

She was still for a moment, and I hoped she'd leave, but instead she sat on the side of the bed and placed her hand on my back. That small touch seemed to unlock something inside me, and I curled in on myself and wept. Mary silently rubbed my back until the worst had passed.

I sat up and reached for her, and she pulled me into a hug. Her cheeks were wet.

Half an hour later, we sat next to each other on the bed, our backs against the wall and our knees tucked under our chins.

"You have to get out of bed, Catherine."

I pulled my legs tighter into my chest, wincing as my right knee protested. "Why?"

"Because you must. It's the way of things. Freddie wouldn't want you wasting away in this hideous room. Polly certainly wouldn't have stood for it."

I closed my eyes, indulging for a moment in the pain I knew would lie just beneath the surface of life for years. But within it was something else. A spark of Freddie, perhaps. I turned my face toward Mary.

"I don't know," I said. "Whatever Polly might say, I think Freddie would have enjoyed young maidens mourning him in such a spectacularly dramatic fashion."

She gave me a small smile. "Yes, but not forever. Your uncle will be here on Monday. It's time to get up."

She looked at me expectantly, and I nodded. I waited for the tears to return, but they didn't. I'd cried all I could cry.

Mary gently but firmly guided me out of bed and helped me into the dress Mrs. Ellerby had brought for me at some point. I held it up. It was one of my winter dresses, a dark charcoal gray. The closest I had to black.

Once Mary was satisfied with the state of my hair, she led me downstairs for the noon meal. Mrs. Ellerby stood when we entered the drawing room and whisked toward me, hands fluttering. She embraced me, soft and round in contrast to the stiffness of her cotton dress.

"Oh, my dear girl," she whispered in my ear. She released me and sniffed, straightening her bodice and smoothing her hair. "Well now. There's been time enough for that." She lifted her chin and gave me an appraising look, which I did my best to meet. "Come here, child."

I followed her to the table she'd set up by her front window, where a mound of black cotton lay. Something like a sleeve protruded from one side of the pile of fabric.

"I guessed your measurements as best I could from that frock you're wearing now," Mrs. Ellerby said, nodding toward my dress, "but I could do with some proper figures."

It took me a moment to find my voice. "You're making me a dress."

"Yes. I didn't think you had anything, since you've not needed any mourning attire since you were a girl, and I was only able to find that one gray dress in your wardrobe. I knew you'd be in need, and well—" She sniffed again and faced the window. I wasn't used to seeing Mrs. Ellerby attempt emotional control, and I knew she did it for my sake. "Well, it was the least I could do, considering."

I touched her arm, turning her toward me, and hugged her again, sincerely this time. "You've always been far better to me than I deserve."

"Nonsense." She stepped back and spent a few moments fussing with the fabric, smoothing it and spreading it out so that I could see its lines. It was nearly done; she merely needed precise measurements in order to complete the bodice. "We'll get more ordered for you straightaway, but you'll need something to get you through the next week or so. Between this and that charcoal you've got on, you should get by."

With quick, efficient movements, she wrapped the tape around my waist, chest, and shoulders, marking the numbers down with a short, dull pencil.

"There," she said when she'd finished. "Let's eat. You could use a good meal."

I ate more of the cold cuts and fresh bread set out on the dining room table than was strictly proper, but for once Mrs. Ellerby didn't chide me. When we were finished with the meal, contentedly sipping tea, she sighed and exchanged a look with Mary.

"What?" I asked.

"I didn't want to say anything until after you'd eaten," Mrs. Ellerby said, looking apologetic.

Mary leaned toward me and laid a hand on mine. "We just wanted to make sure you were ready to hear it."

My teacup clattered back into its saucer. "What's happened? Is it Uncle Gerald? Is it—" I stopped myself before saying James's name and gripped the edge of the table until the skin beneath my fingernails turned white. "Please."

After another quick glance toward Mrs. Ellerby, Mary

squeezed my hand and said, "The ruffians who murdered Freddie and Polly struck again two days ago."

"Who?" The word left my mouth barely audible.

"An employee of Mr. Hale," Mrs. Ellerby said, sending my heart hammering into my throat. "His only employee, I think. Name of Marsh. They found him behind the Laceys' stable Wednesday morning."

My hand flew to my mouth. I remembered the older Scot's kind brusqueness, the feel and smell of his jacket holding me together while the world fell apart around me. They'd killed him, too.

"We think they were after the horses," Mrs. Ellerby continued.

I turned to Mary, hoping she could see the question I could not ask in my eyes. She did.

"The Laceys and Mr. Hale, thankfully, were unharmed, though Mr. Hale is quite devastated by the loss. Apparently they were very close."

I nodded, closing my eyes. *They were.*

∞∞∞

Two days later, wearing the completed mourning dress, I walked toward the cliffs to exercise my leg. The area surrounding my knee was one massive bruise, but there was no damage beyond that.

Uncle Gerald would arrive tomorrow, and I both dreaded and craved his return. I could not imagine what losing his youngest son would do to him, but I also needed him with me.

Freddie's older brothers, David and William, had come from Manchester, where they practiced law, and were staying in Uncle Gerald's home. They'd arrived in time for the funeral, for which I was grateful. I didn't think I could have borne it alone. Polly's son, Daniel, had attended and given me his condolences, which made me cry more than anything else. I'd missed Polly's small, quiet burial during my days in bed, and guilt made my chest ache.

I could hardly bear to think how Uncle must feel, knowing he'd missed his son's final service. I wished I could go to him so he didn't have to make the long trip from Brighton alone, but there was nothing I could do but wait. Nothing any of us could do but wait.

The clouds above matched my mood, low and gray but empty. I walked along the cliff path, listening to the waves crash against the rocks below me, letting the brisk sea wind pull my hair from its pins and tangle my skirt in my legs.

I'd been walking for half an hour, my head down, my thoughts focused inward, when I realized someone sat midway between the path and the cliffs ahead of me. He faced the ocean, his knees pulled into his chest. He looked young and lost, and I sensed that he hadn't heard me, that this wasn't something he wanted anyone to see.

I hesitated a moment but then thought that perhaps he needed someone to talk to as much as I did.

A few feet away, I stopped and said, "James."

He startled and turned, then started to get to his feet.

I held out a hand. "Please. Don't. I wondered if...if I might join you."

He sank back onto the grass. He looked tired, haggard, and I wondered how long it had been since he'd slept. "Of course."

I sat next to him, pinning my skirt to my shins with my arms. For a long while we simply watched the waves roll in and let the wind make our eyes water.

"I heard about Marsh," I said, face to the breeze. "I'm sorry. I liked him."

After a moment, James spoke. "I've known him since I was a boy. He was the only one I knew would believe me about Sarah's death, who would come with me." He took a shaky breath. "We were careful. We thought they might try for us after... He went out to feed the horses at dawn and never came back. By the time I noticed anything was wrong, he'd been lying out there for an hour—"

He broke off, and I looked at him, at the tension in his jaw, his shoulders.

"It's the guilt that keeps me awake at night," I said quietly, holding tight to my composure. "The thought that if I hadn't gone out that night and encountered Ann Claybrook, they might not have come for us."

James shook his head. "It's not your fault." Before I could protest, he continued. "It's mine." He released his hold on his knees and pressed his hands to the ground, as though holding himself up. "If I hadn't come here, if my reckless actions hadn't caught your attention—"

His fingers strained, digging through the grass to the thin, rocky soil beneath. One hand rested in the narrow space between us, and I laid mine on top of it.

"No." I slid my fingers through his, tracing the valleys between his knuckles. "It's not your fault your sister died. It's not," I repeated when he opened his mouth to speak. "It's their fault. You've done only what you had to do, what I or Freddie or anyone would have done in your place."

He turned his face to the sea, teeth clenched, and I touched his jaw with my other hand, gently bringing his eyes back to mine.

I smiled, sad and broken, not holding back any of the emotions I had suppressed for Mrs. Ellerby's and Mary's sakes. "But I know words and logic can do nothing to alleviate this burden, so understand this: you don't bear it alone."

I tightened my grip on his hand, and after a long moment, he curled his fingers around mine.

"You called me James," he said.

We sat, listening to the waves crash below us.

∞∞∞

Uncle Gerald arrived the next afternoon. I ran out of Mrs. Ellerby's house as soon as I heard the carriage, and we clung to each other in the street, not caring who could see. He shook against me, tremulous and fragile, and I felt a pang of fear that he might not be strong enough to survive this. He seemed to have aged twenty years.

His friend, Dr. Worth, had accompanied him, and I gave him a hug too, my gratitude for his friendship to my uncle bringing me to tears. David and William came out of the house and embraced their father, while David's wife hovered in the doorway, wringing her hands.

William pulled Uncle Gerald's trunk from the coach, Dr. Worth fetched his, and we walked up the front path to the house. David and William maneuvered the trunks through the front door, and Dr. Worth and Uncle Gerald followed.

I froze on the porch, my hands suddenly clammy. I couldn't move.

Uncle Gerald paused on the threshold and turned back to me. "Catherine?"

I shook my head, suddenly short of breath. "I can't," I gasped. "I can't go in there. I can't—"

He moved quickly to my side and pulled me into his arms, one hand on the back of my head. I could feel his tears where his cheek pressed against my temple.

"My darling girl," he said, his voice shaking. "What you must have been through. Of course, of course you can't." He pulled back and held my face between his hands. "As soon as I'm settled, we'll all come to Mrs. Ellerby's. You can stay there for as long as you need."

"I'm sorry." I pressed my cheek into his palm. "I want to be here with you, but—" My eyes drifted over his shoulder. I could see through the foyer and down the hall. The dining room door stood open.

"You've been through a trauma," Uncle Gerald said. "We all have, but you most of all. And we all must deal with such things in our own way. You'll come home when you're ready."

He kissed my forehead and slipped inside, and I walked slowly back across the street to Mrs. Ellerby's house, leaving Freddie's father and brothers to mourn him without me.

nineteen

The next day, Mary and I walked down High Street. It was my first stroll through town since Freddie's death. Friends and neighbors nodded as they passed, giving me pitying looks, and some stopped to take my hand and tell me how much they'd miss young Mr. Martin. I tried to ignore the whispers about how the thieves responsible had never been caught, about their strange predilections and the lack of blood on either victim despite their obvious cuts. The truth was too horrible to imagine, and so the villagers filled in the gaps the best way they knew how.

We stopped at the milliner's and admired the new bonnets, then made our way to the Amhersts' general store. A window display of ribbons held our attention for a few minutes, but I noticed Mary's gaze slipping past the brightly colored spools to search the store's interior for Peter.

Leaning closer to the glass, I pretended to study a particularly fine blue satin. "Have you decided when you're going yet?" I glanced up and caught Mary's reflection in the window.

She bit her lower lip, trying to quell a grin. "No, not an exact date, but very soon. Oh, Catherine, very *very* soon."

I straightened and turned to her, making sure she could see the earnestness in my face. “Don’t delay on my account.” She started to shake her head, but I continued. “The worst is passed now, and nothing would make me happier than knowing *you* were happy.”

Mary took hold of my hand and squeezed, then led me into the store.

We had barely decided to focus our false attentions on the bolts of summer muslins toward the back when Peter appeared at my side.

“Miss Chase,” he said with a small dip of his head. “My condolences.”

“Thank you, Mr. Amherst,” I returned, giving him a small smile.

His eyes slipped toward Mary and fastened there. “And you, Miss Hayworth? How are you today?”

“Wonderful,” she breathed. She placed a hand on my arm. “I’ve just learned that the thing I desire most in the world can happen sooner than I anticipated.”

Peter’s eyes widened as he looked at me, and my smile grew.

“That’s…that’s wonderful news, indeed,” he said.

He looked at Mary, and I felt certain that neither I nor the rest of the store existed for either of them in that moment. He took a small step forward and stretched out his hand, letting the tips of his fingers run the length of her arm. Her eyes drifted closed, then snapped open at the sound of someone nearby gasping.

The three of us turned in unison, Peter guiltily jerking his hand away from Mary and hiding it behind his back.

Mr. and Mrs. Hayworth stood in the entrance to the store, identical looks of shock on their faces. With a quick look around to see if the handful of other patrons had noticed, Mrs. Hayworth schooled her features into something a few inches away from composed, nudged her husband in the ribs so he would shut his mouth, and swept toward us.

Peter straightened, squaring his shoulders, but at a tiny shake of Mary's head his determination wavered. I tugged him gently backward.

"Not like this," I whispered. "Not yet."

He looked from me to Mary, his jaw clenched, then nodded and disappeared into the back room. Mary watched him go, catching his eye as he paused in the doorway to give him a small smile, then turned to face her parents.

"Mary." Mrs. Hayworth's hands worried at her reticule, and Mr. Hayworth looked at his daughter as though he wasn't sure who she was. "We need to speak with you. At once. And at home."

"Of course, Mother," Mary replied smoothly. She seemed perfectly calm and collected, and I marveled at this new Mary. "Catherine will join us."

Mrs. Hayworth's eyes flashed at me, hostile, and I stared back. "I'd rather she not."

"I insist." Mary moved toward the door, not looking back to see if we would follow. I exchanged a glance with both of her parents, then followed her out onto the street. Mr. and Mrs. Hayworth trailed behind.

The walk to the Hayworths' house seemed to have doubled in length. Mary looked at me only once, her eyes bright. This was a fight she meant to win.

We entered the house in a silent procession, and Mary led us to the sitting room. She stood in the middle of the room, idly removing her bonnet as we arranged ourselves around her. Mrs. Hayworth perched on a straight chair facing Mary and produced a fan, which she fluttered at her face. Mr. Hayworth paced behind his wife, grumbling unintelligibly to himself. I stood off to the side, an observer, waiting to see when I might be called upon to take part.

"Well?" Mrs. Hayworth demanded.

Mary placed her bonnet on the desk behind her. "Yes, Mother?"

The speed of Mrs. Hayworth's fan increased. "What is the nature of your…attachment to Peter Amherst?"

"We're engaged."

"Engaged!" Mr. Hayworth shouted. His pacing stopped.

"For two years," Mary continued, her voice level. Her gaze sharpened. "I'm going to marry him."

"A shopkeeper?" Mrs. Hayworth squeaked. "Don't be silly."

"I assure you, Mother, my feelings for Peter are anything but silly."

"You will end it." Mr. Hayworth still looked shocked, but anger was slowly making headway in his tone and expression. "I won't have my daughter marrying the son of a common tradesman." He nodded, growing more confident in his belief. "You will end it."

"No." Mary hadn't yet moved or raised her voice, but that sharp look remained in her eyes. "I will not."

Mrs. Hayworth abandoned her fan for a handkerchief.

Mr. Hayworth's face reddened. "You *will*, or I will deny you your annual living. You'll have nothing."

Mary nodded once, slowly. "You're wrong. I will have Peter."

For a moment all three of us stared at her in states ranging from awe to horror. After months of fretting and indecision, Mary had finally made a choice, and I had never seen her so firm.

Her parents wavered. Mrs. Hayworth's handkerchief lowered to her lap, and Mr. Hayworth sank onto the sofa.

"I love him," Mary continued. "He's kind and clever and hardworking, and he'll take better care of me than the richest man in the country, with or without my inheritance. Catherine can vouch for his character." She paused, as though considering something, then said, "She can also vouch for my intention to elope with Peter before the month is out."

After three long seconds of silence, the Hayworths burst into loud displays of emotional protest. Mrs. Hayworth began to cry as Mr. Hayworth shouted over her.

"You'll do no such thing—"

"The *scandal!* Our family—"

"—I'll lock you in your room if I have to—"

"—your brother, all ruined—"

"You have a choice." Mary's voice rang through the room, silencing her parents. "I will marry Peter, but the manner in which I do is up to you. You can either allow us to marry publicly and be seen as indulgent parents who let their daughter make an imprudent match, or you can live with the scandal of my elopement. Because I *will* find a way to elope." She softened. "I love you both, and I know the hurt this causes you. I've struggled with the consequences of this decision for more than a year." She glanced toward me. "Poor Catherine can attest to my dilemma and the dramatics involved. I am sorry—but I have made my choice, and nothing will sway me."

Mr. Hayworth rubbed his eyes with the index finger and thumb of one hand, then looked at his daughter. "No," he said quietly.

Mrs. Hayworth gave him a hopeful look.

"I don't think anything will sway you." Standing, he moved to Mary's side and placed a hand on her shoulder.

"John!" Mrs. Hayworth cried. "Surely you're not going to *allow* her to...to..."

"What choice do I have?" he said over Mary's head. "Only the choice she has given us, and I, for one, would rather not lose my daughter." He gave Mary a stern look. "I am not happy, but I am willing to be convinced."

Mrs. Hayworth rose to her feet, her imperious bearing a testament to her family's standing in Gloucestershire. She laid her fan on the seat of her chair with a sharp click and swept from the room without a word.

Mary flinched, then closed her eyes and straightened, and I could see her grasping for the calm front she'd held throughout the argument. The effort of her show of strength was beginning to take its toll.

"She'll come around," Mr. Hayworth said quietly. He looked at the door through which his wife had left. "Eventually."

"This is the life I want, Father," Mary said.

He studied her for a moment. "Have the boy pay a visit this afternoon. I'd like to speak with him. Then we'll notify the vicar."

Mary kissed her father's cheek. "Thank you."

He nodded toward the door. "Go on, the both of you, before I get angry again."

Mary grasped my hand in hers and ran out the door, not stopping to retrieve her bonnet. Outside her home, she stopped and threw her arms around me, laughing delightedly.

"Oh, I never in a million years thought that would work!" she gasped.

"You were magnificent. All I could do was gape at you

the entire time."

"I was terrified. Look, my hands are shaking." She held them up as proof, her eyes and smile shining. As quickly she raised them, she dropped her hands again. "I have to tell Peter!" Lifting her skirts, she turned and sprinted down the path toward the road. Laughing, I followed.

Instead of going in the front entrance of Amherst General Store, Mary pulled me toward the back of the building. Sacks of various grains were stacked around the back door, and wooden crates lay scattered in haphazard piles. Mary beat on the door with her fist until Peter opened it. His eyes widened when he saw Mary, her face flushed, her smile so bright her face didn't seem capable of containing it, and they widened even more when she threw herself at him, wrapping her arms around his neck and kissing him full on the mouth.

Blushing, I turned to study the grain sacks next to me. Wheat from Hertfordshire.

"Mary!" Peter said. "What on earth—"

"We don't have to elope!" she said breathlessly. "Father gave his permission. We can get married here, properly."

I turned my head just enough to see my friends out of the corner of my eye. Peter gaped down at Mary for a few long seconds, then bent his head and kissed her again. I turned back to the sack of wheat, reading the small amount of text until I had it memorized, then carefully traced each of the words printed on the rough burlap fabric with my finger. I was about to start humming to remind Mary and Peter I existed when Mary spoke again.

"Come to the house this afternoon. Four o'clock. Father wants to speak with you."

"Yes. Yes, of course. Anything he wants." Peter glanced over his shoulder at the store's interior, then took a step back, his hands falling to clasp Mary's. "I'll see you then."

Mary smiled as he backed through the door, releasing her hands at the last moment. She smiled as she took my arm, and we walked slowly back toward her house.

"The two of you are highly embarrassing," I said. "I hope you won't still be that way once you're married."

"I plan to be that way always," Mary announced, her smile undimmed. She was nearly skipping.

We passed the lane that led to Uncle Gerald's house, and I slowed.

Mary stopped. "Have you been back yet?"

I shook my head. "I tried, but I just—" I took a deep breath and looked at Mary. "I need to try again. After all, if you can stand before your parents and tell them about Peter, surely I can do something as small as walk into a house." I forced a smile.

Mary squeezed my hand. "It's not small at all. Do you want me to come?"

"No. No, I'll be all right." My smile came more easily this time. "I'm so very happy for you."

"Good." Mary's look turned mischievous. "Me, too."

We went our separate ways, and in a few minutes I stood before the front door of my home. My hands felt like ice.

David's wife, Meredith, answered my knock. She looked drawn, smaller than I remembered, but her face lit up when she saw me. "Catherine! You don't need to knock, you know that. Come in, come in."

She ushered me inside, and the huge task of stepping over the threshold and into the house was lost somewhere amidst her swishing skirts and the embrace she caught me in as soon as I was inside. The soft bulge of her belly pressed against me, and I pulled away.

"Oh!" One of my hands hovered near her midsection. "Why didn't you say anything? It's unnoticeable beneath your dress."

Meredith blushed and smiled. "It never quite seemed the time." She smoothed both hands over her stomach, outlining its new roundness. "David wants a boy, of course."

"And you?"

"Oh, a boy, too." She looked away. "And we even know what we'll name him."

I swallowed. The dining room door seemed to gape at me from the end of the hall.

Meredith took a deep breath and turned back to me. "The men have all gone for a walk, but they should be back in an hour or so." Her eyes narrowed. "Are you feeling all right?"

"I—" I swallowed and tried again, my eyes drawn toward the dining room. My mind filled with the image of Freddie's hand, pale against blood-stained wood. "I—"

"Have you come to collect more of your things?" Meredith moved toward the stairs, waving for me to follow. "I can help you pack, if you'd like. Mr. Martin has yet to hire a new housekeeper." She turned toward me. "Unless you're coming home?"

I shook my head, feeling my throat tighten. The last time I'd descended these stairs, it had been with a hand full of Freddie's shirt, terrified of what lay below. "No. No, I can't come home yet."

Meredith nodded sadly and continued up the stairs. Grateful for a task, something to occupy me, I followed. As we walked down the hallway toward my room, I found myself pausing in front of Freddie's room. The door was closed.

"Could you start without me?" I asked, my eyes on the doorknob. "I need to..."

I heard her footsteps pause. "Of course," she said quietly.

Her footsteps moved down the hallway, and I slowly reached out and turned the knob.

Freddie's room looked the same as it always had. I wasn't sure what I'd expected; some sort of sign that things had changed forever. The bed had been made, the furniture dusted, the floor swept. I wondered if this was Meredith's work or Mrs. Ellerby's.

I ran a hand across the small desk beneath the window, touching the quill, the ink bottle. A letter from someone named Smythe—a friend from university, I remembered—lay toward one corner as if casually dropped there. I moved slowly around the room, touching a novel here, a candle there, finally stopping in front of the bureau. I hesitated a moment, then slid open a drawer. A stack of shirts lay in two neat piles inside, and I lifted one of them.

Sinking onto the bed, I held the shirt in my hands, rubbing the fabric between my fingers. My cheeks felt wet, and without thinking I pressed the shirt to my face. It smelled like Freddie.

A sob rose from my chest, and I lay on my side on Freddie's bed, my face buried in his shirt.

Meredith found me there some time later, her soft hand on my shoulder urging me to sit up. She held one of Uncle's old medical valises in her other hand.

"I wasn't sure what you wanted," she said, pushing my hair away from my face. "I hope this is okay."

"I'm sure it'll be fine," I said hoarsely.

"The men are back. I told them you'd be down once

you were done packing." She looked at the shirt in my hands. "Are you done?"

I reached for the valise. It was surprisingly heavy. "Almost. Please tell them I'll be down in a few minutes."

Meredith watched me for a few seconds before nodding and leaving the room, quietly closing the door behind her. I sat on the bed until I could take a deep breath without feeling the burn of new tears, then stood. On a whim, I shoved Freddie's shirt into the valise. Before leaving the room, a thought struck me, and I looked through the bureau until I found a pair of worn work trousers buried toward the back, leftover from Freddie's adolescent years of character-building chores in the stable. Once I'd stuffed them into the valise as well, I felt ready to go downstairs.

Uncle Gerald stood at the bottom of the staircase, waiting for me.

"Catherine, you've been crying." He took the valise from my hand.

"It's hard...being here," I said. He wrapped an arm around my shoulders, and I leaned into him as we walked toward the parlor.

David and William greeted me, and Meredith sat next to her husband.

"I'll walk with you over to Mrs. Ellerby's," Uncle Gerald said. "I need to thank her for the fine plate of cakes she brought earlier today."

I felt lighter as soon as I stepped out of the house, and I wondered if I'd ever truly be able to go home again.

When we reached the lane, I saw James walking our direction. Upon seeing us, he quickened his pace and angled toward us.

"Mr. Martin, Miss Chase," he said once he was within

speaking distance. "I hope you're doing well."

"Mr. Hale," Uncle Gerald greeted. "Enjoying the weather?"

James looked up at the sky as though he'd forgotten it existed. "Oh. Yes, very much. Just getting some air."

We lived toward the edge of the village, and there was very little reason to walk down our lane unless you lived there—or wished to visit someone who lived there. I knew he'd come on the hope of seeing me, and I wished Uncle Gerald hadn't insisted on carrying the valise. I desperately needed something to hold on to. The strength of my urge to fling myself into James's arms took my breath away, and I wasn't sure I could hold myself back on my own.

"I wanted to express my condolences, Mr. Martin, on your loss. I haven't yet had the chance."

My uncle bowed his head, his shoulders drooping slightly. "Thank you. My sympathies, in return, on the death in your own household. The same ruffians, I'm told." His jaw tightened. "They'd do well never to return to this village."

James glanced at me, and I had to clench my fists, digging my fingernails into my palm, to keep from stepping toward him. "I rather wish they would," he said, his voice low and dangerous. "I'd like to meet them."

"Indeed." Uncle Gerald straightened. "If you'll excuse us, Mr. Hale, my niece needs to get properly settled, and I need to speak with Mrs. Ellerby."

James's eyes moved from me to my uncle's house, and then to Mrs. Ellerby's. "Of course. I won't keep you any longer." He nodded to us each in turn. "Mr. Martin. Miss Chase."

"Mr. Hale," I whispered, watching him walk away

while my uncle led me up the path to Mrs. Ellerby's door.

twenty

I sat up out of my dream. The night air cooled the sweat on my face and neck as I shook for a moment, my face buried in my hands.

The nightmares were getting worse. Every night I watched Freddie die while the faces of Ann Claybrook and Sarah Hale twisted into grotesque masks. Their laughter still rang in my ears as I sat in Mrs. Ellerby's spare room, the morning glories marching steadily toward the ceiling around me.

My hands curled into fists. I was tired of their laughter, tired of feeling helpless and frightened. Tired of hiding from the dark.

I flung the sheets off my legs and stood in the middle of the room. The light of the half-moon trickled through the window, just outlining the objects in the room. I moved toward the valise that sat in the corner next to the small bureau. I remembered Ann Claybrook's broken body lying in the dirt of the stable. They could be killed, and I thought I knew how.

I didn't know what time it was, but I didn't care. I pulled Freddie's clothes from the valise, where I had left them after unpacking my own belongings. They were much too large for me, but when I'd belted the trousers with a lace from one of my boots and tucked the shirt into them, I felt secure enough. I rolled the trouser legs until I no longer stood on them, then put on my walking boots. After quickly braiding my hair to keep it out of my face, I eased open the bedroom door and crept to the sitting room, where I slipped the fireplace poker from its stand. Returning to my room, I opened the window above the bed and crawled outside.

Crouching in the flowerbed below my window, I took a moment to let my eyes adjust to the night. The moonlight was brighter out here, and I could see well enough to navigate. When I could see as well as possible, I braced myself, took a deep breath, and sprinted for the lane. I doubted I could outrun a banshee, but at least this way they couldn't bewitch me. At least this way I would go down fighting.

I ran, my new anger keeping the fear at bay. I felt almost as though I were daring them to come after me, and I would have laughed were my breath not occupied in keeping my legs moving.

By the time I reached James's cottage, my lungs and muscles felt as though they were on fire, but I didn't slow until I'd reached the front door. The house was dark and silent, but I beat against the door with my free hand, the poker ready in my other, looking over my shoulder every few seconds to make sure I was safe.

Half a minute had passed before I heard noises inside the cottage, and I dropped my hand as the door opened an inch.

"James," I said.

After two heartbeats, the door opened enough for a hand to slip through, grab my arm, and pull me inside.

It was dark in the foyer, but I heard the door latch click,

then the rasping slide of the bolt, and finally the strike of a match accompanied by a sudden blaze of light.

James held the match between us, his eyes frantically searching my face. "What is it? What's happened?" His eyes traveled down my body and widened. "Why are you dressed like that?"

I looked down. We were dressed similarly, a simple shirt and trousers. The open collar of Freddie's shirt extended far lower than the necklines of most of my dresses. I didn't care. "Do you have a candle?"

"I—yes." James moved a few steps away, shaking out the match that had burned down to his fingers and lighting another one. He touched the flame to the wick of a candle that sat on a table near the door, then turned back to me, the candleholder in his hand.

I shook my head. "No. Set it back down."

He hesitated for half a second, then obeyed.

The poker still held at my side, I stepped into him and wrapped my free arm around his neck. Standing on tiptoe, I pressed my nose into the hollow just behind his jaw and breathed him in.

He stiffened, then exhaled in a rush. His arms came around me, pressing me into him, and his head dipped until I could feel his breath against my ear. One of his hands ran slowly up my spine, hot through the thin fabric of my shirt. "Catherine…"

"I want to kill them," I said, my lips brushing the side of his throat.

He tensed again, then slowly disentangled himself and took a step back. "What?"

"I want to kill them." I lifted the poker. "And I think I know how."

He barely glanced at the poker. "Yes, iron, I know. But

what—"

I frowned. "What do you mean, you already know?"

"I figured it out a couple of days ago and went to the blacksmith's. I was on my way back from there when I saw you that afternoon."

I looked past him, toward the door. He'd hung iron horseshoes on the doorframe, easily two dozen of them lining the top and both sides of the door.

"Why didn't you tell me?" I demanded. "Is this some sort of masculine thing, protecting me from vital knowledge?"

He blinked and took another half step back. "What? Of course not. I told you, I just figured it out. Was I supposed to come knocking on Mrs. Ellerby's door and announce it there? Besides, you didn't need me." He gestured toward the poker. "You figured it out yourself."

I frowned down at my weapon. "You could have written a note or something."

"I didn't—I wasn't sure it would be welcome."

I looked up at him. "Don't be daft. You're always welcome."

He smiled. "That's a relief to hear, but I meant the subject."

"Oh." I scuffed my boots on the wooden floor, noticing for the first time that James's feet were bare. For some reason, despite the fact I'd thrown myself at him only a few minutes before, this made me blush. "I suppose I can forgive that."

"I'm very glad to hear it." A laugh lay just beneath his voice. He picked up the candle and took my hand in his. "Come here, I want to show you something that might help with your plan."

"It's not really a plan," I admitted as we moved into the

cottage's kitchen. "More a burning desire."

James glanced at me over his shoulder, an amused look on his face, and I blushed again.

On a large wooden table in the kitchen lay a double-barreled flintlock pistol, the necessary paraphernalia neatly arranged around it. James picked it up and handed it to me. It was heavy.

"Two barrels, two banshees. Marsh fetched it from York for me."

I nodded. "That's why you asked me to come along that night. Marsh was gone, Freddie was ill."

"Yes. I'd already missed three nights. It was stupid of me to ask you, but I couldn't bear to lose another chance at them."

I carefully set the gun back on the table. "It would have been stupider of you to go alone."

"We came out alive, didn't we?"

As soon as he realized what he'd said, his eyes widened and his face paled. I closed my eyes and placed a steadying hand on the table.

"I'm sorry," he whispered. "I didn't think."

I shook my head, then opened my eyes and looked pointedly down at the pistol.

James inhaled sharply. "Right. I'm having iron bullets made, but they won't be done until tomorrow. I had to ask for them specially, as opposed to lead."

I frowned, trying to remember the basic mechanics of a gun. Neither Uncle Gerald nor any of his sons were big hunters. Uncle owned a single musket, older than me, which had never been used in all the years I'd lived in his house. "Will that work? Iron?"

James shrugged. "I've no idea. But if it blows up in my face, we can always fall back on your method." He gestured toward the poker I still held. Somewhat sheepishly, I placed it on the table next to the pistol.

"How did you figure it out?" I asked. "Was it the night in the blacksmith shop or Ann Claybrook's death?"

"Both." He smiled. "I couldn't figure it out—how the horse could kill the banshee when setting her head on fire and stabbing her in the chest did nothing—until I remembered what you said that night, how the creature could only come within a few feet of the blacksmith shop. Then I realized it was the horseshoes that killed her, not the horse."

"Same here, though I had added evidence. The night Freddie..." I swallowed. "I was able to fend her off with the poker. Otherwise I'd have died that night as well, and there'd be four banshees running around."

"I don't think I've ever felt quite so fond of a poker before."

"As well you should. We both owe this simple instrument our lives, because I guarantee I'd have eaten you first."

James looked startled, and I wanted to bite my tongue off.

"I'm sorry. That was completely uncall—"

He pressed his fingers against my lips, and my entire body went still. "Don't be. I'm honored." He smirked. "I think."

He slowly pulled his hand away, and we grinned stupidly at each other for a moment. I wondered if he would kiss me, and a surge of anticipation bloomed in my belly and ricocheted through my limbs.

But instead of reaching for me, James said, "In this mad desire of yours, did you form any sort of plan?"

It took me a moment to find my voice through my disappointment. "Not really. I'm not sure we need one. They want us. They've made that clear. I think if we make ourselves known, they'll come to us."

He nodded. "That's not reassuring at all."

"No, but it's easier."

"Point."

"I suppose you want to wait until tomorrow, though," I said. "For your bullets."

"I think it'd raise our odds."

"Well, then."

"Yes."

We stared at each other, and suddenly I felt half-naked in Freddie's shirt and trousers. I wrapped my arms around my torso and looked down at my feet.

"I'll walk you home," James said quietly.

"All right," I said automatically, then frowned as my head snapped up. "No."

He blinked. "Why not?"

"Because then you'll be alone for the return journey."

He huffed. "We went through this last time. I got home just fine that night."

"They're a bit angrier now than they were before," I retorted. "Seeing as they invaded my home, killed two people I love, and then murdered one of your closest friends a few yards from your door."

"You made it here, didn't you?" He rested his hand on the poker. "I can carry this."

I shook my head. "I shouldn't have. It was stupid." I swallowed. "I can't let you take that risk for me."

"Well, staying here isn't that much safer since, as you pointed out, they're not above breaking into homes."

"Except they probably can't bear to get anywhere near your doors and windows," I said, pointing over his shoulder at the small window set into the kitchen wall. It too was lined with horseshoes. "Interesting décor. Did you clean out the blacksmith?"

He gritted his teeth. "More or less."

We glared at each other for a long second, and then a piece of our argument settled into my chest and made my fingers turn cold.

"Breaking into homes. Like Uncle Gerald's again, or Mrs. Ellerby." I sank into one of the simple wooden chairs that surrounded the table, but as soon as the back of my thighs touched the seat, I sprang up again and caught James's shirt in both fists. "What if they break in again? My family—"

James covered my hands with his. "They haven't struck for several days. I don't know why they're waiting, but I think we're probably safe for one more night. Just one more. Tomorrow we'll end this, one way or another."

I closed my eyes and focused on breathing. "They're more interested in us, anyway, right? They won't care about Uncle Gerald or David or William or Meredith or Mrs. Ellerby or Mary. Right?"

"Right."

I looked up at him and asked, my voice small, "Why did they come here?"

James was silent for a long moment. "Sarah always did love the sea."

We stood like that for a long while, his hands curled around my fists. My forehead slowly drooped until it rested against his collarbone.

"Stay here tonight," he said, gently loosening my grip on his shirt. "I'll take you home in the morning."

I nodded and took a step back, trying not to sniffle.

"Come on." James took my hand and led me into the

cottage's main room. A door in the back wall led to a bedroom. Through it, I could see the end of the bed frame and a low cot hugging the wall. "You can have the bed. I'll take the cot."

I flushed and looked down at my boots. "No. I couldn't possibly—"

"I insist."

"No," I said louder. I released his hand and moved to one of the two surprisingly plush armchairs set before the fireplace. I threw myself into it and took as firm a grip as I could on the overstuffed arms. "I'll be perfectly fine right here."

For a moment, James looked like he might argue, but then his expression shifted to amusement, and he sank into the chair across from me. I relaxed.

"So," he said, "how would you like to pass the hours ahead of us?"

A highly inappropriate answer to that question flashed through my mind, and I blushed again. It really wasn't fair, him sitting there with the neck of his shirt open, his feet bare, and his hair tousled.

James glanced away and swallowed. I wondered if his thoughts were traveling the same path as mine. If so, this evening would get dangerous in a hurry.

I bent forward and worked at the laces of my boots, finally kicking them off. They flopped to the floor near the fireplace, and I straightened to see James's eyes determinedly fixed on the ceiling. It was hard to tell in the candlelight, but he looked more flushed than he had a moment ago. I glanced toward the ceiling but saw nothing but shadows.

Then I remembered the loose, open neck of the shirt I wore, the sharp V that exposed much of my sternum, and realized leaning down had probably not been the smartest idea I'd ever had.

With one hand clutching the top of my shirt, I turned sideways in the chair and pulled my legs into my chest. Bracing my back against the padded surface of one chair arm, I tucked my bare toes between the seat cushion and the other arm.

"I'd like to sleep, I think," I said, adding a silent, *if I can*. "We'll need the rest if we're making our stand tomorrow."

James brought his eyes down from the ceiling and flicked them over me. "Do you want a blanket? Or a fire?"

I shook my head. "I'm warm enough, thank you."

He nodded and reached for the candle. I expected him to rise and head for the bedroom, but instead he pulled the candle toward him and took a breath, preparing to blow it out.

"Wait," I blurted.

He looked at me.

"Can we keep it?"

With a small smile, he set it back on the side table.

I folded my arms and tucked them between my legs and stomach, curling myself deeper into the chair. My head lolled against the chair's back, and I turned it slightly to look at James.

"Are you staying?" I asked.

"Is that all right?"

The size of my smile surprised me. "Yes."

I turned my face into the chair and closed my eyes. It took a while for the smile to completely fade from my lips, but I figured it would take even longer for sleep to find me, if it did at all.

∞∞∞

Sleep must have found me, because the next thing I felt was the brush of fingertips along my forehead and cheek.

My eyes floated open, and I saw James hovering above me. I felt instantly alert but strangely calm.

He knelt next to the sofa, one hand pressed into the cushion at my side to support his weight. His other hand drifted down my neck, his touch as light as a breeze.

I closed my eyes and tilted my head back into the pillow. My hand found the wrist of his supporting arm, and my fingers danced over tendon and muscle as they made their way to the soft skin in the crook of his elbow, pushing his sleeve up as they went. His other hand, firmer now, trailed down my side to my stomach, where it slipped beneath my shirt. His fingers, hot and heavy, splayed over my skin, as though to cover as much of it as possible.

I gasped at the heat, and his head dipped down to press his mouth against mine—

I woke with a start, one of my feet kicking uselessly against the arm of the chair I slept in.

The room was dark, lit solely by the soft, vague glow of pre-dawn that managed to slip through the curtains of a horseshoe-lined window. My breathing sounded loud in my ears, short, fast breaths that matched my heart rate. Every inch of my skin felt alive, and I could feel my clothing, the fabric of the chair, the softness of the blanket draped over me.

Blanket? I started to push it off, more than warm enough, but the realization that James must have fetched it for me after I fell asleep stopped me. Instead, I tucked the blanket under my chin and looked at him.

He slept in his chair, his legs stretched out in front of him, his arms hanging over the sides. His head lolled near his shoulder, and as I watched him, he snored lightly. I smiled and turned back to the window, trying to ignore the urge to comb my fingers through his sleep-mussed hair.

The soft light behind the curtains had begun to brighten, and I knew it was time to leave if I didn't want to be caught having spent the night in James's cottage.

I swung my feet to the floor and laid the blanket aside. I stood and, with one hand carefully holding my shirt closed at my throat, leant over James and gently shook his shoulder.

His eyes opened instantly, and the softness of his smile when he saw me made my skin burst into awareness again.

I took a hasty step back. "It's almost morning."

"Right." He rubbed his face as he sat up, then stretched and yawned. He caught me watching him and smiled. "What?"

I shook my head and turned my attention toward my boots, biting my lip to hide my own smile.

"Boots," James muttered behind me. "That's a good idea. I used to have boots."

I heard him shuffle out of the room as I sat on the hearth and laced up the first boot, then moved to the second. By the time I'd finished that one, he'd returned. Instead of returning to his chair, he squeezed past me and sank into mine.

I looked up at him, eyebrows raised in a mixture of amusement and annoyance, but he merely grinned in response and bent to the task of putting on his boots.

The whole exchange felt very much like something that would have happened between me and Freddie, and a sharp stab of emotion made me turn my face to the fireplace. My cousin had only been dead a week, and not only had I made the sort of advances upon a man that would send Mrs. Ellerby into a coma, I'd spent the night in his company, not six feet from him, in a set of clothes that would destroy my reputation in a heartbeat.

The only remorse I could dredge up, though, had nothing to do with my reputation. I'd never have dreamed of coming to James in the middle of the night if Freddie were still alive, if the banshees hadn't killed him. But by the same logic, I never would have met James if he hadn't followed the banshees to Harwick, and the thought of not having him here with me made my chest tighten in panic.

I pressed my fists into my temples. Those thoughts only led to a spiraling vortex of guilt and grief, and though I knew I wouldn't be done with either for years to come, right now I needed to focus on what James and I could do to make sure the banshees killed no one else.

"Catherine?"

I lifted my head. James held his hand out to me, and I let him pull me from the floor.

"All right?" he asked.

I shook my head but squeezed his hand to let him know it wasn't his fault. "Let's go."

He nodded, and we walked out of the cottage, hand in hand.

∞∞∞

We paused in the woods behind Uncle Gerald's house, much as we had the last time we'd been out all night together.

"I can sneak back to Mrs. Ellerby's house from here," I said quietly. "If I get caught, it'll be better if I'm alone. I can always claim I woke early and couldn't sleep. I'll pass my clothes off as some sort of attempt to protect myself from passing ruffians or something. Better a skinny youth than a lone, helpless woman. That sort of thing."

He nodded, still holding my hand. "They were smart, the clothes. Wear them again tomorrow."

I assumed he was remembering how my skirt had snagged in the hedge the first time we tried to go banshee hunting, but I couldn't help saying, "Why? Just because you like them?"

He gave me that bright, sudden smile that still surprised me when it burst across his face. "Well, there is that," he admitted.

He pulled me closer, and his free hand cupped my cheek, then slid behind my neck. I stopped breathing as he lowered his head toward mine, and then a window in Uncle Gerald's house banged open.

I jumped, barely stifling a yelp, and James pulled me down into a crouch. We watched Daniel, Polly's son, empty a basin of water into the small vegetable patch beneath the kitchen window, then slam it closed again. I winced at the noise.

"Well, everyone's awake now," James muttered. "You should go while you can."

"Yes." But I didn't move.

We looked at each other for a long second, and then I reluctantly stood and let go of his hand.

"Tomorrow?" I asked.

He nodded. "Tomorrow."

"I'm the back window on the west side of Mrs. Ellerby's house."

The corner of his mouth twitched. "I'll be sure to knock."

"Be sure you do," I said with mock severity. "Gentlemen can't just go climbing into ladies' rooms as they please."

James's expression had a very *just watch me* quality that made my stomach flutter, and I turned and sprinted for the back of the stable before I did something very foolish indeed.

twenty-one

The next night, I lay on the bed in Mrs. Ellerby's spare room, wearing Freddie's clothes and waiting.

I'd taken a walk through town earlier, hoping to see James, but instead had been stopped by everyone I knew so they could inform me that Miss Hayworth and the Amherst boy were engaged. Not in the mood to encourage town gossip, I simply replied, "Yes, I know," and moved on, but that didn't stop someone else from stopping me four steps later. The Amhersts' store was packed. I hoped they were at least getting some business out of the entire village cramming themselves inside to gawk.

I fidgeted through dinner with Uncle Gerald and my cousins, then returned to Mrs. Ellerby's home and excused myself to my room early. I couldn't focus on conversation or a book or needlepoint or whatever other meager options were available to me. So instead I dressed in Freddie's clothes and lay down to wait.

I couldn't stop my mind from returning to the previous night. The feel of James's arms around me, his hand in mine. My dream.

I thought Freddie would approve, despite my scandalous behavior. He'd liked James and James had liked him. I thought—I hoped—that Freddie would be delighted by me flinging myself wholly into my burgeoning feelings for James. He was probably up in heaven, laughing so hard at me that he couldn't breathe.

That thought was more comforting than anything else I'd been told since he died.

My mind turned to its other favorite topic of the night —whether James would be able to safely travel from his cottage to Mrs. Ellerby's house. I reassured myself for the thirtieth time since lying down that he had his pistol and its new iron bullets.

Something tapped lightly against my window, and I sat up, holding my breath until I made out James's face peering at me through the glass. I padded quietly to the window and eased it open.

James put both hands on the sill and hoisted himself up, but I shoved him back down.

"What do you think you're doing?" I asked.

He grinned. "Climbing into a lady's room. I knocked first." He eyed me. "At least, I was told this was a lady's room. You don't look much like a lady."

"At your request, as I recall," I said, fighting my own smile. "Help me down."

I climbed out onto the sill and braced my hands on James's shoulders. His hands found my waist and lifted me down. My feet had barely touched the ground before one of his hands rose to cradle the back of my head, and he kissed me.

I made a small, surprised sound, then inhaled sharply against his cheek as a flood of new sensations absorbed my senses. His mouth moved against mine as he pulled me closer, and everything outside the feel of his hand on my back, the taste of his lips, and the shape of his shoulders beneath my fingers disappeared.

He eased back, breaking the kiss but not releasing me. I stared up at him, waiting for my ability to speak to return.

"Oh," I breathed, and he smiled softly.

His fingers brushed down the side of my face. "I wanted to do that before we left. Just in case."

I managed to nod. "Good. Yes. A good idea."

He took a deep breath, then bent and retrieved the unlit lantern he'd set at the base of the house. I could see his pistol tucked into his waistband. He picked up the iron poker he'd leaned against the house and handed it to me. "You left it last night."

I sighed and took my weapon. "Yes. Mrs. Ellerby noticed. She interrogated her poor maid for half an hour. I couldn't think of anything to satisfy her until I could get it back."

We stood looking at each other, neither of us wanting to leave the illusion of safety created by Mrs. Ellerby's flowerbeds. A wave of fear ran through me as I realized we could both die tonight, but my anger from the night before had condensed into a cold determination that quickly reasserted itself. We had to do this. No one else could.

James held out his hand. "Come on."

I slipped my fingers into his, his hand already so familiar, and nodded. My other hand tightened around the poker.

"Where should we go?" I asked as we crept around a tree and into the lane.

"I've been thinking about that. I'm supposedly in town to buy the Markham place, as you know."

I nodded, remembering how Freddie and I had questioned him at the Laceys' party. That felt like months ago.

"I figured I should probably make a show of going to

look at it. Do you know it?"

"Yes."

"You remember the large, sloping lawn behind it that leads down to the creek?"

It had been several years since I'd been to the old Markham estate, but I remembered the large, open space James referenced. The village children—including Freddie and I, ten years ago—often played cricket there. The estate sat on the edge of the village, separated from it by the creek and several hundred yards of forest. If we could get to it, it would be a good place to make a stand.

We had a mile's walk ahead of us, first.

Neither of us spoke, too busy trying to watch everywhere at once. My fingers ached with the intensity of my grip on the poker, and James had awkwardly tucked the lantern beneath one arm so he could hold my hand and his pistol at the same time.

Just outside the village, we left the relative safety of the road and stepped cautiously into the woods. The trees blocked the moonlight, making it nearly impossible to avoid tripping over fallen branches, but we didn't dare light the lantern. A little noise felt safer than a light.

I hugged James's side as much as I could without hampering his movement. It felt like hours had passed before we reached the creek. We jumped across it, our pace increased by silent, mutual consent. Another quarter mile of forest, and we'd be at the Markham estate.

By the time we reached the edge of the trees, we were running. We burst out of the woods and into the clearing, and didn't stop until we stood in the center of the wide lawn that sloped from the manor house to the woods.

We spent a few moments panting, looking wildly around us, before letting ourselves calm down. On one side of us stood the stables, the roof half caved in. On our other side, an overgrown rose garden, wild and impenetrable, like something out of a fairy tale. Behind us the house, before us the woods and creek. Fifty square yards of open space surrounded us.

I let go of James's hand just long enough to push a few strands of sweat-soaked hair off my face. When I reached for him again, he laced his fingers into mine with as much desperate eagerness as I felt.

"No point going any farther, I think," he said. "We won't find a better place." He lit the lantern and placed it on the ground.

"No," I agreed. "And we won't have long to wait, either."

I pointed toward the rose garden. The silhouette of a woman was visible against the white rock of the path. She walked toward us.

Still holding hands, we faced the coming banshee. I wondered if she'd followed us or if she'd simply always been here. It didn't seem to matter. I shifted my grip on the poker.

Into the circle of light cast by the lantern stepped James's sister.

"Sarah," he breathed. His hand twitched in mine.

"Hello, James," the banshee said, moving a step closer. "I've missed you." The satin dress she wore had a wide neckline, and her brown hair hung well past her shoulders. Where the moonlight touched her, she looked like a porcelain goddess, beautiful and flawless, skin and hair gleaming.

I could feel James shaking. "Oh, God, Sarah," he said, his voice half a sob. "I'm so sorry."

"I'm not." She held out a hand, beckoning him. "Let me

show you."

His fingers went slack, and he dropped my hand. With a dull thud, his pistol fell to the ground.

"No. No!" I cried, grabbing his arm. "James! Wake up. Please, James, no. Please!"

He ignored me, stepping toward his sister. She smiled at him, inviting and warm, and he took her hand.

"No," I said again, my voice sounding weak to my own ears.

Sarah Hale stroked her brother's cheek, then trailed her fingers down his neck. I remembered how easily she'd slit Freddie's throat. I remembered the detached look on her face as she watched him sink to the floor, his life pouring out of him.

And I remembered the poker in my hand.

I gripped it in both fists and stepped toward the siblings. As the banshee curled her finger and began to draw a cut down James's throat, I swung the poker into her back.

The barb sank into her flesh, and she arched back and screamed, an inhuman howl. As she staggered backward, her arm lashed out, and the back of her hand struck me across the face.

I hit the ground hard, and everything went black for a few seconds as pain overwhelmed my senses. A roaring sound drowned out my hearing, and I could feel nothing but the throbbing fire in the side of my head.

Slowly the world came back into focus. I could feel the grass beneath my hands and face, could hear the hissing of the banshee nearby. I struggled to get to my feet, but the earth spun beneath me, and I couldn't make my legs obey.

A foot shoved at my ribs, rolling me over, and I looked

up into the livid face of Sarah Hale. The sky seemed to swing behind her. I tried to crawl away, my feet shoving uselessly at the ground. I had only moved a foot or two, my breath coming in panicked sobs, when she snarled and reached for me.

She lifted me effortlessly, her nails digging into my shoulders, and wrapped one hand around my throat.

"We would have made you one of us," she hissed. "Part of our eternal sisterhood. But now I think I will simply snap your neck." She leaned closer, baring her teeth. "And then I will have James, and my remaining sister and I will kill everyone in your village. Know that, little Catherine Chase, as you die."

Her hand tightened, cutting off my air.

An explosion tore through the night.

Sarah Hale's eyes widened, and she released me. I collapsed to the ground at her feet, coughing, one hand to my neck. I looked up at her. Her hands hung by her side, her eyes still wide. She slowly turned to look at James, who stood a few paces behind her, pistol raised. A wound in her back, just over her heart, oozed thick, black blood.

"James?" she said, her voice small and confused.

His arm shook as he slowly lowered the pistol.

Her knees buckled, and James dropped the gun and leapt forward, catching her. They sank to the ground together. James hugged her to his chest, his hand fluttering over her hair, face, shoulder. She pushed against him, trying to break free, but he held her tighter, sobbing her name. Her nails tore into his chest, drawing blood, and raked over his face, carving companions to his existing scar.

Finally she weakened, her hands lying limp against her stomach and the grass, and James bent his head, burying his face in her neck.

And with her eyes on the moon above, Sarah Hale died in her brother's arms for the second time.

twenty-two

I knelt in the grass a few feet away from James and his sister, my hand covering my mouth, frozen by the horror and grief of the scene before me.

Then I heard the swish of fabric behind me, and terror swamped every other emotion. I turned my head.

The final banshee stood just out of reach of the lantern's light, looking at me sadly.

I scrambled to my feet and took two hasty steps backward. She didn't move. She simply watched me.

I felt instinctively that she was ancient. I had seen her only once before, the night James confronted her near the woods behind my home, and then only from afar. She was small, a full head shorter than me, with a dark complexion—olive skin and thick, black hair that hung past her waist. The deep green of her dress seemed to shimmer, as though reflecting the stars.

Her gaze, so calm and heavy, quieted my fear. I could feel her sadness, as tangible as the ground beneath my feet. It tugged on my soul, and I took a step toward her.

She looked past me, to where James held his sister's body, and her sadness intensified. "You have taken my companions," she said slowly, her voice carrying a soft northern brogue I found soothing. She turned her head and looked into the distance. "I left my home in search of sisters, weary of my solitude. But now I am alone again." She looked at me, and I caught my breath. "Will you join me?"

I opened my mouth to say *yes*, but a strangled sound behind me caught my attention. I looked over my shoulder. James stared at us, Sarah lying limply across his lap. He shook his head but didn't seem able to move.

"Come," the banshee said quietly, pulling my gaze back to her face. "Dance with me beneath the stars, and you can have him. I will save him until you are ready, and then he will be yours completely."

Yes, I thought, the word ringing through me. *Yes, I want him.* I closed my eyes as the banshee's hand brushed my face, and I felt as though I were floating. I'd never been so light, so beautiful. I wanted to dance forever.

I heard my name somewhere in the distance, but I couldn't focus on it because loneliness suddenly filled my soul, dwarfing me with the vast stretch of eternity. I saw the empty expanse of the highlands stretching before me, the endless monotony of existence. I felt the searing brightness of Sarah Hale, who shone as though she were her own star. Her energy, her desire to see the world, was overwhelming. In a small village by the sea, a girl bubbled over with life and was claimed as well. While waiting for Ann to adjust to her new existence, Sarah discovered her brother's presence in the village and refused to leave until she'd drunk from him. I felt his vengeance, his danger; an urgent desire to leave filled me, but Ann took Sarah's side. They were young, reckless, and now they were dead. They were dead, but I—

Then it stopped. The images, the memories—gone. I was no longer floating, no longer dancing.

I blinked, swaying on my feet, and saw James and the banshee tangled together, rolling down the slope of the lawn. Pain blossomed at the base of my neck, and I realized I was bleeding. As awareness slowly came back to me, I grasped what had just happened and began to shake.

Several yards away, James shouted as the banshee tossed him away as though he were a child. She stood, her movements almost sedate, and reached for him. He scrambled away, legs and arms shoving against the ground as he tried to find his feet and run, but the banshee caught his arm with one hand.

"James!" I moved toward them, not sure what I could do unarmed, when a glint in the grass caught my attention. The pistol. The double-barreled pistol, which still had one shot left.

It lay where James had dropped it, a few feet away from Sarah Hale's body. I lunged for it, but my legs gave out, still weakened by the banshee's spell, and I fell.

Crawling, I turned my head toward the banshee and James and watched as she twisted his arm and hauled it up. He bit back a cry, and I realized it was his injured arm. She pulled higher, and James rose onto his knees. The banshee's other hand gripped his chin, lifting his face to hers.

"I see I should have killed you after all, that night. At the time I thought to have mercy, as in a few short decades you would be dead anyway. I thought to show mercy in gratitude for your sister's companionship. But you have killed her, so I have no more need of mercy."

She slid her hand to the back of his neck and forced his head down, yanking his arm higher. James struggled against her, but he couldn't get his feet beneath him. Though she was only half his size, she restrained him with ease.

He knelt at her feet, head bowed, a sacrifice.

I reached for the pistol, my hand clumsily trying to find its grip without the help of my eyes, which were locked on the struggle before me.

The banshee pressed her thumbnail into the skin of James's wrist until blood began to flow, then lowered her mouth to the wound. He thrashed harder, beating at her legs and arm with his free hand, but she hardly seemed to notice.

My fingers slipped around the butt of the pistol and tightened.

The banshee watched me calmly over James's twitching hand as I stood and raised the gun. It had been years since I'd fired one, and my arm shook so badly that I didn't trust my aim. I took a few steps forward until I was sure I couldn't miss.

Her eyes fixed on the gun, and she pulled her mouth away from James's wrist. Blood ran over her fingers and down his arm.

"You can feel it, can't you?" I said, my voice trembling as much as the rest of me. "You can feel what this is. This is what killed Sarah."

She was only a few feet away. I could see the moon reflected in her eyes. "Ah," she said quietly. "Then you will be my end."

"Yes." The trigger felt cold against my finger.

"It's been so long..." The banshee's gaze drifted toward the sky, then snapped back down to me. "Are you sure this is what you want?" she asked, and the euphoria of my earlier enthrallment filled me. She wanted me. We would be together forever, watching time pass like a river or a breeze. For a moment, I could hear the stars sing.

Then James said my name, and the spell broke. I glanced at him, and the banshee tightened her grip on his neck. He gasped and bent lower, his shoulder twisting at an angle it wasn't meant to withstand.

"I could kill him," the banshee said. "So easily. You aren't fast enough to stop me."

The aim of my pistol wavered. "Please," I whispered. "Don't."

She studied me for a moment, then said, "Very well. A mercy in gratitude."

And she released him.

James collapsed onto the grass, then rolled to his feet and stumbled toward me, holding his shoulder. When he reached my side, I felt his hand on my arm, but I couldn't look at him.

The banshee and I faced each other, the pistol spanning the gap between us. She clasped her hands in front of her, one of them glistening with James's blood, and closed her eyes.

"I've waited a long time for this," she said quietly.

For a long moment I couldn't move, couldn't breathe, but then two words floated to the surface of my consciousness. My muscles stilled and relaxed, my aim steadied, and the peace of the night sky settled over me.

"Sleep, Elaine," I said and pulled the trigger.

The iron bullet tore through her throat, splattering the bodice of her medieval gown with thick drops of black blood. Her eyes opened as she sank to her knees, and she looked at me one last time. I felt nothing.

She sagged sideways, her eyes drifting closed, and fell with a soft sigh. She didn't move again.

twenty-three

"Oh, God, your face," James said.

He gently touched my temple, and I gasped as fire seemed to spread down my cheekbone. I finally tore my eyes from the dead banshee and looked up at him. I couldn't decide if I wanted to cry or not.

"The whole side of your face is turning black," he said. "Did she hit you?"

I didn't need to ask who he meant. I nodded, but he didn't see it. His eyes had moved to his sister's body. His arm fell back to his side, and he clenched his fists. I turned his face back to me.

"It wasn't her," I said, though I wasn't sure that was true. "Not anymore."

He shook his head, his eyes closed. He started to shake, and I pulled him toward me. Face buried in my neck, arms wrapped around my waist, he sank to his knees, taking me with him. I held him as he had held me after Freddie died, one hand in his hair, feeling the waves that ran through him.

When he had quieted, he pulled away, rubbing his hands roughly across his cheeks, and I saw the blood covering most of his forearm.

"Your wrist!" I caught his injured arm and pulled it

toward me, examining the wound. The cut in his wrist was deep, more a puncture than a slice, and still bleeding, but it seemed to be slowing. I pulled my shirt from the waistband of my trousers and ripped a long strip from the bottom of it.

James chuckled, the sound rough. "Patching me up again."

I wrapped the strip snugly around his wrist and tied it off. "I'm getting rather good at it, I think."

Satisfied with my bandage, I looked over the rest of him. The shallow cuts on his face and chest had stopped bleeding on their own, but the one on his neck still oozed slightly. I ripped off another section of my shirt and folded it until I had a thick rectangle of fabric, which I pressed to his throat. I brought my other hand up to the opposite side of his neck, cradling his jaw, so I could apply pressure to the wound.

My eyes drifted up to his, which were raw and open, filled with the same emotions that still stormed inside of me. But something else resided there, something I was just learning to recognize. Feeling strangely bold, perhaps from the giddy realization that we had survived, I whisked the thumb of my stabilizing hand against his jaw line.

He seemed to snap. His uninjured hand slid around the back of my neck and pulled my mouth to his. This kiss, unlike the one beneath my window, felt hungry and desperate, and I found myself more than capable of matching his intensity. My fingers fisted in his hair, my mouth moved with his, and I couldn't seem to get close enough.

By the time we separated, gasping for breath, I sat in his lap. James pressed another simple kiss to my lips, then rested his forehead in the curve where my neck met my shoulder. We sat wrapped in each other for several minutes until James turned his head, and I knew he was looking at his sister.

"We need to bury her," he said.

"Both of them," I agreed.

Reluctantly, we untangled ourselves and stood.

After a few heartbeats of hesitation, James knelt and lifted his sister into his arms. I couldn't do the same for the banshee Elaine, so I was forced to drag her into the woods. I felt strangely guilty about this and couldn't keep my eyes from straying back to the horrible wound in her throat.

We laid the bodies side by side in the woods behind the Markham place, and James went back for the lantern and to search the stable for a forgotten spade. I sat several yards from the banshees, my arms around my knees, and tried to see the stars through the leaves of the trees. The sky in the east had started to turn gray. Dawn was coming.

∞∞∞

The burials didn't take long. James spread dead leaves over his sister's grave to mask the disturbance in the soil, then set an oddly shaped stone at its head. When he stood, our hands found each other.

"She was lovely," I said quietly. "I wish I could have known her."

"So do I." He was quiet a moment, then said, "How did you know the other's name?"

"She—she told me. I'm not sure how, but I just knew

her name, just as I knew her loneliness and sorrow, her need for companions." I hesitated, not sure if I should continue. James turned to look at me. "She could hear the stars sing," I said. "She felt time move around her, leaving her behind, but she also danced with the moonlight." I looked at Elaine's grave, nearly invisible beneath the leaves covering the forest floor. "Whatever they were, whatever horror was involved, I think there was beauty, too."

A breeze whispered through the tree branches above us. I could see the leaves in the growing morning light. James squeezed my hand, and something inside me relaxed.

We left the woods, walking silently toward Mrs. Ellerby's house. At her gate, James pulled me into his arms again.

"Mmm," I said, my head against his chest. "I understand now why Mary and Peter were always sneaking out to see each other. It's not fair that I can't do this whenever I want."

"You could, you know." He adjusted his hold on me, dipping his head so that his mouth hovered near my ear. "Catherine, I—"

I jumped as a sharp bang echoed through the night.

"Catherine!" Mrs. Ellerby shrieked. "Where have you been? What do you think you're doing?"

She stood on her porch, a tower of righteous indignation wearing a nightcap. Uncle Gerald stood just behind her, his mouth hanging open. I guiltily extracted myself from James's embrace.

"And with a *man!*" Mrs. Ellerby continued, her voice rising in octaves. Her eyes widened as she took in my attire. "And *dressed* like a man! Oh! Oh, Mr. Martin. I feel faint."

She sagged against the doorframe, but Uncle Gerald ignored her. He rubbed a hand down his face, then scrubbed at the bald spot on top of his head. "You'd better come inside, Catherine," he said. "You too, young man. Before the whole village hears us."

I bit my lip to stop myself crying. Too tired and shocked to argue, we filed into Mrs. Ellerby's parlor and obediently sat on the sofa. Uncle Gerald paced in front of us as Mrs. Ellerby bustled about the room, lighting candles and lamps.

"Mrs. Ellerby checked on you an hour ago," my uncle said, his hands clasped behind him in a fist. "She found you missing and your window open. She immediately came to fetch me. Can you imagine our fear? The certainty that I'd lost you as well?"

"I'm sorry," I whispered, my eyes burning. "I didn't think—"

"Clearly not. Your cousins are out searching for you. We can only hope they also return unscathed."

I bit my lip and looked down at my hands.

"Sir," James started, "this isn't what—"

"Not a word from you, young man," Uncle Gerald said sternly.

Mrs. Ellerby brought a candle over to the small table at the end of the sofa, and my uncle stopped in front of me, his face stricken.

"Catherine!" He gently turned my face to the light and pressed at my bruised temple and cheekbone. I winced. Releasing me, he surged to his feet, and I shrank back from his anger. "Did *he* do this?" he asked, his voice low and even. He didn't bother acknowledging James with so much as a glance.

Near the fireplace, Mrs. Ellerby wailed.

"What? Of course not, Uncle!" I stood to face him, but at his look, I sank back onto the sofa. "He saved me from much worse."

"Worse?" Uncle Gerald closed his eyes and took a slow, deep breath. "I think perhaps you'd better tell me everything, Catherine."

"What is there to tell?" Mrs. Ellerby demanded. "She's snuck out for a midnight tryst with this scoundrel. She's ruined!" She turned away, crying into a handkerchief.

I nearly rolled my eyes at Mrs. Ellerby's sudden change of heart where James was concerned. But her use of the word *scoundrel* had given me everything I needed to get James and I out of this situation socially unscathed.

"Sir," James said, starting to stand.

With one hand, I lightly pressed him back down. "No, Mr. Hale," I said firmly. "While I appreciate your sense of heroism—and owe it my life—I can't let you save me now. It's my own folly that has brought me to this place, and I must own it." I stood and looked my uncle in the eye, hoping that after this night I would never need to lie to anyone I loved ever again.

"Catherine, please," Uncle Gerald said. "I'm not sure if I should be frightened or angry."

"You're entitled to both." I took a deep breath and fiddled with the cuffs of Freddie's shirt. "I...I snuck out of my room tonight because I couldn't sleep. I meant to be back before anyone noticed I'd gone. I just needed to be outside, beneath the stars. I walked down to the creek, then wandered along it for a while." I closed my eyes, hating myself a little. "Then a man seemed to materialize in front of me, a stranger. I tried to run, but he grabbed me, hit me."

"Oh, Catherine," Uncle Gerald said, sinking into a

chair.

I turned to look at James. "But then Mr. Hale came. And he saved me."

James blinked once. "I—I couldn't sleep either. She was near my cottage, and I heard her scream."

Uncle Gerald bent over, his elbows on his knees. He lifted his head to look at me. "We saw you embracing."

I froze. I'd forgotten that.

"She was weak from the shock," James said, standing. "I had to carry her from the woods. I set her on her feet at the gate, and another wave of faintness hit her. I merely wanted to keep her from falling and am afraid that in my overprotective state I may have overstepped my bounds." He bowed his head to me. "I hope you can forgive me, Miss Chase."

"Of course," I murmured.

Uncle Gerald looked at us both for a long moment, then stood. "I think, considering the circumstances, we can overlook the misconduct this once." He held a hand out toward James. "Thank you, sir, for my niece's life."

"My duty and my honor," James replied.

Uncle Gerald turned to me. "As for you..."

Two tears ran down my cheeks. "I never should have left my room. I'm so sorry."

He opened his arms, and I nearly fell into them. Mrs. Ellerby sniffled.

"Just...don't do it again," Uncle Gerald said.

"No."

Mrs. Ellerby sniffled again. "What happened to the man?"

I shook my head. "I don't know. He just ran off."

"Do you think it was the murderer, coming back for another go at us?" Mrs. Ellerby's voice held a familiar undercurrent of excitement—she had scented gossip no one else had yet heard.

"Mrs. Ellerby, really," Uncle Gerald scolded. "I'd prefer not to think about such things tonight." He looked toward the window and the light gathering there. "Or this morning, rather."

"Well, whoever he was, I hope you gave him a good thrashing, Mr. Hale," Mrs. Ellerby continued, tightening the sash of her dressing gown.

"Er, yes." James gave me a helpless look.

"I doubt he'll ever come back to this village," I said, trying not to smile.

Mrs. Ellerby nodded in satisfaction. "Serves him right."

Uncle Gerald peered again at my bruise. "I don't like the look of that contusion. Mrs. Ellerby, could you stoke the fire, please, and bring more light over here by the sofa? I'm going to fetch my medical bag. I'll just be a few minutes." He moved toward the door.

"I should go," James said, standing. "I don't want to intrude any more than I already have."

"Don't be silly," I said. "You can't leave." I felt Mrs. Ellerby and my uncle look at me and added, "Not with that nasty cut on your arm."

"You're hurt as well?" Uncle Gerald crossed the room and held out a hand.

James showed him the blood-stained fabric tied around his wrist. "Miss Chase was kind enough to bandage it for me. I'm afraid the man had a small knife."

Uncle Gerald's eyes narrowed as he took in the scratches on James's face and neck. "And these other cuts?"

"Running through the woods."

Uncle Gerald nodded and studied the bandage on

James's wrist. "It's well done. I won't remove it until I get back with my supplies." He looked at me and smiled. "My Catherine always would have made an excellent doctor."

I blushed. "It's just a bit of cloth."

"It stopped the bleeding and kept Mr. Hale from experiencing any number of unfortunate side effects of blood loss. It *was* well done." He laid a hand on top of my head for a second, then left the room.

James and I reclaimed our seats on the sofa while we waited. Mrs. Ellerby set three more candles on the small table next to me, then moved to the fireplace. She reached for the stand of implements, then threw up her hands.

"That blasted poker is still missing!" She looked around the room as though it might be leaning against a chair and didn't notice the small choking sound I made. I exchanged a quick look with James, who smirked at me. I couldn't believe I'd forgotten the poker again. We'd have to search the Markham grounds later and sneak it back in before Mrs. Ellerby fired her help.

"Do you want some tea?" she asked. Without waiting for an answer, she hurried toward her kitchen. "It'll do you good. Could use a nice strong cup, both of you."

When she was gone, I stood and moved to the fireplace, staring down into the glowing embers.

"Catherine?" James said.

I wiped tears from my cheeks. "I'm sorry. I'm just so tired of lying. I feel like all I've done since this whole thing started is lie."

He came up behind me, standing so close I could feel his warmth, and ran his hands up and down my arms. "It's over now. They're gone, and we're safe."

"Yes, but at what cost?" I rubbed more tears away, but others simply took their place. "I'll never get Freddie back, your sister is gone. And now you'll leave as well, go home."

"Well, yes." He paused, and I felt him shift his weight. "Though I was rather hoping you'd come with me."

I turned and looked up at him, my mouth open.

"I know it's fast," he said quickly, "but nothing has to happen tomorrow, or even this summer. In the meantime, I'd like you to meet my parents and see Edinburgh. That is, if you want—"

I caught his face in my hands and kissed him.

For the second time in an hour, a shriek startled me, and I jumped away from James, tripping over the hearth and nearly falling into the fireplace.

Mrs. Ellerby stood in the doorway, a tray of tea things shaking dangerously in her hands. James leapt forward and took it from her, setting it carefully on the nearest flat surface.

"I knew it. I *knew* it!" Mrs. Ellerby said, pointing a finger at me, then James, then me again.

"What's going on?" Uncle Gerald asked, appearing behind her in the hallway, medical bag in hand.

"I caught them! I caught them in a flagrant display of—of—" She swooned backward, and Uncle Gerald was forced to catch her or be knocked over. He half-dragged her into the room, and James helped him prop her up on the sofa. She moaned and fanned at her face.

"What's happened this time, Catherine?" Uncle Gerald asked, setting his medical bag on the ground.

I sighed, too tired for anything but the truth. "She walked in on me kissing James."

Uncle Gerald's gaze sharpened and flicked toward James. "James, eh?"

"Yes."

"I see. And how long has he been 'James'?"

Mrs. Ellerby made a strangled noise. "Oh! She's been sneaking behind our backs this whole time. Sneaking behind dear *Freddie's* back! Her fiancé!"

I looked at the ceiling and took a deep breath. "He was not my fiancé."

Mrs. Ellerby wailed. "Listen to her! Talking about her poor dead cousin that way!"

In two strides I stood next to the sofa, glaring down at Mrs. Ellerby, my hands clenched at my sides. "How dare you?" I spat. "How dare you dictate how I think of Freddie? I knew him better than anyone, and I watched him die. I loved him as much as it is possible to love someone, but we *were not engaged*."

She blinked twice, then recovered enough to huff and look at my uncle. "Are you going to let her speak to me this way?"

Uncle Gerald regarded me with a seriousness touched by realization. "She's right."

Mrs. Ellerby nodded triumphantly, then wavered. "Wait—what?"

"Catherine's right. I always hoped—but she and Freddie were never actually engaged."

I took a couple of steps back and found myself at James's side. He gave me a small smile and nodded. Our hands found each other.

I turned to my uncle. "But James and I are."

Mrs. Ellerby covered her mouth with a hand. Uncle Gerald eased himself into a chair and said, "Then I'll rephrase my earlier question. How long have you been engaged?"

I glanced up at James and smiled sheepishly. "Um, about five minutes."

Four seconds ticked by on the mantel clock, and Uncle Gerald's mouth twitched. Two seconds later, he burst into laughter.

"Mr. Martin!" Mrs. Ellerby said. "Get hold of yourself. This is no laughing matter. Catherine's reputation is still in tatters."

"Why?" Uncle Gerald challenged, the mirth draining from his face. "The only people capable of ruining her are in this room. I certainly don't intend to tell anyone what occurred tonight. Do you?"

Mrs. Ellerby's mouth clicked shut, and she sat back into the sofa. I thought about repeating one of her favorite directives about ladies not sulking, but I felt bad for yelling at her, however liberating it had been.

"I don't know what's happening to the young women of this village," Mrs. Ellerby muttered. "First Miss Hayworth attaches herself to that Amherst boy, and now our Catherine is running off with some Scot."

"She's hardly running off, my dear woman," Uncle Gerald said, retrieving his medical bag. "And you'll forgive me for feeling somewhat indulgent after losing my son. I see no reason to separate Catherine from her young man as long as things proceed in the accepted way from this point on." He pinned James with a look. "Which they will, yes?"

"Absolutely, sir," James responded crisply, straightening.

"There, Mrs. Ellerby. You see?" Uncle Gerald repositioned a lamp and settled into his chair. "Now come here, Mr. Hale, and let me take a look at that cut of yours."

∞∞∞

Half an hour later the sun was firmly established in the sky, and I walked James down the path to Mrs. Ellerby's gate. With my hand on the latch, I hesitated.

James's fingers on my chin turned my face up to him. "I'll call on you later today," he said in a low voice. He smiled, his fingers brushing my throat as he dropped his hand. "Good morning, Catherine."

I leaned up to kiss him, but he glanced at Mrs. Ellerby's house and pulled his head away.

I fell back onto my heels with a jarring thud and frowned. "Bollocks."

He laughed, an unfettered, delighted sound. "Are you unsatisfied with our new arrangement, Miss Chase?"

"Yes," I grumbled. "Aren't you?"

"Not in the least. After all, what's a few more months?" He dipped his head, and his voice deepened. "I've been in love with you for ages."

He chuckled at my soft gasp. "And how long is that?" I asked.

His eyes filled with mischief. "Oh, at least a week."

I laughed and clasped my hands behind me so I wouldn't touch him.

"Besides," he continued. "I have a feeling we'll manage admirably. I'm sure you know all the best secluded spots around the village."

"Oh, yes," I agreed, smiling hugely. "And I'm such a fan of walking."

"Me too."

The sun warmed my back as it climbed the sky. James opened the gate and stepped into the lane. After quickly squeezing my hand in farewell, he walked toward the Laceys' home and his cottage. I watched him go, leaning on the open gate, swinging it back and forth with one foot.

He turned the corner, and I sighed happily. If he had been there, Freddie would have made fun of the lovesick look on my face. Mary certainly would when she saw it later that day.

I straightened reluctantly. I needed to go inside before one of our neighbors spotted me in men's clothing. Mrs. Ellerby had given me one of her dressing gowns in an attempt to reclaim my feminine modesty, but the trousers were still plainly visible beneath the hem, as she was a few inches shorter than me.

I turned to enter Mrs. Ellerby's house, then changed my mind and walked across the lane, pushing through the gate to Uncle Gerald's instead.

It was time to go home.

Julianne Sharpe is an American author who loves fantasy stories set in our world. She lives in the northern United States with her husband and two dogs, where she gets very excited about wildlife and is trying to learn how to garden. *A Lady's Guide to Monsters and Moonlight* is her first novel.

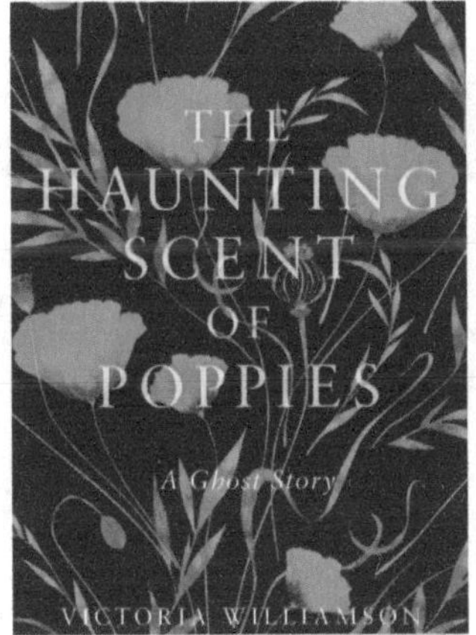

Also available from Silver Thistle Press

silverthistlepress.com

www.ingramcontent.com/pod-product-compliance
Lightning Source LLC
LaVergne TN
LVHW030122160826
845673LV00019B/2913

* 9 7 8 1 9 1 7 7 9 4 1 4 5 *